Bronwyn Scott is a communications instructor at Pierce College in the United States, and the proud mother of three wonderful children—one boy and two girls. When she's not teaching or writing she enjoys playing the piano, travelling—especially to Florence, Italy— and studying history and foreign languages. Readers can stay in touch on Bronwyn's website, bronwynnscott.com, or at her blog, bronwynswriting.blogspot.com. She loves to hear from readers.

SEDUCED BY THE PRINCE'S KISS

Bronwyn Scott

MILLS & BOON

First published in Great Britain 2018
by Mills & Boon, an imprint of HarperCollins*Publishers*
1 London Bridge Street, London, SE1 9GF

Large Print edition 2019

ISBN: 978-0-263-07881-7

MIX
Paper from
responsible sources
FSC
www.fsc.org   FSC™ C007454

This book is produced from independently certified FSC™ paper to ensure responsible forest management. For more information visit www.harpercollins.co.uk/green.

Printed and bound in Great Britain
by CPI Group (UK) Ltd, Croydon, CR0 4YY

To Scott and all the adventures still to come.

Chapter One

Shoreham-by-Sea, West Sussex—March 1824

Spring had come again in all its glory: blustering winds, lashing rains and always the peculiar English dampness that conspired to keep a person indoors far beyond the body's patience for inactivity—at least *his* body's. Stepan Shevchenko braced himself against the sea winds buffeting the bluffs. He peered through the eyepiece of his spyglass, searching the empty horizon.

Nothing yet.

He collapsed the spyglass with a frown. Still, it was far better to be out here amongst the elements than inside where he'd been for months. He had little tolerance for the indoors. He craved constant exercise, constant adventure, despite his efforts to tame himself to the more sedate rhythms of an Englishman's life.

Two springs now he'd spent in Britain and yet in all that time he'd proved only that one could take the man out of Kuban, but one couldn't take Kuban out of the man. The wildness of Kuban with its mountains and rivers called to the wildness within him, something he buried deep at his most primal self, something he'd been careful to suppress. It had become a secret identity, known only to him and those who knew him best: Nikolay, Ruslan, Illarion and Dimitri. Certainly, no one in London who did business with Prince Stepan Shevchenko would guess at it. To them, he was all that was *proper*. A boring word for someone whom many thought a boring man.

He preferred it that way. Proper was a very good cover. So good, in fact, he could even hide the wildness from himself. Sometimes, he almost believed the façade. But on days like today, when the wind blew through his hair, and the rain soaked his face, he knew better. He was still wild at heart; always running, always raging.

The horizon shimmered, the emptiness interrupted by the appearance of sails. Stepan smiled and lifted the spyglass again. It must be her—his ship, one of them. Through the eyepiece he sought out the name on the prow; the *Lady Frances*, a ship well known to be sponsored by Prince Stepan Shevchenko, bringing the latest Kubanian luxuries to London: lacquered trifle boxes with carefully painted scenes of Kubanian life on their lids, delicate birch wood carvings and the ever-entertaining Matryoshka dolls. A sense of tentative gratification rippled through him at the sight of the ship, followed by a clench of anticipation deep in his stomach. He moved his glass to take in the space behind the *Lady Frances* but the remainder of the horizon was empty.

Wait for it, he counselled himself. Impatience often bred unnecessary worry. He should not be concerned. Not yet. It was a good sign the *Lady Frances* was here. There *was* a satisfactory profit in her cargo once the duties were paid and a satisfaction of another sort, the sort that came from surrounding oneself with reminders of home. If he could not go to Kuban, he could bring Kuban to London. It was a type of cure for an odd homesickness for a place he'd not expected to miss, a place that didn't hold good memories, but haunted him none the less now that he could never go back. But a man did not get rich, not like he had, on importing knick-knacks to decorate ladies' parlours. No, the *Lady Frances* wasn't the real prize. She was merely the decoy.

His anticipation growing, Stepan focused on the empty space left in the *Lady Frances*'s wake. Wait for it…wait for it…five minutes went by. Then ten. There was movement. His adventurer's heart leapt. The thrill never got old. Slowly, a second ship came into view. It was here! The *Razboynik* held the true profit—casks of undiluted vodka straight from Ekaterinador and duty-free, thanks to his ingenuity and specially engineered barrels. Without the vodka there was no profit in it otherwise. No adventure, either, and no cause that justified the risk. For him there must be all three. Stepan reached into his pocket, trading his spyglass for a mirror and flashed a brief signal out across the water. That single flash meant: 'All is safe, come in from the sea.'

Stepan heard his horse nicker from his picket and felt a presence behind him. He smiled without turning, knowing full well who it would be, his land-crew chief, Joseph Raleigh. 'I swear, Joe, you can smell a ship a mile out to sea.' He chuckled as Joseph came up beside him. Stepan passed the young man the spyglass.

'It's a beaut, milord.' Joseph grinned, peering through the eyepiece. 'What I can smell is profit. The boys are rarin' to go.'

By 'boys', Joseph meant the crew that would gather to unload the *Razboynik*, all of them adolescents ranging from fourteen to seventeen, all of them orphans figuratively or literally. Growing up, Stepan had been both. Some were from London, gathered up during his visits, others were from the area. There were those in society who, if they knew, might condemn him for employing 'children' in illegal work. But these were boys who'd seen hardship, who lived with it every day, boys who'd been reduced to doing far worse than diluting vodka in caves before he'd found them. At their age, these boys needed guidance and help, but they also needed their pride. They wouldn't take charity.

He knew, he'd been their age and in their situation before, never mind that he'd been raised in a palace and they'd been raised on the streets.

Context didn't prevent one from being lost and rudderless. Like them, he'd been headed towards a life of shiftlessness before he'd been found, a boy not interested in school, only in running wild in the great outdoors. A balanced life needed both freedom and structure. Stepan would pay forward the favour Dimitri had done him if he could. One didn't need to be poor to need direction. The pitfalls of being an orphan were no respecters of station.

As for the smuggling—well, everyone did it. There wasn't anyone in Shoreham who wasn't connected to 'free trading' in some way, either as merchants or consumers or employees. That made it a fairly safe 'industry'. Folks were less likely to turn in their friends and their own suppliers of goods they couldn't afford by other means. There were the politics of it, too—this was a way to stand up to an unfair government that taxed goods beyond legitimacy. It was a way to stand up to greed, to a system sustained by standing on the backs of those who could least afford to support the weight, while the system ignored those in the most need: widows, children, orphans, broken men home from war and farmers who could no longer afford to farm. To Stepan, smuggling was protest. When the system changed, he would change.

Joseph shut the spyglass and handed it back. 'Shall we go down, milord?'

Stepan pulled a pouch of coins from his pocket. 'Make sure everyone who works tonight gets their share. I'll see you later.' He would ride down in a moment to meet the *Lady Frances* at the docks. While he was respectfully and publicly paying the duties on her cargo, the *Razboynik* would put in unnoticed to the quiet cove below the bluffs. Joseph Raleigh and the land crew would stow the vodka and small packets of spices in the caves. Then, they would spend the week preparing the vodka for transport from Shoreham to London, where Stepan had managed to make Kubanian food, drink and artefacts the latest rage. The women wanted their knickknacks, the men wanted their vodka.

It was a good arrangement, one that had increased his fortune and satisfied his need for adventure. The arrangement was neat, but not too neat. There was, after all, a margin for risk. Multiple aspects of his 'business' could be discovered at any time. The caves where he stored his treasure were not his own. They belonged to the estate of Preston Worth, whose wife, Beatrice, was a friend of Dimitri's wife. Worth and his family were not always in residence. The man's work took them to London a good part of the year as it did now and, when it did not, Worth was a civil prevention officer intent on ridding the coast of smugglers while one roosted in his very own nest. The irony of it appealed to Stepan nearly as much as the risk.

Preston wasn't the only threat. There was always the potential the coastguard would discover his illicit little enterprise. Little or large wouldn't matter to the King's men. The penalty for smuggling was still the same: hanging or, if one was lucky, transportation.

Not that Stepan worried about either overmuch. If anything, the penalty for discovery challenged him to be more creative. A good smuggler these days couldn't rely on simply outrunning the British as one might have done in the past. In the modern era, a good smuggler had to outsmart the soldiers. Thankfully, Stepan was very smart. His new casks with their secret compartments were proof of that. Even if the *Razboynik* had been stopped, he doubted the excise men would have found anything of concern.

Stepan turned from the bluff and strode to where his horse waited. They would ride to the docks and then the hour back to Little Westbury and the hospitality of Dimitri Petrovich. He didn't mind the long day in the saddle or even the rain. He had plenty to occupy his thoughts. He was already planning his next delivery. *That* ship was due next month and would require more thought than this one. The *Razboynik* was a practice run of sorts to try out the decoy and the new casks. The other ship, the *Skorost*, carried an enormous vodka cargo along with more spices and precious Russian saffron. The stakes were infinitely higher. Planning excursions kept his mind busy. It was better to think about how to land contraband than to think about other, less feasible things, like the unattainable Anna-Maria Petrova, Dimitri's vivacious sister.

There was nothing but disappointment and heartbreak down that road. If anything were to come of his fantasies in that direction, transportation and hanging would be the least of his worries. Dimitri would have him drawn and quartered, and that would be after Dimitri had him castrated. He'd always admired Dimitri's tenacity when it came to protecting his family. Stepan just never wanted that tenacity turned in his direction. He valued Dimitri's friendship too much, and well, to be frank, he valued certain parts of his anatomy, as well.

Stepan smiled ruefully and swung astride his horse. He had smuggling to soothe his agitated soul. It gave him purpose and a cause. It kept him out of the house a good part of the day and out of Anna-Maria's energetic orbit. For the sake of all parties concerned, he'd concluded long ago that Anna-Maria was a passion best indulged at a distance.

She saw him coming the moment he turned down the long drive towards the house. Hmmm. Where had he been this time? Anna-Maria stood carefully to the side of her gauzy white bedroom curtains where no one could see her and pondered her question. She'd made something of a study of Stepan in the long winter months he'd been with them in Little Westbury. It had begun as a way to pass the time until spring, until she could go to London and make her debut. She was nineteen and by rights she should have gone to London last year, but she'd been too new to British shores in her brother's opinion. This year, she could hardly wait. Finally, her life could begin. Anything would be more exciting than the country.

But until she could go to London, her brother's friend made an interesting enough subject. There was an air of mystery to his absences. He left mid-morning and returned late each evening just in time for dinner. Anna had entertained the notion of trying to rise with him in the mornings, but the earlier she rose, the earlier he rose, until he was leaving well before his usual mid-morning departures. She'd experimented with that variable for a week before she gave up trying to pace him.

She watched Stepan ride up the drive, so straight in the saddle, his hands and legs moving imperceptibly to guide the big horse. Stepan's riding was refined. He might not be a cavalry officer like Nikolay, but he rode just as well. She'd grown up watching him ride. Stepan, like the others, had always been in her life, just as her brother had. If her brother acted more like a father to her, his friends acted more like uncles. Nikolay, Illarion and Ruslan were the friendly sort of uncles. Affection came easy to them. They'd been the ones to pull her braids, to tease her, to tickle her and make her laugh. Stepan was more reserved, hardly ever indulging in horseplay even when she was younger. When she was growing up, Dimitri had explained in terms a six-year-old could understand that Stepan didn't know how to be part of a family. They had to teach him.

If so, Stepan still didn't know. He'd grown more reserved the last few years, more distant, not only emotionally, but now physically. He and the others had spent most of last year in London at her brother's town house. She'd missed all of them. Together, they'd been her family, but she'd missed Stepan most. Regardless of how stoic he was, she'd grown used to his presence. He was always there, a fixture she could count on, less mercurial than Illarion, more even-tempered than Nikolay. She'd been excited when Dimitri had told her Stepan was coming for the winter.

She thought she'd have Stepan all to herself for nearly four months! But when he'd arrived, he'd been more aloof than ever and had spent many of his days like this one—gone.

The realisation steeped the sense of mystery. What or who drew the stoic Stepan out into the cold and the rain? Below her on the drive, Stepan dismounted and gave the reins to her brother's groom. Anna smiled. That was her cue. She would greet him and ferret out his secrets; maybe she would even coax a smile from him. Out of all her brother's friends, Stepan smiled the least and worried the most.

Stepan stood in the entrance hall, unwrapping a muffler as she sailed down the stairs, all air and light teasing. 'Where have you been? Who have you seen?'

Stepan looked up. She'd startled him. 'Are you my mother now?' It was not an unkindly chiding, but it was still chiding. There was no mistaking that he *was* scolding her.

'Someone needs to be if you're going to be out all day and come home soaking wet.' She took hold of his muffler and finished unwrapping it. 'Shall I call for a bath?' She shook out the wet wool, droplets splattering the hardwood floor. Stepan peeled off his greatcoat, making it clear he didn't want any help. 'Where's Tate? Shouldn't this be the butler's job, Anna-Maria?'

'I beat him to it, and it's *Anna*, as I've told you before,' she reprimanded him with a smile that she knew made the most of the dimple to the right of her mouth. The few boys in Kuban she'd been allowed to meet had thought her smile was her best quality. She hoped the young gentlemen in London would, too.

Stepan didn't. Perhaps he didn't even notice it. 'Your name is Anna-Maria and has been since the day you were born.'

Anna shrugged and gave a toss of her dark curls. 'I prefer Anna, it sounds more English.'

He noticed *that*. His dark eyebrows winged upward at her reasoning. 'Why ever would you want to be *more* English?'

She put her hands on her hips and faced him squarely. 'Perhaps for the same reason you cut your hair.' In Kuban, he'd worn his hair longer like Nikolay and Illarion. They had kept theirs, but Stepan had cut his immediately upon arrival.

It had now grown to the point where he could pull it back as he did today.

'What would that reason be?' Stepan's grey eyes narrowed. He did not like being challenged or forced to reveal anything private.

'To fit in, of course,' she answered honestly. Then she grinned. 'And because it's more exciting. Anna-Maria is a nun's name. Anna is more sophisticated.' She pronounced it with a short *A—Ahnnah*. It sounded foreign, but not too foreign, she thought.

Stepan gave her censorious look. 'Being more exciting is hardly what your brother wishes for you.'

She made a face. She knew that all too well. Dimitri, well meaning as he was, would keep her hidden in the country for ever if he had his way.

Stepan made to move past her to the stairs, his wet greatcoat draped over one arm. 'If you will excuse me, I will go and clean up before supper.'

'No, I don't think so.' She stepped in front of him, her skirts brushing his leg. 'You're not going upstairs until I have a smile from you.' Did she imagine he stepped back? She pressed forward again, her hands playfully gripping the lapels of his jacket. 'I've decided, *you* must pay a toll,' she teased.

Stepan's jaw tightened. 'What might that be?'

She tried another smile. 'You must answer my question.'

'And if I don't answer?'

'Then I get to guess.'

'Very well, you may guess. Quickly, though, I don't want to catch a chill. A few minutes ago you were concerned about that.' He was impatient in his barely restrained intolerance.

Anna forged on. She wasn't oblivious. He was dismissing her, swatting her out of the way as if she were no more than an irritating fly. The sentiment sat poorly with her. She wanted to shock him into paying attention to her, to prove she wasn't an annoying fly. She said the most outrageous thing she could think of. 'Were you with your mistress?'

His grey eyes went flinty, his expression stern with reprimand as he removed her hands from his lapels. 'That is hardly a ladylike guess,' he scolded.

'I know you all had them in Kuban. I'm not a child,' she protested.

'I *know*,' Stepan growled. There was something dangerous in his tone as he made to move around her, but she was entrenched now. This had become about more than goading a smile from him. She would have his acknowledgment and she would have it now. Determined, she countered his move, blocking him at the foot of the stairs.

'You have to answer. Am I right?' she challenged, although a piece of her didn't want to be right.

'Where I was is *none* of your business and you're wrong. I *never* agreed to answering. That was your rule alone.' He moved again. This time she let him pass. She wasn't in a mood to play any more. Anna watched his departing back march up the stairs, shoulders as straight and as unyielding as ever. Her mind worked over its own answer. *Did* Stepan have a mistress? The others had taken lovers by the scores in Kuban. Their affairs had been legendary. She'd used to overhear them talking with Dimitri late at night when she was supposed to be tucked up in bed, safely out of earshot. None of them would have dared to mention anything of that nature to her directly. But Stepan? If he'd had a mistress, he'd kept it very quiet.

She preferred not having abject proof of such a liaison. Stepan was hers, had always been hers in a way the others had not. Any one of them would have fought for her, but it had been Stepan who had come for her the night they escaped. It had been Stepan who had taken her up before him on his big horse and wrapped his cloak and his arm about her and galloped off into the darkness. She had not been afraid. There was never a need to be afraid when Stepan was with her. He was her constant fixture, always there.

Anna wandered into the library. Not much had changed since Kuban in that regard. Stepan was with her still. The others had married and gone their own ways; Nikolay was in London with his riding school, Illarion and Dove still away on their never-ending honeymoon travels, and Ruslan was who-knew-where. She suspected Stepan knew, though. He was their unofficial *adahop*, their leader. He knew everything. She stared absently at the fire, her thoughts focused inward. It had not bothered her to lose the others. She'd been happy for them, she'd been swept up in their romances and their weddings. Her dashing 'uncles' deserved true love in the new lives they'd fashioned for themselves. But in all fairness, she didn't feel that charitable towards Stepan. She'd never thought about losing him that way, that one day he'd find someone.

It wasn't that she didn't want Stepan to marry and have a family of his own, it was simply that she'd never thought of him doing it, of leaving her. Perhaps he already had. Who did he see in London when he wasn't here with them? How did he spend his days? His nights? Did a pretty Englishwoman already hold his heart and his attentions? Anna wished she had not spoken those hasty words out loud on the stairs. They'd conjured up a host of new, unsettling thoughts and she couldn't stop thinking about their implication: one day Stepan *would* leave her.

Chapter Two

He should leave. It was the one thought Stepan returned to time and again over the excellent roast beef supper that night. He could rent a house of his own—perhaps he could even contact Preston Worth about renting his house with the caves beneath it in Shoreham. Wouldn't that be convenient, to smuggle vodka from a prevention officer's own home? The risk-taker in him rather liked the idea. But then, he'd be dining alone and these suppers at Dimitri's would disappear.

Stepan took another swallow of the wine, an exquisite, full-bodied burgundy, and surveyed the table. These were occasions he loved to hate or was it hated to love? Each night Dimitri and his wife, Evie, served a piece of paradise;

warmth and security presented in a delicious, hot meal and comfortable conversation with local guests. Every aspect of the meal was a reminder of what his life would lack without Dimitri. This was not a scene he could replicate on his own. He had no family other than the one Dimitri had adopted him into two decades and one year ago. Ever since he was ten, he'd basked in the borrowed light of Dimitri's familial glow. To walk away from that was no small thing, but neither was his sanity.

Tonight, dining with the Squire's family was no exception. Perhaps he even felt that glow more keenly given the direction of his thoughts. While there was a price for leaving, there was also a price for staying: watching Anna-Maria dazzle the table every night, constantly bracing himself for her sudden appearances like the one in the entrance hall today, a feminine ambush of smiles and silk coming down the stairs or popping into a room at any time, conjuring up reasons to spend hours a day away from the house, knowing that Anna-Maria was oblivious to all of it.

Stepan filled his glass again. Why shouldn't

she be oblivious? He was twelve years her senior. He'd known her since she was born. He'd seen her skin her knees. He'd seen her cry when her 'pet' frog of one day escaped from his jar. He'd even seen her as a stubborn six-year-old stamp her foot in a temper when Dimitri had refused to spoil her with a porcelain doll. He was privy to the best and the worst of her. He was like a brother to her, or perhaps an uncle just as Nikolay and the others were. Why should she even be aware of how he looked at her now?

Across the table, Anna-Maria was teasing the Squire's son. Tonight, she shone in a gown of cerulean blue, a simple crystal heart about her neck and her dark hair piled up high—something Evie was letting her practise this winter before going to London. The poor boy smiled and blushed, unable to take his eyes from the radiant creature talking to him and yet not knowing what to do with her.

Oh, mal'chik, Stepan thought, *you are in over your head. I have been with the most sophisticated women of the Kubanian court and I am barely afloat. She is captivating, vivacious, pas-*

sionate in her tempers... She is dangerous and she doesn't even know it.

As she had been today on the steps, her hands twisted into the lapels of his jacket, her body so close to his that he could feel the heat of her, the light brush of her breasts against him.

Anna-Maria might look upon him as an uncle or brother, but no uncle or brother would ever entertain such thoughts. Stepan took a long swallow of wine, which was getting better with each glass. His awareness of her shamed him. It made a hypocrite of him. He'd always thought of himself as forward-thinking. He'd been one of the first to protest the repressive and archaic laws in Kuban that compelled girls into arranged marriages at young ages without providing them a voice or a choice in the matter. He'd seen girls as young as fifteen wed to men in their fifties. He *did* reason with himself that this was hardly the same. At thirty-one, he was in his prime like many well-born Englishmen who waited until their thirties to marry and took brides ten to twelve years their junior. But that didn't make the situation more palatable to Stepan. He knew the general reasoning behind it: the younger the better when it came to producing the next heir and moulding an unformed mind. He refused to assess a woman's value in the same way he would a brood mare.

Even with these arguments, he hated himself for the attraction. He could not say when his feelings had changed, when he'd become aware of her in the way a man is aware of a woman he desires. He was doubly careful with her now, with Evie and Dimitri, too. What would they think if they knew? Dimitri wanted more for Anna-Maria than an exiled prince.

The Squire reached for the carafe at Dimitri's informal table—no hovering footmen here. Everyone served themselves. 'The wine is excellent, Petrovich. Wherever do you get it?'

Dimitri smiled and nodded towards Stepan. 'Stepan has a connection, a French vintner by the name of Archambeault who ships to him.'

Monsieur Archambeault was otherwise known as Ruslan Pisarev, former Kubanian revolutionary, now a happily married, soon-to-be owner of a small but profitable winery in Burgundy. Dimitri's eyes met his at the mention of their friend. Ruslan did not want to be found by the world, at least not by his real name. It was one of their secrets, one of the many things that had bound them together over the years. Stepan loved Dimitri as a brother. Dimitri had given him a family when he'd had none, sharing his own father with him, and hope when he'd had even less. Dimitri had given him a reason to seek out the freedom he claimed to want. Without Dimitri, all those things might have remained dreams only.

In return, he'd given Dimitri unquestioning loyalty, ushering the Petrovich family to safety in England and leaving behind the only life he knew—a life full of privilege but lacking in affection. Dimitri had given him so much. He could not repay his friend by coveting his sister, especially when he knew how much Dimitri had given up in the raising of her.

In theory, Stepan wanted all the best for her, too. At a distance, he could embrace the knowledge she was in London having a Season without having to experience it in person. He wouldn't have to witness her flirting with London's young beaux the way he had to watch her charm the Squire's son tonight. He wouldn't have to watch her dance in the arms of gentlemen with titles more legitimate than the honorific he bore. Yes, it would be best to leave. He wondered if he'd find the discipline to do it. After all, he'd simply be exchanging one type of hell for another, the only difference being that one hell held Anna-Maria in it and the other did not. It was hard to say which one was worse. Perhaps hell didn't have varying degrees, only varying interpretations.

There was brandy after the meal and the requisite half hour of polite conversation with the ladies after that while Anna-Maria played the pianoforte. All in all, it was a very satisfactory country evening, the sort that usually filled him with a soft contentment, a domestic denouement of sorts to the adventure of his days. But tonight, Stepan had little to contribute and he was glad to see the Squire's family go. Anna-Maria shut the door behind them shortly after ten, with a laughing farewell to the Squire's son and a promise to go riding as soon as the mud cleared. She turned, a beaming smile on her face, her dark eyes dancing with mirth.

'Be careful with him,' Stepan said sternly, too sternly. Part of him, the jealous part, wanted to wipe that smile off her face. 'You will overwhelm him with your boldness.'

'My boldness?' Anna-Maria challenged, turning the force of her smile on him. 'What are you suggesting, Stepan?' Indeed, what was he suggesting? That she was too easy with her favours? It was hardly what he intended.

'Nothing, only that he is young and inexperienced.'

'And I am, too,' Anna-Maria retorted. 'Much to my regret.' She shot a look at her brother. 'I can't even go out riding without an escort.'

'The country is a big place, Anna,' Dimitri answered wearily. This was an ongoing argument. Dimitri's gaze met his sister's in a timeless sibling staredown.

Evie intervened, linking an arm through the younger woman's. 'Anna, come and help me check on the baby one last time for the night.'

Stepan followed Dimitri's gaze up the stairs, watching the two women. Despite his exasperation with his sister, a soft smile played on Dimitri's face. How many times had that smile been followed by the words, 'there goes everything I love'?

Not tonight, however. Dimitri sighed. 'The sooner she gets to London, the better. Perhaps I should have sent her last year even though she'd only just arrived.'

Stepan shook his head, unwilling to let his friend second-guess himself. 'No, she needed time to adjust, we all did.'

'I just want her to make intelligent decisions. She's so vivacious that I worry...' Dimitri let another sigh communicate all the things he worried about: Anna-Maria running off with the first man who showed her any adventure, Anna-Maria falling in love with the first man to kiss her. Dimitri shrugged as if he could shake off the weight of that worry and fixed his attention on Stepan. 'You, my friend, were distracted tonight. Is the winter getting to you, too? The walls closing in? Just two months left and it will be better. We can go up to London. The change of scenery will have us appreciating Little Westbury within weeks.' Dimitri chuckled.

'Actually,' Stepan said, 'I was thinking about not going up to town with you at all. I was thinking I'd stay here, perhaps rent out Preston Worth's house at Shoreham for a few months.'

Dimitri looked surprised and disappointed. 'You'd miss Anna's debut. I am sure she's counting on you for a few waltzes.'

'She'll be surrounded by so many young men, she won't need me to dance attendance on her.' He smiled over the pain the realisation caused him. Like the others, she would be launched into a new life. He would be left completely behind.

'That's what I'm afraid of,' Dimitri argued with a laugh. He clamped a hand on Stepan's shoulder in fraternal camaraderie. 'She'll be surrounded by young fools like herself, champing at the bit for a taste of freedom in the big city. I was counting on you to be the voice of wisdom, to help her keep her head and navigate society with decorum.'

He'd only thought the country was torture. London would be a whole other level of private agony. Hell was proving to be a complicated place. 'We'll see,' Stepan said neutrally. He started up the stairs, but Dimitri wasn't done talking yet.

'How's business? I heard the *Lady Frances* came in today. I hope there wasn't trouble?'

Dimitri was still fishing for the reason behind his distraction.

Stepan shook his head. 'Everything was fine, just a lot of paperwork. Seems like there's more every time.'

Dimitri gave a snort. 'In this part of the world, people ignore the paperwork and smuggle it all in.' He grinned at Stepan. 'Maybe you should try it some time.'

Stepan gave a non-committal laugh. 'Maybe.' West Sussex was a known haven for smugglers with its access to London roads. One could hardly live here and not be aware of smuggling. But Dimitri had no idea how close to home his remark had hit. 'I'm not sure how Preston Worth would feel about a smuggler renting out his house.'

Dimitri shrugged at the supposed conflict of ethics. 'It would make winters in the country more interesting.'

Oh, it does, Stepan thought and continued up the stairs before the conversation went any further. Did Dimitri know? Was this his way of feeling out the subject? Stepan had tried very hard to keep the smuggling operation secret. If he was discovered, he alone would bear the consequences. He wanted none of his friends incriminated or used as leverage.

In his room, Stepan undressed and stretched out on the bed, planning his day. Tomorrow, he'd leave early and spend the day overseeing the unloading of the *Lady Frances*'s cargo at the harbour in Shoreham. Then, on the way home, he'd stop by the caves and see how the spirit distillation was getting on. That should keep him busy and out of the house and away from Anna-Maria until well after supper.

Chapter Three

Ledgers and lading papers might keep him out of the house, but they were not the most entertaining. Stepan pushed back from his desk at the dock warehouse and strode to the window, the room's one amenity. Below him, the pier was bustling, his men sweating in the cold air as they hauled trunks of cargo from the hold to the warehouse where it would wait for wagons to take it to London. He'd been at the ledgers for hours now. He flexed his cramped hand. His body was begging for physical activity. Perhaps he'd go down and help with the hauling. That would give his muscles something to do.

He'd just decided it when there was a soft, hesitant knock on his door. 'Come!' Stepan answered, watching the dark head of his clerk peer around the corner, still hesitant. Oliver Abernathy was a slim, timid young man, one of his rescued boys from London with a good head for numbers.

'There are gentlemen to see you, milord.'

Stepan glanced at the appointment diary lying open on his desk. 'They do not have an appointment.' Not that they needed one with Abernathy letting everyone who stopped by interrupt his work. The boy might be good with numbers, but he was a terrible gatekeeper.

'One is a military officer, milord,' Abernathy offered in protest as if being an officer came with the privilege to arrive unannounced.

There seemed no getting around it. By now, the gentlemen would have concluded he was indeed in. 'Very well, send them in.' Stepan surveyed the austere office. 'On second thought, I will come out.' He took a last wistful look out of the window. He would not be hauling cargo today. He straightened his coat and went to take care of business.

'Gentlemen! To what do I owe the pleasure of your visit?' Stepan strode out of the office, all smiles and bonhomie, taking each man's hand in turn with a firm grip. The one man in the blue coat of his station, Stepan knew: Carlton Turner, the customs officer. The other, dressed in a red coat, he did not. 'I don't think I've had the pleasure, Captain, is it?' Stepan said, taking in the man's uniform and noting the gorget. He noted other things, too, like the tight lines about the man's mouth, giving it a harsh quality that matched the dark eyes. This was not a kind man. Was the harshness simply from the rigors of military life or something else, deeper? Darker?

'Your Highness, may I introduce you to Captain Denning? Captain Denning, this is Prince Shevchenko, lately of Kuban. That's his ship you've been admiring this morning.' Turner made the necessary introductions. 'Your Highness, the captain has been assigned to Shoreham on business and I wanted him to meet some of the key importers he'll need to work with.'

Stepan did not miss Turner's deft positioning of the conversation and was immediately on alert. He didn't mind Carlton Turner. Turner was a stuffy man, always a stickler for protocol, but reasonable beneath the fussiness. Stepan knew how to deal with him. As long as things were shipshape on the surface, Turner didn't bother to probe deeper. But the man had been around a while; he knew the limitations of his authority. Captain Denning didn't give the first impression of sharing that understanding.

'I find business goes well with venison pie and ale this time of day,' Stepan offered with a gesture towards the door. 'May I invite you both to dine with me? It's just past noon and I'm famished. The tavern up the street isn't fancy, but the owner's wife is a good cook.' If circumstances were throwing him together with this Captain Denning, he needed to know more about this newcomer and decide if the captain posed a threat.

Food meant small talk and a chance to size one another up. Stepan kept the captain talking through the flaky venison pie. The man was from Derbyshire in the East Midlands, the younger son of a baron. He'd served against Napoleon in his late teens. But those were just facts. Context was everything and Turner was providing it.

Turner joined the conversation, clapping Denning on the shoulder. 'He was relentless, keeping his troops on the field and holding ground against all odds in Spain.' Turner's tone suggested the comment was meant as an accolade, but the sharp glint in his eye when he met Stepan's gaze suggested the remark was meant as more. A caution, perhaps? Until he knew otherwise, Stepan would take it as one. This was a man to whom the goal was all, the price of attaining the goal negligible.

Denning was ambitious and desperately so. Military work was slow these days with no war to fight. Consequently, advancement was, too. There was little opportunity to prove oneself, yet Denning held on to his commission when others had given up and sold out. Here was a tenacious, canny man who would stop at nothing to achieve his goal.

Stepan could have dealt with that. He understood officers, his friend Nikolay having been one in Kuban. But that was not the sum of Denning. The captain was more than determined. He was also cold. His determination sprang from ruthlessness, not relentlessness as Turner had couched it. The difference was there at the corners of his eyes where faint, early lines fanned out; there were lines, too, at the grooves at the sides of his mouth. This was an exacting man who drove those around him as hard as he drove himself. Perhaps an admirable quality in an officer on the battlefield, but a dangerous quality, as well.

Another round of ale came and the plates were cleared. 'Tell me how I can be of service to you, Captain.' Stepan gave permission for the conversation to move towards business now that they'd eaten.

'A complement of my men and I will be staying at the barracks on New Barn Lane in order to investigate reports of smuggling and act accordingly should anything be found.' Denning sat back on the bench, leaning against the wall with satisfaction. 'I hope you and the other upstanding importers in the area will join with us.' He gave a cold smile. 'It's hardly fair that you pay a legitimate tax on your goods when others do not. Everyone should be accountable to the same rules and I am here to enforce that accountability.'

Except when those taxes are unnecessarily high, Stepan thought.

What wasn't fair was the government placing high taxes on goods and making trade in them prohibitive to all but a small wealthy class who could afford the fees. That wasn't free trade in his mind. Trade, the right to do business and make a livelihood should be open to all, not just the prosperous. Outwardly, Stepan gave a cordial smile. There would be time enough to alienate the captain, he thought wryly. 'Enforce? That sounds like a very menacing word.' He'd lived under a Tsar who'd also used that word, to his detriment. That Tsar was now dead, shot on the front lawn of his palace by his constituents.

'Of course, compliance would be preferred,' Turner broke in. 'If you were to hear of anything, we'd want to know.'

Stepan gave a neutral smile, aware the captain was watching him. 'I'll help in any way I am able.' It was not entirely untrue. He would just not be very able.

Then the captain fired his real salvo. 'Good. If you see or hear of anything I should be aware of, send word to the barracks. I understand Shoreham is a popular landing point because of its access to the London roads. We will be redoubling land patrols, which I think is the best way to catch any activity, and we'll continue to coordinate with the navy to patrol the coastline from the water. With luck, we'll have the rotters cleared out by May.' *Enforce* indeed. The captain was only a step away from martial law.

'Best of luck with that, Captain,' Stepan replied in all honesty. 'Gentlemen, if you'll excuse me, I have ledgers calling my name.' He made the polite noises of leaving and maintained a sense of affability until he was back in his office. Only then did he let his thoughts run over all he'd learned. The captain had an unenviable task, not only for himself, but for the town, as well. Shoreham would not respond positively to the captain's methods.

Smuggling in Shoreham had existed for centuries. It was unlikely the captain was going to curb it in a couple months. But Derbyshire, further inland, wasn't known for its smuggling routes. What did a land man like Denning know about the culture of smuggling? To root out the 'rotters', as Denning put it, would require rooting out whole villages. But that didn't mean Denning's efforts could be disregarded. When Stepan met with Joseph Raleigh tonight at the caves, they had some planning to do along with their distilling. If Denning was going to impart information about his troop's movements, Stepan was certainly going to make good use of it. It was going to be a late night.

What in the world kept a man out this late when he'd already spent the entire day at the docks? The question haunted Anna-Maria with increasing intensity as the hours after supper dragged by. She'd tried to prompt some insight out of her brother as the family had relaxed by the fire, but if Dimitri knew anything, he was close-mouthed about it. Her father had merely glanced up from the newspapers after her third attempt and fixed her with a censorious stare. 'A man's business is his own. A woman respects his privacy,' he said in that scolding tone Anna-Maria knew too well. The man had spent his life reprimanding her when he bothered to notice her at all.

Evie had softened the harsh words with a

smile. 'Don't worry about Stepan, my dear. He knows his way home and so does his horse.'

Anna didn't bother to correct Evie's assumption, although it did make her feel a bit guilty. Truth be told, she was not as worried over Stepan's lateness as she was curious about the reason for it. If the others shared concern or curiosity about Stepan's prolonged absence tonight, they didn't show it. They gave up the vigil at half past nine, leaving Anna-Maria with her book.

It was well after eleven when Anna heard Stepan's horse in the drive. Hurriedly, she sat and picked up the book she'd laid aside an hour ago in favour of pacing the front parlour. Pacing kept her awake. If she read, she might fall asleep and miss his return, miss her chance to badger him about his whereabouts. And he would win. She would not give him the satisfaction of outlasting her.

Anna selected a random page in the middle of the text and pretended to read. This had become a competition when he hadn't come home for supper and Evie had held the meal for him, proof that she and Dimitri had not known he'd be so late despite their lack of concern over it. Anna gave her skirts a final fluff as footfalls sounded in the hall. She counted in her head: one, two, three steps until he'd pass the doorway to the sitting room. On cue, Anna lifted her head with slow surprise as if she was only just now aware of his presence. She managed a polite smile. 'Oh, you're home.'

Stepan leaned against the door frame, looking somewhat less stoic than usual. His hair was damp and tousled from night-riding, his greatcoat undone, and his eyes were…softer…instead of their usual hard granite. Tonight, they were like quicksilver moonbeams. 'You waited up for me, Anna-Maria.' He smiled. He never smiled unless provoked to it. And he smelled faintly of alcohol.

That's when she knew. 'Stepan Shevchenko, you're foxed!' Anna rose in chagrin. She'd waited up for him and he'd been out drinking and who knew what else!

'I wouldn't say "foxed" exactly, Anna-Maria. More like "a trifle disguised", as our friends the English would say,' He gave her a wide grin. 'I've been drinking with the customs officer and *his* friend, Captain Denning. You should see the shape I left *them* in.'

'Well, they didn't have an hour's ride in the dark,' Anna chided. But she was secretly mollified. He'd spent the day at Shoreham, doing paperwork regarding his shipment of Kubanian knick-knacks and drinking with customs officers. Still, it didn't explain where he went every day. 'I suppose this means you'll be at home tomorrow, then,' Anna said with sweet nonchalance. Ships didn't come in all the time and neither did paperwork. Surely he'd taken care of all those administrative loose ends today with the hours he'd put in.

'Oh, no.' Stepan pushed off the door frame. His body language said he was heading upstairs. Leaving her. 'I've got to arrange for the cargo to go to the London shops and the private buyers. I'll be busy for days yet. You'll be lucky to see me at dinner.'

Something inside her deflated. Dinner was more exciting when Stepan was there to talk politics with her brother and father. It diverted her father's attention away from her. 'Men have all the fun.' She pouted. 'I'm bored, too, you know. *I'd* like to get out of the house for hours.' An idea struck and she brightened. 'Take me with you. I have a fair hand. I can record items for you and I love seeing all the pretty things that come in.'

Stepan shook his head. 'The docks are no place for a young lady. Dimitri and your father would never allow it, especially with your debut coming up so soon. Besides, you can look at the pretty things right here at home.' He reached inside his coat pocket and brought out a brown paper–wrapped package.

She took the package with delight. For a moment, she forgot to be mad at him. 'For me?' She unwrapped it and lifted out the small trifle box with its carefully painted lid. It was done in ice blues and lavenders, depicting a snowy Russian lake scene. She smiled. 'It reminds me of the lake at our winter home.' She seldom thought of Kuban fondly. Her life there had been…mixed, not all of it pleasant. There were plenty of bad memories to go with the good. But most of the good memories centred on the Petrovich winter estate. She put the box down on a side table and looked up at Stepan. He was so very tall up close. 'Do you remember the ice-skating parties? How we would drink hot chocolate from the samovar on the lake bank? The deer that would come down to the edge of the ice?' In her enthusiasm, she reached for Stepan's hands and drew him out to the centre of the room with her. 'Do you remember how you used to spin me?'

She was twirling now, taking him with her in her whirlwind of a circle. 'We'd lean outwards and throw our heads to the sky as we spun!' Anna laughed, tossing her head back.

'Hush, Anna! You'll wake the house,' Stepan scolded, tugging at his hands. She let go, her smile fading.

'You used to be more fun, Stepan. At least slightly. I wouldn't go as far as to say you've ever been a load of fun.' She could scold, too.

'We all used to be a lot of things.' Stepan bent his dark head in a stern, deferential nod, part reprimand, part apology. 'I beg your pardon. It was not my intention to ruin your fun. Goodnight, Anna-Maria.' He squared his shoulders and walked past her, out of the room.

Anna stomped her foot on the carpet where no one could hear. She hated when she did that, when she drove him off in her stubbornness because she had to have the last word. She spied the box and snatched it up. 'Stepan,' she called softly, stopping him on the stairs. She waited until he turned and she had his full attention. 'Thank you for the gift, it's lovely. I'm sorry.' She wanted to say more. She was sorry for running him off, for always challenging him. 'I don't know why I do it,' she lied. She knew. She did it to needle him, to jar him out of his stoic reserve in hopes of seeing what lay beneath all of that, although why it should matter so much to her, she didn't know.

Stepan nodded. 'It's nothing more than winter megrims, Anna-Maria. We've all been indoors too long.'

Not you, she wanted to argue, but she caught herself in time. Arguing would get her nothing. 'You're sure I can't come with you tomorrow? Father and Dimitri won't mind if they know you're there to protect me.' She didn't think that was entirely true, but Stepan could persuade them if he wanted to.

That was the problem. He didn't want to. He all but ignored her request, his voice quiet and strict as he continued up the stairs. 'I don't think it's a good idea, Anna-Maria.' So much for getting him out of his stoic reserve.

Anna crossed her arms. Fine. She'd come up with a better idea, anyway. He hadn't said she couldn't come, just that she couldn't go *with* him. He'd said nothing about following along behind. A plan took shape. It would be easy enough to do. Evie and Dimitri were taking the baby over to Claire and Jonathon Lashley's for a day of visiting. Her father was going along, too. They would leave in the morning. She'd have the day to herself. It would be the perfect opportunity for a little unsupervised adventure.

At least it would have been, if Stepan was actually where he'd said he'd be, Anna reflected sourly late the next morning. She was damp and cold after a rather soggy ride to the Shoreham docks, only to discover Stepan was not there. No one, apparently, had seen him yet and no one was expecting to. She stood in the shipping offices, shaking droplets from her wool riding habit and feeling foolish while she gathered her thoughts. She needed a contingency. She was reluctant to simply turn around and go home. She didn't relish the thought of another hour of riding in the drizzle, but neither could she simply go on standing in the middle of the offices while Stepan's clerk pitied her, his thoughts written plainly on his homely face about the sort of woman who came to the docks alone. It was embarrassing, really.

Anna was regretting her inability to follow Stepan directly. She'd not been able to leave when he'd left—which had been at sun-up. But she'd thought nothing of it at the time. He was going to the docks. She could simply follow later after Evie and Dimitri had left. But now, she had no idea where he was. She looked about the little waiting room. There wasn't much, just a stove, a chair, the counter where the clerk worked, guarding the door to Stepan's private office, and a loudly ticking wall clock. She flashed the clerk a smile. 'I'll wait a bit, if you don't mind?' It wasn't really a question. She pulled the chair towards the stove. She could warm up and, with luck, Stepan would come striding through the door at any moment.

The heat felt good as she ran through possible

explanations as to why Stepan wasn't here yet even though he'd had a three-hour head start. Perhaps he'd had a delivery to make? Perhaps it was nothing so benign. Perhaps his horse had thrown a shoe and he was holed up at a smithy somewhere along the road. Even worse, maybe he'd gone home and even now was sitting comfortably in front of the fire, warm and dry. There was some irony in that, while she was cold and cross and still faced an hour's ride home. Or perhaps he'd not told her the truth last night. He'd never intended to come to the docks today. The latter was seeming more likely as the minutes ticked by.

When she'd been there the better part of an hour, she had to admit he wasn't coming. It did pique her curiosity, though. If he wasn't here, where had he gone and why couldn't he tell her about it?

She rose and the clerk eyed her from his ledgers with wary suspicion.

'Could you possibly check his schedule diary? Perhaps I could meet him at whatever appointment he has?' Anna asked sweetly, dazzling him with a smile that made the poor clerk blush.

He cleared his throat. 'Mister Shevchenko is a private man, miss. I do not keep his calendar for him.' There was a polite reprimand for her nosiness.

Would tears work? Anna wondered. They used to work a charm on Dimitri. They'd never worked on her father. 'It's just that I've ridden so far,' she dissembled, looking down at her hands. 'I would hate to turn back without seeing him.'

'Oh, now, miss, don't cry!' The clerk sounded genuinely horrified. 'Perhaps I could take a peep at his calendar, after all.' He bustled away and returned shortly, wringing his hands. Bad news, then, Anna thought. 'I am sorry, miss, there are no appointments in his diary today. As I said before, we are not expecting him.'

No appointments he wanted any record of, at any rate. Now she really did have to leave, there was no point in delaying. A glance out the window affirmed the drizzle had stopped. If she was lucky, the ride home would only be cold, but she had plenty to think about. Stepan had a secret. Was it a secret lover as she'd rashly guessed? Or something else? A little smile played on her lips as she walked back to her horse. Whatever Stepan was hiding, he didn't want anyone knowing about it. Except that now, someone did know and that someone was her. For once, *she* had some leverage on *him*.

Chapter Four

'You lied.'

Stepan stopped in his tired, muddy tracks, the words cutting through the preoccupation of his thoughts. A lamp flared to life in the front parlour revealing Anna-Maria bent over the flame as she replaced the glass chimney, affirmation that he had not escaped. When he'd ridden up, the house had been dark and he'd known a moment's relief. He wouldn't have to face her, wouldn't have to disappoint her, wouldn't have to be tempted by her. Last night had been rather disastrous, in that regard. On top of the ale he'd drunk at lunch with the officers there had been the vodka sampling he'd done in caves when he'd visited the boys, all of which had induced him to sentimentality. He'd given her that silly box. Her eyes had gone soft and his body had gone hard.

'What, per se, have I lied about?' It was late, later than it had been last night. She should be abed, yet if he was honest there'd been disappointment mixed with his relief when he'd seen the dark house. A perverse part of him *liked* sparring with her. It was all he could have of her, this rather odd guilty pleasure.

She came towards him. 'You lied about where you were today.' She paused, letting her eyes rake his appearance. 'You were not at the shipping office. In fact, Mr Abernathy informed me you had never planned to be there today. Your appointment diary was empty.' She crossed her arms over her chest, her eyes blazing with grim satisfaction. She was waiting for his rebuttal. More than that, she was waiting for his explanation.

But she'd left herself open to a rather healthy counter-offensive. Stepan arched his eyebrow. 'You went into Shoreham alone after I warned you about the docks last night?' There was so much to be appalled with he wasn't sure where to start. Did he start with the fact she'd 'followed' him when that could have exposed the entire operation? Or that she'd taken such a risk in travelling alone? That Abernathy had gone into his office and looked in his diary? He'd thought his young clerk was above reproach. 'What did you bribe Abernathy with to sneak into my office?' Stepan asked. 'I'll have to have words with him, perhaps dock his pay so that he learns his lesson.'

'No!' Anna cried. 'It wasn't his fault,' she begged.

'Oh? What exactly compelled him to look in his employer's diary?' Abernathy knew better. 'You didn't offer him money, did you?' Stepan hoped not. If Abernathy could be bribed, it boded ill for the whole scheme. He would have to let the young man go.

A vice tightened in his chest. *Please don't let it have been for money.* He didn't want to believe he couldn't take the street out of the boys.

'No.' Anna-Maria shook her head. 'I have no money, you know that.' He heard the resentment in her voice. Money meant freedom. He knew it better than anyone. 'I just...' She looked away from his stern gaze.

'You just what?' Stepan pressed, the vice in his chest easing a bit. He'd still have to talk to Abernathy about this breach, especially with Captain Denning in town. They couldn't afford traitors, even small ones.

'I smiled at him a bit. When that didn't work, I sat in the waiting room for an hour hoping you'd come in.' Anna-Maria bit her lip and gave a relenting sigh. 'Then I got impatient. I might have used tears,' she admitted with a quick rejoinder, 'but it's *your* fault. I never would have needed to do it if you'd been there in the first place. *You* told me you were doing accounts.' She was tenacious in her anger. Heaven help a husband if he ever ran afoul of her.

At least it had taken Abernathy an hour to succumb. That did say something about the boy's resolution. 'Since when do I answer to you, miss, about my whereabouts?'

She gave him a long look that swept him from head to toe and lingered on his boots. 'Since you can't admit where you've been and come home with wet sand on your boots.' Her gaze caught his. 'That's not the mud of Little Westbury.' She stepped close to him, too close. He could smell the scents of lemon and lavender on her and she could smell him. She reached up on her tiptoes and sniffed near his ear. 'Wind and salt, Stepan? If I didn't know better, I'd think you'd been to the seashore.'

She cocked her head, her sharp mind assimilating the information. 'You *were* in Shoreham today, just not at the office,' she accused with an authority that rivalled a barrister, 'which leads me to conclude you were indeed with a woman.' Anna-Maria gave a toss of her head. 'You're having an affair.'

'It is not your business, Anna-Maria,' Stepan warned. Did the minx not know when to stop? No gently bred young girl called out an older man on his private affairs. No gently bred girl was supposed to know about such things and, if she did, she was to pretend she did not. But Anna-Maria was all dark-haired defiance as she stood with her hands on her hips, her eyes flashing. He'd have liked to scold her and say defiance did not become her, but it did. She was magnificent in her accusations and he was a powder keg primed to explode after three and a half months under the same roof with her. A woman could not provoke a man thusly without consequences.

He stalked her, encroaching on her space as she did his, making her aware of him with every step, of his height, of the piercing intensity of his gaze. There would be gentlemen in London who would make her aware of much more if she wasn't careful.

Anna-Maria took a step backwards, her eyes glinting, but wary now. Good. She should be wary. A man aroused was a dangerous creature. Her back was to the wall and she could retreat no further. Stepan rested an arm above her head, his gaze intent on her face. 'This is what you wanted, isn't it? To jar me out of what you call my complacency? To break my stoic reserve?' His eyes lingered on her mouth, 'Well, now you've done it, my sweet girl, and there is a price to pay for waking the sleeping dog.' Anna-Maria's gaze dropped. 'Are you prepared to pay it?' He would be toyed with no longer.

He captured her mouth in a hard kiss meant to demonstrate his point, but Anna-Maria wasn't ready to admit defeat. Her mouth moved beneath his, opening in answer to his press. Her body moved against his. He intensified the kiss, his hand at her neck, keeping her close, as he claimed deep access to her mouth, his tongue testing and tasting her. What a heady elixir it was to drink of her naïve boldness, the innocent curiosity waking in his arms.

He had not expected it to go this far. He'd expected her to be frightened long before his body roused, but her curiosity was fast outpacing his ability to keep his body in check. Soon, the masculine hardness of his response would be in evidence. Perhaps it would be for the best that she encounter all the consequences of her behaviour. This was not a harmless game she played. She gave a sudden gasp. The moment he felt her hesitate, he stopped. He pulled back from their embrace, creating much-needed space between them.

Her eyes were wild and questioning, her hair had come down from its pins and her lips were puffy. She looked precisely like what she was: a beautiful woman halfway seduced. If Dimitri were to walk in at this moment there would be no explanation other than the truth: that he'd kissed Anna-Maria up against the sitting-room wall. Never mind he'd felt prompted to do so after months of provocation or that he'd done it out of some misguided notion of teaching her the finer points of dealing with gentlemen. Stepan didn't think those arguments would go far with Dimitri.

Anna-Maria smoothed her hands over her skirt. He gave her time to gather her shaken composure. That was his second mistake. The first had been giving in to her game. He saw that now. Whatever advantage he might have gained in his ambush was lost when she raised her head and met his gaze. 'Why did you do that? What did you think to prove?'

He should have pressed his advantage when he'd had the chance. 'You've been flirting with me.' He waved a hand when she tried to protest. 'Admit it, Anna-Maria, you've been cutting your teeth on me all winter and why not?' Stepan growled. 'There's very little appropriate male society to practise on in these parts.' He was rewarded with a slight flush creeping up her cheeks. The little minx didn't like being caught out. 'Be warned, Anna-Maria, I am no green ham-handed boy like the Squire's son, willing to be led about by the nose because a pretty girl smiled my way. Neither am I a dissipated gentleman with finer clothes than manners who would not have stopped this evening.'

Her eyes narrowed. 'Is this your way of saying I should be thanking you for the experience?' She was far too saucy for a girl who'd just been delivered her comeuppance.

'It's my way of alerting you to the lesson that desire is power—a sword to be wielded, a currency that can be bartered by any man or woman. Be careful, Anna-Maria, you are a beautiful woman and a susceptible one. You are not fully aware of the weapon you possess in your face alone.' To say nothing of her body, of the passion that coursed through her.

Stepan's hands fisted at his sides. He was deuced uncomfortable with the direction of this conversation. This was why young girls needed their mothers. Mothers were supposed to teach those lessons, not nominal uncles. Least of all him. What did he know of family? Of mothers and daughters and preparation for marriage? He knew nothing even of fathers and sons. His own father had decided he wasn't worth raising well before he'd reached adulthood.

Anna-Maria gave him a wry smile. 'I think

there might be a compliment in there somewhere for me. I will pretend there is. I will pretend you called me beautiful and that my beauty wasn't an insult or a plague to be protected against as my father suggests.' She laughed harshly. 'Would you prefer it if I went around veiled so that I would not be a Jezebel enticing men to their doom?'

'I was being honest.' Which, apparently, he couldn't be without having his words come back to haunt him. He'd not meant to imply she was to blame for a lack of male self-control. Nor had he meant to align himself with the cruel opinions of her father. He owed the old man a debt of gratitude. The man had been nothing but gracious to him, treating him as a second son, yet Stepan could not condone the way the man treated his daughter. He'd had the nagging suspicion over the years that if Anna had been born male her mother's death would have been forgiven.

'I thought we'd left such old-fashioned nonsense behind us in Kuban,' Anna-Maria argued. 'I thought you believed a woman should have the same freedoms in society a man had?'

'I do,' Stepan protested.

'Unless that woman is me?' She pierced him with a stare. He knew impending defeat when he heard it. He wasn't going to win this.

'You should talk to Evie about these things.' He stepped back, looking to retreat the field.

'Evie doesn't know about "these things",' Anna-Maria snapped. 'How could she? She has two parents who raised her. She's lived the entirety of her life in Little Westbury surrounded by safety and love. Her parents saw to it, her friends saw to it and now my brother sees to it. Their child will grow up with the same.'

'Lower your voice,' Stepan cautioned. 'You'll wake the house.' The warning was inadequate and frankly a non sequitur. He chose not to address the wistful envy behind her words. It was an envy he knew well. How many times had he held Dimitri's infant son and thought the same? Dimitri's boy would grow up never knowing a lack of affection, never doubting his worth, his acceptance.

Anna-Maria did not heed his request. She was angry now and she was exacting revenge for his madness over the kiss. 'Evie is not like us. She knows nothing of being raised without parents, without a family, of being looked upon as an inconvenient nuisance by one's own father.'

'You had Dimitri,' Stepan reminded her. He would not tolerate his friend being maligned. At twelve, Dimitri had taken on the responsibility of caring for a newborn and he'd never laid down that burden. Nor did he like the reminder of those painful similarities between them.

'But for the single variable of my brother, both of us would have been entirely alone,' Anna-Maria said sharply. 'Why won't you admit that we're more alike than the others? That we're both lost souls, surrounded by people who have found theirs.'

'You are not lost, Anna-Maria,' Stepan countered argumentatively even as the words caught him by surprise. Was that how she saw herself? He'd not once thought the vivacious Anna-Maria, the beloved centre of her brother's life, a girl who had everything, felt lost. The very image of Anna-Maria being lost cut at him. He and the others had joined Dimitri in that fight years ago to protect Anna-Maria from the cruelties of their world, from the hurt of a father who did not acknowledge her existence because her life had stolen the life of the woman he loved. For her to feel lost implied their efforts had been for naught, that the fight had been lost along with her—a fight for which Stepan had fought harder than the others because he knew first-hand what awaited her if they were not victorious. He had a twelve-year head start on her. He already knew what it was to grow up empty, passed from nanny to nanny, tutor to tutor, valet to valet, growing up with the trappings of wealth and physical security, but not real security—the security of knowing one had love and a family and a place where one would always belong.

'Don't be a selfish bore, Stepan. You're not the only one who gets to be lost.' Anna-Maria huffed and pushed past him. 'It's late and I'm going to bed. You can stay down here and wallow in your "lostness" or whatever else it is you spend your time doing.'

He wanted to shout after her that if he was staying up it was her fault. He'd planned to come home and seek his own bed, but she'd been lying in wait, baiting him. His honour would not allow her to bear all the blame for his detour. A real gentleman accepted his own complicity in such things. He was as much to blame for his own wakefulness as she was. He'd been fighting the urge to kiss her for weeks. Tonight had supplied an exigence and an excuse for his behaviour. Now, that kiss would always be between them.

Stepan helped himself to brandy in a decanter at the sideboard and poked the fire Anna-Maria had forgotten to bank. He took a chair and rested his boots on the fender of the fireplace. Tonight's incident and yesterday's meeting with Captain Denning were further proof he needed to move out. Leasing Preston Worth's home in Shoreham was looking like a better option by the minute. He'd sent a message to London two days ago after he'd mentioned the idea to Dimitri. With luck, he might hear back tomorrow. Distance wouldn't erase the kiss, but distance could mitigate it.

Stepan sighed and took a long swallow. Even brandy couldn't sweeten the taste of regret. He should not have done it. He'd kissed his best friend's sister! What the hell was wrong with him? Yet in those moments, she'd not been Dimitri's sister, but a woman of her own identity and free will. She'd kissed him back with a wildness that matched his own. Perhaps that was the real source of his guilt. He ought to fully regret what he'd done and he didn't. There. He admitted it. He did not *entirely* regret it.

With any other woman, he'd be asking himself the question of what next? Now that they'd opened negotiations, so to speak, what was his next overture? But this was Anna-Maria. She was not one of Kuban's sophisticated women of the court. The question of what next was moot. There was no 'what next' beyond moving to Seacrest, moving away from her and the temptation that there might be another kiss, that he might be tempted to create a 'what next' scenario. One kiss could change everything, but only if he let it. He wouldn't let it.

He drained his glass, his conscience mocking him.

You could kiss her a thousand times and it wouldn't change a thing. You have nothing to offer her. She is love and light. What do you know of those things? She'll want a family once her wildness settles. How can you expect to be a better father than your own when you have nothing to go on? She'll want you mind, body and soul until she realises how dark those places are, that you can't be saved. Then the regret will be all hers. You can only disappoint a woman like Anna-Maria—a woman who wants more than your meaningless title, your ill-gotten wealth and a few nights of pleasure from a man who isn't capable of anything more.

For all those reasons, and for other reasons like his loyalty to Dimitri, he needed to leave. Tomorrow would be nothing short of torture. It would be full of waiting, and it was unfortunately imperative he do that waiting here: waiting for the letter from Preston; waiting to hear word from Joseph Raleigh that the ankers of vodka were ready to move to London. He would do better to worry about those ankers than Anna-Maria.

Denning's men were still arriving, still settling in. Major routes would be watched first. It was too bad Denning couldn't have waited another month to establish his diligence. Stepan would have preferred the *Skorost* coming in without the coastguard and the army on alert, but at least it would give him something to think about. Tomorrow, he could keep his mind busy planning how to handle his ship's arrival.

* * *

The morning got off to a decent start. He'd been able to bury himself in Dimitri's study, but Evie had other plans for his afternoon. After lunch, she cornered him into partnering Anna-Maria for dancing lessons in the front parlour, saying simply, 'you're the best at the waltz.' Now, all the furniture was pushed back and Evie sat ready at the pianoforte. She smiled at Stepan. 'It will be all the rage in London. Anna needs practice.'

'She should dance with Dimitri, then. He's a fine waltzer,' Stepan tried to demure, casting a raised-eyebrow plea in Dimitri's direction where he sat on the sofa pushed against the wall and played with the baby.

Dimitri looked up with a grin, his finger caught in the baby's tiny grip. 'I'm busy, as you can see. Besides, I'm not sure sisters and brothers want to waltz together.' He made a face. Anna-Maria laughed. But Stepan did not. He didn't find the allusion to the less platonic aspects of the waltz funny in the least given what had transpired in this very room last night. It went without saying that those elements of the dance would be on his mind today.

Anna-Maria swept forward, mischief in her eye as she took his hands and tugged him to the centre of the room. 'Of course he'll do it. Stepan thinks lessons are very important, don't you, Stepan?' Her eyes flashed, agate and sharp. She was still exacting revenge for last night. She put her hand at his shoulder and held her other one up. 'Now, where does this hand go, exactly?'

Stepan made a low growl and grabbed her hand. 'In mine, like this.' She moved close against him and he readjusted her away from his body, flashing her a dangerous stare. 'There must be space between us or the matrons at Almack's will never give you vouchers. Remember, when you waltz, more than your dress and your dancing ability are on display. Your morals are on display, as well.' He sounded like a prig. He liked to waltz, loved the feeling of flying. But he could not afford such a luxury with Anna-Maria in his arms. It would tempt him too far.

She pouted. 'What's the fun in that, then? I thought the waltz was *supposed* to be scandalous. You make it sound like a nun's dance.' Stepan threw another look at Dimitri, hoping his friend might have changed his mind about helping. Dimitri only shrugged and jostled the baby, tapping his toe as Evie began to play.

The fates were toying with him. This was what he deserved for last night: an afternoon in hell, waltzing Anna-Maria and her pointed remarks around the front parlour as his best friend watched, oblivious to his agony. It would have been better if Anna-Maria had been a horrid dancer, if she'd stepped on his toes or tripped on her hem. It would have been better still if holding her in the dance didn't trigger memories of holding her last night, if every time he passed *the wall*, he didn't think of what they'd done there. Last night might very well have ruined this room for him for ever. Anna-Maria's secret smile every time they sailed past said she knew it, too.

Salvation came in the form of Tate bearing the post far too late into the afternoon to make a difference. The damage of dancing was done. Anna-Maria was looking flushed with victory as they came to a whirling halt. 'A note for you, milord,' He passed the salver to Dimitri and then to him. 'And one for you as well, milord Stepan.'

Stepan broke it open—it was from London. He scanned it quickly, a smile taking his face.

Anna-Maria was on tiptoes looking over his shoulder. He shifted the paper away while Dimitri scolded, 'Anna! Let the poor man have his privacy.'

'Why? It's clearly good news,' Anna-Maria teased with a smile directed at Stepan.

'It *is* good news.' Stepan announced to them all, 'Preston Worth has written. I am able to lease his house in Shoreham until August. Effective immediately.'

'August!' Anna-Maria cried in disbelief. 'You don't even need a house for that long. You have to be in London for my debut.'

'I am afraid business will keep me from the Season this year,' Stepan said truthfully. With Captain Denning in town, he could hardly leave the boys unchaperoned and unprotected.

Anna-Maria looked at him, stormy eyes condemning his decision. He felt like a cad. His relief was coming at her expense. 'Come now, my dear, there will be hundreds of young men to dance with you. I will not be missed, you'll see.' He glanced out the window, gauging the remnants of daylight. There was an hour or two left. He could make Shoreham before too much darkness had settled in if he left soon.

'No, I won't hear of it.' Evie left her spot at the pianoforte, guessing at his plans before he spoke them. 'You are not leaving tonight. We will have a farewell dinner and you can set out in the morning. It's only fair to the servants at Seacrest who likely just got word of your coming today. They need time to put their best foot forward. They can't have a prince descending on them without notice.'

Evie was right, of course. It wasn't fair. Stepan relented. He'd endured this long; he could endure one more night. He smiled at Evie. 'One last night of your hospitality, then, before I am out from underfoot and you can get your lives back to normal. No doubt I've overstayed my welcome.'

Evie stood on tiptoe to reach his cheek with an affectionate kiss. 'Never, Stepan. All of Dimitri's friends are welcome here for as long as they like.' But not all of Dimitri's friends were infatuated with his sister. Stepan suspected that would change his welcome drastically if Dimitri knew.

Chapter Five

Anna-Maria poked at her peas, pushing them around the plate. The first day after Stepan left had been bad. Things had gone downhill since then. The house was too quiet. There were no sudden openings of the front door due to an unannounced return from parts unknown, no chance of catching sight of him riding down the drive, so straight, so irritatingly perfect, no energising spats to look forward to. Worst of all, there were no bone-jarring kisses. She'd done nothing but think about that kiss since he'd ridden out. It had been wild and arousing in ways unlooked for and it had been her first. Did he realise that? Had that played a part in how quickly he'd departed? Had his leaving been her fault? Had she pushed him to it as certainly as she was pushing her peas now?

A fork clattered against china from across the table. 'Damn it, girl, will you stop sulking and eat your dinner?' Her father glowered. Anna-Maria gave her peas another shove just to be perverse.

'You'll hardly catch a husband with manners like that.' Her father huffed. 'You'll shame us all in London.'

'I don't want to catch a husband, not right away at any rate.' Anna-Maria tossed her head and slid a defiant glance in Dimitri's direction. 'I want to dance until dawn and drink champagne. I want to live a little bit. Besides, who cares if I push my peas around tonight, there's no one to see, there's no entertainment for miles. I've been stuck out in the middle of nowhere...' She bit her lip as Evie looked down at her plate. She'd gone too far with her remark. Little Westbury was Evie's home, her parents were here, her friends and her husband's work. Evie had never made her feel anything but welcome.

Her father pointed his spoon at her. 'You are an ungrateful wretch,' he said, 'all the sacrifices that have been made for you—'

'Father, that's enough,' Dimitri broke in, soft-voiced but stern with the authority of the head of the household. Always, he had been the peace-maker. No wonder he and Evie were so well suited. Evie was a peacemaker, too. Not like her. Sometimes, Anna-Maria thought she required drama to make life interesting. Not for the first time, she wished she were a little more like her brother who thrived in the seclusion of country life.

'I am sorry, Evie. I didn't mean…' Anna-Maria apologised.

Evie dismissed her efforts with a polite shake of her head. 'No offence taken. You are young and vivacious, it's only natural you'd want to surround yourself with activity.' Evie glanced at Dimitri. 'We could all use an outing. Why don't we plan something? Maybe a day with Liam and May before they go back to town?'

Anna-Maria liked May, she was one of Evie's more scandalous friends, having had a mad af-fair with her husband before they married. May had, in fact, been younger than Anna was now when it had occurred. But, a day spent talk-ing about babies wasn't exactly the sort of out-ing Anna had in mind. She wet her lips, a plan forming. 'Why don't we go to Shoreham and see how Stepan is settling in?' Anna looked over at Evie. 'We could take him some of Cook's bread and the lemon biscuits he likes so much and we could advise him on the house. He doesn't have anyone to help him run such a large place. The servants will run roughshod over him,' she argued shamelessly. There was nothing Evie liked as much as rectifying a domestic crisis.

'I don't know.' Dimitri seemed dubious. 'It's a long way for the baby,'

'It's only an hour, maybe two, by carriage, but your carriage is equipped with every luxury,' Anna argued. 'We'll all take turns holding the baby and he'll sleep most of the way.'

'That settles it.' Evie decided the issue with a smile at Dimitri. 'We'll go and see how Stepan is getting on.' She rose. 'Anna and I will go and talk about what to take with us, while you two enjoy your after-dinner port.' She beamed at her father-in-law as if he hadn't tried to disrupt her dinner with a fight.

'You are too generous with him,' Anna chided once they were alone in the sitting room. Evie had the baby at her feet and her ever-present needlework in her hands—the perfect picture of domestic bliss.

'Nonsense. He is a broken man. He has suffered much in his lifetime and he deserves our consolation.' Evie flashed her a brief smile as she threaded her needle. 'As do you, my dear. He has suffered, but how he treats you is inexcusable. Dimitri and I are both aware of it.'

'I killed the woman he loved.' Anna-Maria shrugged as if the fact meant nothing to her. She should be immune to it by now. After nineteen years of hearing the story, of being reminded her mother died giving birth to her, it shouldn't affect her.

'You were a baby. You had no control over that.' Evie bit off the thread and gave her a considering glance. 'You're missing Stepan.'

'As we all are.' Anna fussed with her own stitching, a simple handkerchief. The house seemed empty without him. Even being absent so much, he'd managed to stamp the house with his presence. His coat was gone from where it usually hung on the hooks by the front door. Dimitri's boots looked forlorn where they stood alone without Stepan's beside them. Anna had slipped into his room, thinking it would help her loneliness. It hadn't. The room he'd occupied looked positively sterile now that he'd gone, the bedcovers pristine and unwrinkled, the bureau uncluttered by personal effects. It was as if he'd never been there at all.

Evie gave her a sharp look when she was too silent too long. 'Are you certain this trip to Shoreham is only about helping him set up house?'

Anna's hand stilled. Evie went on. 'I watched you waltzing with him the other day.' Anna froze completely. The other day. The day after *the* kiss. What had Evie divined? What was there *to* see? That somehow, at some time, her relationship to Stepan had taken on an edge that she could hardly define? 'Are you sure your request doesn't have anything to do with the New Barn barracks being full again?' She gave Anna a conspiratorial wink. 'Dimitri tells me a Captain Denning has come to Shoreham with a company of men to catch smugglers. There will be assemblies and plenty of men to dance with while the countryside waits for spring.' Evie cocked her head. 'Perhaps they would be more interesting to practise on than the Squire's son before London? Consider it a trial run.'

Anna smiled in relief and grabbed at Evie's line of reasoning. 'The garrison does have its own appeal.' It wasn't the only appeal, however, but she could hardly give voice to those other reasons. She could hardly explain them to herself, not when so much suddenly lay unresolved between her and Stepan. With a single kiss, the world had upended itself. She only knew that she wanted to be near Stepan, whether he needed her or not. Where that need had sprung from she wasn't sure. The kiss had done more than jar him out of his complacency. It had somehow jarred her out of hers—a complacency that had been content to study him through windowpanes and at the distance of a dinner table, a complacency that was content to needle him. Now that she'd got a response, she was no longer content in mere needling. The rock had been turned over and instead of solving the intrigue, it had merely increased it.

Evie leaned forward. 'I'll see if I can persuade Dimitri to let you stay on in Shoreham, to help Stepan with the house.'

Anna shook her head, pessimistically. Her hopes faded. 'How will we ever do that? He won't even let me go riding without a proper escort, let alone live with a man.' It was a poor choice of words. It said far too much about how her view of Stepan had changed in the last week.

The comment earned her another sharp look from Evie. 'But that man is Stepan. It's not as if you're living with a stranger. He's practically family,' Evie argued.

Not really family, though. One did not kiss family like that, Anna thought. Over the course of the winter, he'd gone from being a childhood fixture to a curious mystery, to being a flesh-and-blood man with deep-seated emotions he strove to hide, along with an ability to shatter one's world with a single kiss. She should want to run from that intensity, but she found she only wanted to run towards it, to see where it led.

Evie was too deep in her plans to notice her misstep. 'You can take Mrs Batten, our house-keeper. She has a sister in Shoreham. She'll enjoy the chance to visit. I'm sure the Worths have their own housekeeper, so this will free up plenty of time for Mrs Batten to keep an eye on you. She'll be able to give you household management instruction, too. I'm sure Stepan wouldn't mind the assistance, or the company if he's as busy as he says he'll be.' Evie laughed. 'Men don't know how much they take a hot meal for granted at the end of a long day until it's not there for them.'

'Of course.' Anna nodded and gave her attention to her embroidery. She was starting to doubt her eagerness to go to Shoreham. Mrs Batten was highly capable and a moral termagant to boot. And then there was the issue of just how 'glad' Stepan would be to see her, especially when Evie apprised him of the plan for her to stay more permanently—hot meals at the end of the day notwithstanding.

In the end, Dimitri's carriage went home from Shoreham one occupant short of what it had come with. Anna-Maria stood on the steps of Seacrest with Stepan waving them off, a curious loneliness rising in her stomach when the carriage was out of sight. It was silly, really. Dimitri and home were just an hour away. She could ride over whenever she liked, yet, as dusk settled, home might have been a thousand miles away. Stepan had not been glad to see them, at least not her. He'd been cold and stand-offish since their arrival. He and Dimitri had closeted themselves away, leaving her and Evie and the redoubtable Mrs Batten to their own devices. Those devices had involved meeting with the household staff—a staff far more elaborate than the five servants who helped Evie at home. They'd drawn up lists for foodstuffs and a weekly menu of meals. They'd gone over the linens and found most things to be in order. Preston's wife ran a good house, anything that needing shoring up was due only to Stepan's abrupt arrival.

'Regretting your decision to stay already?' It was the first direct comment Stepan had made to her all day. It seemed he was intent on ignoring not only the kiss, but her, too.

She shook her head. 'No, I'm just thinking of other times I watched Dimitri drive away,' Of the time he didn't come back. He'd sent a letter instead informing her of his decision to give up his title, his life, and stay in England to marry the daughter of a baronet. Stepan had been with her then. Dimitri had entrusted Stepan and Ruslan with the details of their quiet departure from Kuban. Only that departure had not been so quiet. Nikolay had been arrested and Illarion would have been next. Stepan had suddenly found himself not only with one young girl and an old man to whisk off to safety, but also a gravely wounded cavalry officer and a poet wanted for libel. Stepan had never faltered no matter how difficult the duty.

Stepan sighed. 'They all drive away one way or another.' He must be thinking of the others: of Illarion, Ruslan and Nikolay. He missed them, she realised. He was always so strong, so stoic, it was hard to imagine he had softer feelings, as well. But she knew better now, didn't she? Now that he'd kissed her. That kiss had exposed him to her as much as it had exposed her. He did feel, he did yearn, he did hurt. Beneath his hard shell, Stepan Shevchenko was human after all. Such a realisation should have made him less heroic to her, but in fact it did not. It only increased the mystery of him, a stark reminder of how much she didn't know and how much there was yet *to* know.

Stepan gestured towards the open door. Somewhere deep inside, a servant was lighting the lamps. A warm glow beckoned through the dusk. 'Come, Anna-Maria. Dinner will be on the table soon and we can discuss exactly what you've got yourself into.'

Did she understand that by extension whatever she'd got herself into she'd got him into, as well? Stepan poured himself another glass of wine, studying Anna-Maria in the candlelight of the dining table: the glossy dark waves of her hair, the fine line of her nose, the soft curve of her jaw, the stubborn point of her chin. She was a beautiful woman, empirically, a quality heightened when she smiled, putting the sensuality of her mouth on full display. She was smiling now as she motioned to his nearly untouched plate.

'Do you not care for the venison pie?'

He'd only taken a few bites. 'No, on the contrary, it's quite delicious.' It was the best meal he'd had since he'd left Dimitri's and he knew it was thanks to Evie and Anna-Maria, who'd given Cook instructions and direction. He'd been too busy with the ships to pay attention to the house. As a result, he'd eaten cold meat and bread since he'd left Dimitri's, or eaten at the tavern. But he wasn't going to admit that to Anna-Maria. It would only give her justification for staying. He took a bite to pacify her. 'Why are you really here, Anna-Maria?'

'Because you need someone to look after you.' Anna-Maria took a sip of wine, looking over the rim with a coy glance. 'Cook told us you haven't eaten a decent meal all week or left any instructions.'

So much for not admitting that, then—but she'd made a tactical error. Stepan chuckled. 'You didn't know that until you arrived, though.' He leaned close over the table. 'Somehow I suspect this little jaunt was all your idea. What prompted you to leave Little Westbury?'

She looked him squarely in the eye. 'I'm bored. Why should you get to have all the fun? You need help and I can help with the house and the books, and in return you can squire me to the assemblies. I can practise for the Season on the officers in town.'

Heaven help the British military. Heaven help *him*. There wasn't a part of Anna-Maria's speech that didn't drive a spike of fear into him. The last things he wanted were for her to get her hands on his books and for her to be waltzing around Shoreham with the very people sworn to bring him down. A deadly game was about to get underway in earnest. He couldn't afford to be distracted or to have his crew distracted. He'd already spoken to Abernathy about his earlier breach. He had a lot to oversee as it was, without worrying about what she might accidentally uncover: the hidden staircase leading down to the caves, ledgers left out on an office desk. He'd have to live very carefully in both action and association. That would be a whole other layer of distraction to consider. At Dimitri's home there'd only been the distraction of her. Now, the distraction was double.

'Well, say something?' Anna-Maria prompted expectantly. 'You don't seem pleased about it. *I* thought it was a rather good trade for your services.'

'I don't,' Stepan answered bluntly. Perhaps if he could scare her off, she would reconsider. 'I didn't ask for your help. I am managing in my own way and I don't have time to escort you to military assemblies.' He gave her a strong look.

'Dimitri told me the real reason you wanted to come. You want to dance.'

Her brother made her sound like a silly-headed flirt. Anna-Maria set down her glass with enough force to make the wine slosh over the rim, and sat back in her chair, arms crossed over her chest. 'You don't have time or you simply don't want to? While we're being honest, why don't you like me? You used to, at least I thought you did.'

Stepan groaned. What he didn't have time for was *this*—doing maintenance on a relationship that wasn't supposed to exist. 'I do like you, Anna-Maria; you know I care for your family very much,' he placated, trying to sound brotherly and uncle-like when he didn't feel either in the least.

'This is not about my family, it's about *me*,' Anna-Maria challenged. 'You've been ignoring me all winter. At first, I believed you went out for business or for an affair. I let myself believe that for months, but now I think it's something else. Either you don't like me or—' she pierced him with a hard stare '—you're afraid of me.'

Now, *his* blood was starting to boil. 'Afraid

of you? Whatever gave you that idea?' It was preposterous. He was a smuggler. He risked the noose or transportation with every shipment. He'd smuggled his best friends out of Kuban with warrants from the Tsar on their heads, for which the penalty was treason. He was not afraid of a nineteen-year-old girl.

'You kissed me and you ran. You couldn't get out of my brother's house fast enough.' Anna-Maria laid out her evidence.

'I kissed you to teach you a lesson. Nothing more. Don't go attaching girlish fantasies to it.' He did not want to talk about the kiss. It had been a piece of ill-advised foolishness on his part. He'd drawn too near the fire with it.

'Fine. The kiss and your leaving are mere co-incidence.' Anna-Maria studied him with her whisky eyes. 'If the kiss was not the reason for your hasty departure, then Shoreham was. What's so important about being here?' This was precisely the type of enquiry he wanted to avoid. He didn't want her poking around his business interests any more than he wanted her poking around inside his head.

Stepan rose. 'I must claim a gentleman's prerogative for discretion in order to ensure the privacy of all parties involved. It's been a long day. I need to retire.' He needed to be down in the caves helping Joseph get out the last of the half ankers of vodka and other goods before Denning had his troops organised.

'Prerogative? Discretion? Those are very English words, Stepan. I don't recall you ever being so enamoured of the British. Weren't you always the one that said the British had the same oppressions Kuban did, they only dressed them up differently?' Anna-Maria had risen, too. 'You've changed. You're becoming one of *them*.' She nearly spat the word and her vehemence caught at his attention.

Stepan stiffened at the cut. 'Them' didn't mean British gentlemen, but a far larger grouping of men in general: men who used their power to keep others down. 'I am still the same as I've ever been, Anna-Maria.'

Constant and true to those he loved even when they demanded too much from him.

He wanted to say more. He wanted to defend himself against her misguided slander, to explain he was fighting for justice and power for the downtrodden, that right now a crew of boys depended on him for their livelihood, for their slice of justice, but there was no time. Joseph was expecting him and there was work to be done. Arguing philosophies with Anna-Maria would have to wait. 'Perhaps the change you see is in yourself.' He gave her a bow and departed, already regretting his words long before he heard the shattering of crystal against the dining-room wall.

Chapter Six

How dare he insinuate the fault was hers! Anna knelt on the floor, a napkin in hand as she carefully picked up the crystal shards of her shattered goblet before a servant came in and witnessed her folly. She should not have thrown the glass any more than Stepan should have spoken so harshly to her. Perhaps she should not have come. Her motives hadn't been entirely pure. She'd come for herself and in doing so, she'd made Stepan miserable, although why it should matter so much to him that she was here she didn't fully understand.

She wrapped the glass pieces in the napkin and set it on the table. Shock over the violence of what she'd done began to sink in. She'd never thrown something, never wantonly destroyed anything. The force of her response was illuminating. She cared about Stepan's words far more deeply than she would have guessed. Not because he'd accused her of changing—that much was true. She *had* changed. How could she not have after the journey she'd been through? The life she'd been through and the reality that she was coming of age? For her, it was a natural time of change. To assume otherwise was to be naïve or in denial.

No, what had been illuminating was what those words revealed about him and her *together*. After all this time, after all the years and adventures they shared, they didn't know each other at all. He didn't know the woman she was becoming any more than she knew the man he'd become—the man who preferred to be alone, who preferred to keep his own secrets. That was assuming they'd ever known each other at all. What had she known of the boy her brother had brought home beyond his quiet reserve? And what did he know of her? Did he know her dreams? Her hopes? Her fears? She didn't know his. But she could. Anna blew out a breath. They had to learn one another again, learn one another perhaps for the first time.

She *would* apologise to Stepan, but not just yet. Despite her realisation, her anger was still too hot to seek him out. She would see to it that the goblet was replaced, too, even though it would mean asking Dimitri for money. He wouldn't deny her, but that didn't make the prospect of asking any more palatable. Some of her anger flared again at the thought, taking the form of hot tears at her own impotence. Some things were changing, but not everything. There was some change that was apparently beyond her. She would *not* cry inside this house, not where anyone could see, not the servants and not Stepan should he return from wherever he'd gone. Outside. She needed to get outside.

Anna-Maria found her way to the veranda. It ran the length of the back of the house and commanded an unadulterated view of the ocean beyond. It also paid for that view by taking the brunt of the weather. The wind was strong out here. Tonight, she welcomed its power as she gripped the stone balustrade, letting the wind dry her tears before they could fall.

It wasn't fair. She didn't *want* to ask Dimitri for money even if she knew he'd give it to her. She wanted her own money just as she wanted her own life and the power to make her own decisions. *These* were the things England had promised her and had so far not delivered.

Two years! Two years of waiting and nothing had changed. She would be twenty next month, older than the debutantes she would meet in London. The difference seemed like a lifetime. She'd escaped Kuban so that her life could start, but *nothing* had started. Worse, nothing had changed. She'd been tucked away in the country living in a manner far too reminiscent of how she'd lived in Kuban. If this was all there was, why had she bothered to leave? Why had Dimitri bothered to rescue her at all?

In her more rational moments she understood she could not have remained in Kuban. She would have been married to the Pasha's son and spirited away to a foreign land. She'd no more be in Kuban right now if she had stayed than she was right now. She understood, too, Dimitri's hesitation in launching her into London society; she'd needed time to practise her English, to learn English ways, to polish her manners, to learn forms of address. They had also needed time to ensure they were safe.

Flaunting an escaped princess among the ballrooms of London after twice breaking a royally arranged betrothal agreement was hardly discreet, even if her cousin Yulian had been glad enough to step into the breach and offer himself to the Pasha's daughter instead. If Kuban wanted her back, it wouldn't be hard to retrieve her. But she was safe now. Time and Ruslan's efforts with the recent Summer Revolution ensured no one would be looking for her ever again. In that regard, she had her freedom.

In all fairness, she understood her brother's protective reasoning. But tonight, she didn't want to be fair. She wanted to be entirely free. During all those long nights in the mountains, sleeping on the ground, eating cold food for fear a fire would give them away, fearing discovery, fearing she would wake up and be told Nikolay had died of his wounds, she'd never imagined England would be like this.

England had been the Promised Land, a place where she could be free to discover herself. England would be a place where she could live out from under Dimitri's sheltering thumb and her father's unforgiving censure. Not that she'd had any idea what she'd do with that freedom. But she'd wanted to explore the possibilities. Might she paint or draw? Might she ride like Nikolay? Might she write like Illarion? Might she discover some heretofore unknown passion that was entirely her own?

The night she'd fled, anything and everything had seemed possible. Hope of the impossible had buoyed her throughout that journey. She didn't feel that way now. She felt more sheltered than ever. Anna-Maria looked up at the stars. Not for the first time, she envied Stepan and the others their maleness and the freedom that went with it. When they'd arrived, they all had spent a few months in Little Westbury with Dimitri. By that first winter, the men had gone to London to look around. Only Stepan had come back to Little Westbury and tonight he'd borne the brunt of her dissatisfaction for all of them. It was hardly an endorsement for Stepan to return to the house while she was still up. She couldn't blame him if he avoided her like the plague.

* * *

'You'll have to avoid the main roads like the plague,' Stepan instructed Joseph as they distilled the last of the raw vodka. The work was hard, lifting heavy kegs, but he welcomed it as a much-needed distraction from his emotions. Dinner with Anna-Maria had not gone well. He would leave it at that for now. He'd have to apologise. No matter his frustration, there was no excuse for speaking to her like that.

'Denning will have his men in place, watching the obvious routes. He won't have discovered the secondary roads yet.' With luck the captain never would, but that luck would depend on how loyal the population of Shoreham was to their smugglers. It only took one informant to break the chain.

'Aye.' Joseph nodded thoughtfully, looking older than his seventeen years. 'We'll manage. We could take on some more bat men. I know some fellows we can trust.' Bat men had the job of protecting the tub men if anyone dared to interfere with the transport.

'I prefer stealth over force.' Stepan cautioned, 'Force is obvious and can be tracked. Bat men can be recognised.' He wouldn't risk anyone facing hanging on his account.

'Force may become a necessity if this Captain Denning can't be reasoned with.'

'You mean bribed?' Stepan chuckled and cracked open another cask. 'He didn't seem the bribable sort, I'll say that much for him. He's a very determined fellow.' More than determined. He would exact cruel retribution from anyone he caught.

Stepan stood, stretching his back, and surveyed the cavern. The half ankers that would be worn by the tub men were nearly full and only a few casks remained for distilling. Soon, he wouldn't have an excuse for staying out of the house and avoiding Anna-Maria. But it was late and he could hope she'd gone to bed. 'Can we move the ankers tomorrow night? I think the sooner the better, given the circumstances.' He would have preferred to have used a wagon, but the winter mud combined with the weight of heavy casks would have left a wagon mired on boggy roads before it had gone a mile, a sitting duck for the excise men.

'We can go tomorrow night.' Joseph rubbed at

his chin. 'The hardest part will be getting out of town. The place is crawling with soldiers, even if they are disorganised at the moment.'

Stepan thought for a minute. 'You need a distraction.' A slow smile spread across his face. 'I think I know just how to kill two birds with one stone. We'll wait one more night, Joseph, and move the vodka and spices while the barracks dance. A welcoming assembly is planned for them this Friday. I've been invited, of course, as have the troops. I'll keep Denning busy while you and the boys move the cargo.'

Joseph grinned in agreement. 'It's the perfect distraction. I'll keep guards posted tonight and tomorrow to make sure no one comes sniffing around in the next thirty-six hours.' Then his brow furrowed. 'That's only one bird, though, milord. You said two birds with one stone. What's the other?'

Stepan gave a wry smile. 'I owe a lady a dance.'

A lady. Anna-Maria. One and the same. Stepan climbed the steps to the house, the wind howling around the stone tunnel encasing the stairs—all one hundred and sixty of them. He could not gloss over the reality. Anna-Maria was no longer a little girl in braids, or the wide-eyed adolescent who'd ridden in the saddle before him without complaint on the gruelling trek out of Kuban. That girl was gone and in her place was a stunning, passionate young woman too head-strong for her own good and too tempting for his.

Was she aware of it? Of the current that ran between them? Did she understand the sparring between them was not truly out of anger, but out of that nebulous something called chemistry, a subconscious attraction? They were testing each other, trying each other, like a buck tries a doe, chasing her to ground over the course of a few days before mating. And like a worthy doe, Anna-Maria wasn't afraid to play hard to get.

Whether or not she was doing it deliberately was another question, as was whether or not she wanted him to catch her. She'd made it clear she wanted to be caught by no one, not just yet. In light of that declaration, he had to be the re-sponsible one, as always. He had to protect her dreams, whatever they were, from anyone who posed a threat to them, including himself. In-cluding *her*. Had she stopped to consider what

a flirtation with him might carry as a consequence? Or, in true Anna-Maria fashion, had she
simply thrown herself into it headlong without
a thought for the results?

At the top of the stairs, Stepan paused, hand
on the knob, before going in. He felt guilty for
having left her so long tonight. Regardless of the
tension between them, she was alone in a strange
house with no company. Alone was something
Anna-Maria had no experience with. Wasn't that
what she'd been trying to tell him tonight on the
front porch? Unlike him who was far too familiar with being alone, Anna-Maria had always
been surrounded by people. He would have to
apologise for that, too; perhaps a shopping trip
was in order. Perhaps he could take her into town
for hair ribbons for the assembly? He'd placated
women in such a way before, usually with prizes
more substantial than hair ribbons. In Kuban,
placation had come with jewels: a pretty diamond tiara or a ruby bracelet.

No. He would not classify Anna-Maria with
those women. Those women had been mis-
tresses, not ladies. Buying and selling had been
part of the negotiation between them. He would

not reduce Anna-Maria to that. She would want his words, his sincerity, not hush gifts. Inside, the house was dark. Alone or not, Anna-Maria had found her way to bed. His apology would have to wait until morning.

Stepan rose early, vowing to do his apology right. He propped the invitation to the assembly at Anna-Maria's plate where she would see it when she came down for breakfast and he put aside his morning obligations to wait for her. He was nonchalantly reading his paper and drinking his coffee when she came down. He glanced up with a smile. Anna-Maria looked fresh in a gown of apple-green wool trimmed in white cotton lace at the collar and cuffs, her hair tucked in a neat chignon at her neck.

Stepan rose, determined to be on his best behaviour. Dimitri would expect it of him. Dimitri had entrusted his sister to him. He needed to start earning that privilege. 'Good morning. I trust you slept well? I am sorry business kept me out so late last night. It was inexcusable of me on your first night here.'

'I did sleep well, thank you.' Her eyes landed

on the invitation. 'What is this?' She opened it, her gaze scanning the contents. Stepan had expected her to smile, to see her face explode with joy. But her brow furrowed. 'The mayor's assembly? Stepan, you don't have to do this.' She shook her head as she set the invitation aside. 'I should have stayed up last night and waited for you so that I could apologise right away.' She took her seat. 'I behaved badly and I spoke out of turn. You have responsibilities here and I have imposed on them for selfish reasons. I was frustrated and I took it out on you. You don't have to make it up to me.'

He'd never thought an apology could be so... stunning. Whatever lingering remnants of girlhood he might have attached to her were vanquished with her words, the words of a mature, grown woman who was aware of her actions and took ownership of them. She had always been beautiful to him, but this was a beauty that went beyond the skin. He felt as if he were seeing her for the first time.

How well did he know Anna-Maria?

It was a heady and dangerous sensation to think the girl he'd once known had changed into a woman he had yet to discover—that he *wanted* to discover.

'Then we are both forgiven,' Stepan said, nearly rendered speechless by the revelation. For a few moments, time was suspended as they regarded one another over the breakfast table. Meanwhile, her plate was still empty, he realised belatedly. His manners had left him entirely. 'Coffee?' Normalcy would return with routine actions. He reached for the pot to pour. 'You said you were frustrated last night. About what?'

He moved to take her plate, loading it with eggs and ham. If she could play the lady, he could play the gallant gentleman. She was not just the sister of his friend, she was a guest in his home, rented though it was. The nascent beginnings of a different fantasy teased the corners of his mind—a fantasy where he had a home of his own and a wife at his breakfast table. No more fictions where homes were leased for a temporary sense of place, or families borrowed from friends.

A home of his own. A family of his own. The impossible.

She met his gaze, startled by the question. 'It's

hard to explain. I'm not sure I can.' She settled her napkin in her lap, but he would not let her dismiss her thoughts.

'Try me.' He found himself impatient for the answer. What dreams, what hopes might she reveal? What might he learn?

'I am eager to go to London, that is all. So much time has passed since my arrival in England and nothing has changed. I feel as if I am falling behind somehow, or perhaps I feel I've been left behind.'

Stepan nodded. 'I remember Nikolay saying the same thing to me when he met Klara.' It was not only Nikolay. Stepan felt it, too, that restlessness that came with watching others launch. He felt it more so now that the others had settled into their own lives.

He'd spent years cobbling together a makeshift family of friends to fill the void of his own non-existent family, and now even that was gone. There was no one left to watch over. Except his boys in the caves. Perhaps that's why they meant so much to him. He was filling the void. But Anna-Maria didn't have such a void to fill. 'You're surrounded by people who love you: your brother, Nikolay, Illarion.' He waved a hand meant to include all her brother's friends. 'You've not been left behind.' All their wives included Anna-Maria in their circles when they visited.

If anything, Anna's circle of friends had grown to include Evie, May, Claire and Klara. She had a faithful correspondent in Beatrice Worth. And she was a doting, loving young aunt with all their children. She would make a remarkable mother. His chest constricted at the image of Anna-Maria with a dark-haired toddler at her skirts, another baby in her arms. He pushed the image away, excusing it as a tag-along remnant of his earlier impossible fantasy. Such things had always been impossible, but he was a smuggler now and that put the fantasy even further out of reach.

She shook her head. 'It's not the same. Everyone has gone on to find their own freedom and I have none. I can't even pay for that glass I broke without asking my brother.' Her tone was bittersweet.

'You needn't ask him then. I will settle with Worth…'

He realised his mistake before she spoke. 'No, that's just it. I don't want a man to settle anything for me; not you, not Dimitri. I want to settle things for myself. Being here in Shoreham is the first time I've been free.'

'It's the first time you've been alone,' Stepan corrected.

'One is the price for the other, is it not?' she asked pointedly, her gaze fixed on him. 'It's the price of your freedom.' For a moment he felt exposed, as if she saw too much of him against his will. What would he do if she guessed at why he had to be alone? Then she softened. 'Even here, I am not really alone. I am with you.' She did not mean for it to be insulting. 'And the worst of it is, I don't know any more what it means to be with you.' She looked away, suddenly shy in the wake of her boldness.

With him. If she only knew what those words did to him. 'You are with me as you've always been with me.' True lies indeed. But how could he possibly acknowledge the change between them without upending the precarious world they clung to? Without disappointing Dimitri who was counting on him to keep Anna-

Maria safe? Without disappointing her? And yet the curiosity remained. What would it be like if she were truly 'with him'? For her own sake, he could not press her to find out. She wanted freedom. He could not give her that. Being with him would strip her of all chance at freedom. Eventually, she would add that to the list of things she'd never forgive him for. She wanted to fly and he had to let her.

Stepan cleared his throat and tried for levity. The water was too deep for him here. If he lingered in these thoughts he would drown. 'As for the immediate future, I hope "with me" means you'll come to the assembly. I have to go. I am an esteemed importer in these parts. I need a lady by my side if you could be enticed?'

She gave him a saucy smile, the one he was used to. 'Well, if it's a favour to you, I will go. But...' she paused, emphasising the 'but' with teasing fervour '...you will owe me.'

Stepan nodded. 'I will owe you, most sorely.' He pulled a purse from an inside pocket. 'You might need a few things for tonight. If so, you may accompany me to the docks, if it suits, and then take the carriage to the shops.' It wasn't truly freedom. She'd be spending his money and Mrs Batten would be with her, but it was a start. He knew for a fact Anna-Maria had never gone shopping alone. In Little Westbury she'd always been surrounded by Evie and Claire and their friends. And Little Westbury had little to offer in the shopping line. As the nearest Channel port to London, Shoreham would naturally have a larger selection.

Anna-Maria beamed and scooped up the purse. 'If it suits? You know perfectly well that it does.'

Chapter Seven

Tonight she was going to dance! Anna held her pink skirts in one hand and took Stepan's hand with her other as she stepped down from the carriage, careful to avoid mud on her slippers, a soggy reminder that this was not London, not by a long shot. The discordant sound of musicians tuning their instruments streamed out of the well-lit tavern, as people bustled inside in high spirits: men in dark evening wear like Stepan, or in the brilliant red coats of officers; women in gowns of a variety of colours: pastel muslins for young girls, deeper colours for the matrons. To be sure, the gowns lacked the fancy trimmings of London fashion and the tavern assembly room lacked the grandeur of a London ballroom, but to Anna-Maria it was perfect.

Stepan's hand was steady at her back, reminding her to keep a rein on her own high spirits as she impatiently waited their turn in the receiving line. She wanted to dance! 'Soon,' Stepan chuckled at her ear, divining the reason for her impatience as they inched forward. Stepan reached for the dance card dangling at her wrist. 'Shall I claim my two dances, then, before they're all snatched away?' He wrote his name beside the first set and then for a waltz later in the evening. There was no sense in letting Evie's lessons go to waste. 'Ah, look, it's our turn.' He ushered her forward. The mayor was a portly man used to good living, his wife likewise. Both were pleasant and exceedingly pleased at having a prince attend their function. They practically fawned over Stepan, and Anna had to hold back the urge to laugh. Didn't they know he was just Stepan? 'Have you met Captain Denning yet, your Highness?' The mayor turned to the scarlet-clad man on his left.

'Yes, we've met.' Anna sensed Stepan's posture tensing as he greeted the man and made the appropriate introductions. 'Captain, may I present Anna-Maria Petrova, lately of Little Westbury?' The captain took her hand and bowed over it.

'It is a pleasure, Miss Petrova. I trust you are enjoying the sea air?' The captain's eyes lingered on her and she felt a flush creep into her cheeks at the attention, which seemed a touch too much for an introduction, but Anna was flattered all the same. The captain was a handsome man in an austere sense and had a commanding presence in his uniform.

She felt the pressure of Stepan's hand at her back. Perhaps he sensed the slight impropriety, too. He was eager to usher her along, but the captain stepped at such an angle that movement was prohibited.

'Before you go, permit me to claim a dance, Miss Petrova.' The captain was all gallant charm as he reached for the card. Stepan stiffened behind her. Only when the captain was done signing did he step back and allow her to pass.

'You were surly with the captain,' Anna commented as they entered the crowded room.

'He is less gallant than he appears,' Stepan answered in low tones. 'I don't like you dancing with him.'

She tossed him a smile. 'It's only one dance, I wouldn't worry.' Her dance card filled up swiftly after that as Stepan moved them around the perimeter of the room, introducing her to his associates. Truth be told, the attention *was* flattering. Men were eager to claim a dance and everyone was so polite—even the captain had been nice despite Stepan's misgivings.

The musicians struck up the opening of the first set, calling all dancers to the floor. Stepan bowed and offered his arm. 'It's our dance, Anna-Maria.' His eyes held hers for a long, steady moment and the thrill of awareness coursed through her. The message of his eyes was unmistakable. Tonight, she was his—his to escort, his to protect, although from what she couldn't imagine here in the safety of the dance hall. They took their places at the head of their group as the music started. She curtsied to him. He bowed to her and they moved into *le tour de deux mains*, hands intertwining as they danced around one another in stately precision, Stepan's grey eyes intense on her own.

'You look stunning tonight. I don't think I've

told you yet. I should have mentioned it sooner. It's no wonder your card is full.' He smiled.

It occurred to her how handsome he was when he smiled. His face was transformed; he looked young. He *was* young, she reminded herself. Stepan was only thirty-one. If they'd stayed in Kuban, he would just now be taking up his official place at court. But it was easy to forget when he frowned. 'You should smile more,' she said as they came together again. 'You're rather handsome when you do.'

'And you are a consummate flatterer, Anna-Maria. I suppose I'll do.'

'You'll more than "do" and you know it,' Anna shot back. 'You're quite the finest man in the room, redcoats notwithstanding.' She meant it lightly, but the air about them charged with her words and she had the distinct impression she'd put a pink-slippered toe over an imaginary line she wasn't supposed to cross. Stepan's grey eyes burned like charcoal as they made the final figure of the pattern and he relinquished her to a new partner.

But the awareness raised by his touch, by his gaze and by her words didn't leave her. She was more conscious of him than ever. Her gaze slid to him even as she made conversation with her new partner. Stepan was indeed the handsomest man in the room, his broad shoulders and long legs shown to perfection in well-tailored dark evening clothes. Pristine linen peeked from beneath the paisley silk of his silver waistcoat, an expensive but not ostentatious opal stickpin winking in the folds of his cravat. Stepan cleaned up well.

Perhaps that was where the awareness sprang from—the novelty of being dressed up, of being out in society such as it was in Shoreham. When was the last time she'd seen Stepan dressed for an evening out? Not for ages. Likely not since Kuban when he would have stopped by their home to gather Dimitri up for a palace ball. And yet, part of her knew better. The awareness sprang from something deeper than the novelty of simply dressing up. It sprang from the realisation that if she was his for the night, then the reciprocal was also true. He was hers. He'd led out the first dance with her to make it clear to all present. For the night, they belonged together. Whatever that meant. She didn't want to take the idea out and examine it too closely for fear of discovering it meant very little indeed. Instead, she smiled, and laughed and danced with all the spirit she possessed. She refused to spend a moment of this wonderful evening worrying about what happened when the clock struck midnight and they became ordinary Stepan and Anna-Maria once more: the stoic man and the unwanted house guest.

Stepan discreetly checked his gold pocket watch. Five minutes before midnight. Joseph Raleigh would have the caravan of tub men and their protectors on the move by now. In his mind's eye he could track their progress through the winding trail up the Seacrest bluff and into the twisty back paths of Shoreham to where the rough country lanes met up with the main road to London. They would meet with no resistance tonight. Every officer was here dancing away the night and impressing the merchants' daughters. Everything was going like clockwork, or nearly everything.

Stepan grimaced as Anna-Maria danced by in the arms of Captain Denning. He'd wager Denning wasn't thinking about smugglers right now. The only thing he was thinking about was how to whisk her away for some privacy. Denning acted entirely enthralled by Anna-Maria, which didn't make him unique, Stepan mused. Every man in the room had been captivated by her. Including himself. He'd been captivated the moment she'd come down the stairs this evening, that pink muslin whispering against her ankles as her skirts belled about her. Pale pink made some women look uncommonly girlish. Not so with Anna-Maria. The pastel shade was the ideal foil for her walnut-dark hair and porcelain-smooth skin: the perfect rose. On a matching ribbon about her throat was strung a crystal heart that caught sparks of the light as she danced. It was a simple piece of jewellery, but she wore it with elan, as if it were diamonds.

She passed by again, laughing at something the captain said, her eyes merry as she flirted. Stepan's temper rose irrationally. Never mind that she was quite the distraction for the captain. He didn't like the thought of her flirting with Denning, perhaps as she'd flirted with him? Was she telling the captain he was the handsomest man in the room? Was she telling him how well he looked in a smile? The captain wasn't worthy of those attentions any more than the naturally vivacious Anna-Maria was guilty of his condemnation.

He recognised the sentiments were beneath him. Jealousy was for an insecure man and his reaction was influenced by his own bias. The captain was his sworn enemy, a man who stood at odds with his own agenda.

Stepan crossed his arms, fingers impatiently tapping against his biceps. This dance had gone on interminably. It hardly seemed fair when his own quadrille with Anna-Maria had sped by hours ago. Finally, the dance ended and couples departed the dance floor as new couples took their place. But Anna-Maria and the captain did not come. Stepan counselled himself to caution. He needn't leap to conclusions, but he could stride towards them. He crossed the room at discreet pace and made for the stairs. At least with the assembly room, there was only one way in and one way out. Downstairs, he asked the barman if a couple meeting their description had gone out.

'Oh, aye.' The barman smiled and jerked his head towards the inn yard. 'The captain said the lady needed some air.'

Stepan nodded his thanks and headed towards the door. *Now* he could jump to conclusions. He knew what the captain was thinking. He was a man, after all, and he knew how men thought when they had a pretty girl in their arms, but what had Anna-Maria been thinking to go outside in the dark with a man she barely knew? Outside, he gave his eyes a moment to adjust to the lack of light in the inn yard. Dimitri would kill him if anything happened to Anna-Maria or her reputation before they could get her to London. He quartered the yard with his gaze, catching a flicker of light from the right corner and the lilt of feminine laughter. Thank goodness for small things like crystal heart necklaces that flashed in the dark.

Stepan strode towards the flicker, determination growing with every step. Good Lord, the captain had his hands all over her, at her waist, at her neck. Stepan wasted no time. 'Step away from the lady, sir. She's under my protection.' He would ask only once with words. If he had to ask twice, the second time would be with his fist.

'Stepan!' Anna-Maria drew back from the captain, startled at the intrusion and had the good sense to look somewhat abashed. Not nearly penitent enough for Stepan's tastes, however. He was entirely cognisant of the fact that the captain hadn't exactly been forcing his attentions on her.

'I hope you are feeling better?' Stepan enquired, for the sake of saving face. 'The innkeeper said you were taking the air.'

'I am quite fine,' Anna-Maria retorted stiffly, but she came to him. Good. The further away she was from the captain the better.

Denning shot Stepan a sly look. 'A thousand pardons, I had not meant to keep her outside for an undue amount of time.' He made a small bow in Anna-Maria's direction. 'Your servant, miss. If you'll excuse me, I'll take my leave.'

Alone with Anna-Maria in the dark, Stepan let his anger boil over. 'What were you thinking?' he asked through gritted teeth, trying to keep his voice down.

'What were *you* thinking?' Anna-Maria snapped. 'I did not need rescuing.'

'Yes, you did. He had his hands all over you! In another few moments who knows what he might have tried.' This was exactly what he'd feared would happen when she'd shown up on his doorstep wanting to dance and meet people.

'He might have tried to kiss me,' Anna-Maria said in sarcastically exaggerated shock. 'A kiss! Oh, sweet heavens, that is the *worst* crime imaginable. No one steals kisses but the lowest of men and the loosest of women. Oh, what levels of depravity.'

'Stop it!' Stepan hissed. 'You're mocking me.'

'Yes, I am,' Anna-Maria answered evenly. 'We did come out for air because *I* asked him. I was feeling a bit light-headed in there with all the heat. And, yes, he might have kissed me, but I wouldn't have minded.'

'I would have.' Stepan scowled. 'You can't go around kissing men, Anna-Maria. You know better than that. It wouldn't have been tolerated in Kuban and it's not tolerated here. Girls caught kissing gentlemen can end up married whether they will it or not.'

She scoffed. 'I hardly think every girl who steals a kiss in the dark ends up compromised.' Anna-Maria paused and then let out a huff. 'Then nothing's changed but the miles. England is no different than Kuban. Except perhaps for men.'

Stepan blew out a breath. He did not want to be having this discussion here in the middle of an inn yard at midnight. Strains of music floated outside, reminding him of what he really wanted and that was to be indoors with Anna-Maria waltzing. He'd paid his dues tonight. He tried a complete about-face. 'That's our cue, Anna—shall we forget this nonsense and go inside? I believe this dance is mine.' He offered her a smile in the dark.

'No.' Anna-Maria's answer was definite. 'Call for the carriage. I want to go home. You cannot buy me off so easily. Do you think all you have to do is dangle a pretty prize in front of me and I'll forgive you?'

Stepan recognised a losing battle when he saw one. There would be no waltzing. He knew Anna-Maria well enough to know she would not relent when she had something on her mind.

It would be better to have her say it in the privacy of the carriage than out here where she could cause a scene he might have to explain to Dimitri later. He waved to the coachman to make ready. 'I do not think you're simple, Anna-Maria.' Hardly simple. Just the contrary. She was as complex as the crystal heart she wore about her neck, multifaceted and ever-changing with the light. She kept a man on his toes.

She was silent as he helped her into the carriage. He would settle for the silent treatment. He would gladly let her be alone with her thoughts since he didn't relish being the whipping boy for whatever was eating at her. He suspected it was more than just being caught outside with the captain.

The coach lurched into motion and so did Anna-Maria. He was not going to get off easy. 'Are you the only one who gets to kiss me?'

Stepan coughed. 'What sort of question is that?'

'One that requires an answer, as most questions do.' He could feel her bristling from her seat.

'I kissed you to teach you a lesson about poking sleeping dogs,' he reminded her tersely. He rather wished she hadn't brought up that kiss.

'You treat me just like Dimitri does, like I am still a little girl.'

At the words, Stepan's control snapped. 'No one in that assembly hall tonight thought you were a little girl.' Least of all him. She'd tortured him, dancing by all smiles in other men's arms, making *them* laugh, making them want her. She had no idea of her effect on them or on him. She flirted without trying, with her eyes, her smile, with an unconscious touch on a gentleman's sleeve. He'd have to tell her to stop that. She touched men far too often in conversation and while men might like it, the gossips in London would not. They'd make a meal of it.

He felt her hand on his arm now. 'Does that summation include you, Stepan?'

'Does it matter?' He was on full alert. She was moving, leaving her seat and coming to his. Not just his seat, but his lap. 'What are you doing, Anna-Maria?'

'By my calculations you owe me.'

Ah, his silly words from breakfast. He'd known he was going to regret those the moment he'd spoken them. His eyes dropped of their own accord to her lips, his voice hoarse. 'What do you want?'

'A kiss.' She wiggled on his lap, her arms going around his neck. 'If you're the only one allowed to kiss me, you'd best get on with it.'

Chapter Eight

One final thought crossed Anna's mind as Stepan's mouth took hers: she might have asked for this kiss, but Stepan had started it in full compliance. His mouth pressed to hers, rough and demanding, the clean pine and starch scent of him surrounding her as she answered with equal ferocity, each of them perhaps exacting their own payment for an evening filled with equal parts pleasure and proving: her proving that she was more than a little girl and him proving... What? She had no idea, but whatever it was, he was intently giving it his all.

She moaned as Stepan's hand moved to the base of her throat, his mouth dropping to her neck, where he sucked hard enough at the tender skin to wring a startled gasp from her. She'd never imagined people doing such things, marking each other in such ways, and she found the exercise exhilarating. Spurred by Stepan's efforts, her own teeth found the lobe of his ear in exquisite retaliation. He groaned as she nipped at him, experimenting with her own power. He did not let her experiment for long. His hands were on the move, sliding up over her muslin bodice, the flats of his palms coming over her breasts, pressing against the peaks of her nipples, his thumbs beginning to stroke them and frustratingly so. The intimacy of his touch, of his caress, was not nearly enough.

She cupped his jawline in her hands, framing his face for her kiss, her mouth taking his in full, her hands moving to undo the exquisite tangle of his cravat, exposing a piece of his bare skin, small as it was. She placed a kiss to the bare triangle at his neck, a wicked thought taking her: she wished he was naked, that she was naked, that his hands touched real flesh, not just curves cased in muslin and cotton. It suddenly seemed a poor facsimile of what could be.

His hands cupped her breasts and she trembled, warmth pooling low inside at her core, delicious and thick like English treacle. She gave a soft, low sigh of pleasure and let her body sink against Stepan's, her softness against the rigid hardness of his, proof of his manhood pressed to her thigh. Their earlier roughness had dissipated into something deeper, something darkly alluring and more intoxicating than retribution. They'd gone far beyond rough play. She was not a girl any longer in the places where they played now, their mouths on each other, their hands exploring where they caressed through layers of wools and muslins. Anna would have lingered in that sensual darkness if not for the carriage jolting to a stop in front of the house and putting an end to it. The ride home seemed much shorter than the ride to town.

Stepan withdrew, setting her aside, and exited first to give her time to gather her composure. It was a nice sentiment, although a useless one. Her composure was scattered to the four winds. There would be no gathering it, but she could at least straighten her clothes and create the illusion. When she was ready, Stepan helped her down with enviable aplomb. His face was set in its usual formidable stoic lines. Only his eyes, burning like embers in charcoal, hinted at something more tempestuous. One would never guess moments earlier he'd had his hands on her breasts, his body pressed to hers with evidence of his desire at her leg, their breaths coming in mutual pants and sighs as they pushed each other to the edges of sanity.

His cinereous gaze held hers, his hand briefly caressing the heart at her neck, momentarily reminiscent of other intimate touches. 'You should have pearls. Not a bauble on a ribbon,' he murmured in low tones, rife with sensuality that turned her insides to treacle once more. She half suspected he would kiss her, there in front of the coachman. Instead, he stepped back, gave her a bow and excused himself. 'Your pardon if I don't see you inside. I have some late business I must see to.' He climbed back in the coach, gave the signal and was off. At midnight. To do who knew what, leaving her standing in the drive after *all that*.

Anna-Maria drew her wrap tightly about her shoulders, letting her mind take its time in assimilating what had just happened. He'd kissed her senseless. He'd done *more* than kiss her. He'd touched her, he'd caressed her and she'd touched and caressed him, and then he'd dropped her off and driven away as if it were of no consequence. To do what? Or was it to see someone? A cold nugget settled in the midst of the warm heat at her core. Had he left her to seek out a mistress, perhaps the woman he'd spent the long winter days with when he wasn't at Dimitri's?

She felt hot and cold all at once at the thought. Anna pressed her hands to her cheeks, hardly daring to believe Stepan would kiss one woman and leave her for the bed of another. Yet, where else would he be going this time of night? Or perhaps he was simply giving himself time and her time, as well. Heaven knew what had happened tonight deserved some consideration. Anna climbed the steps to the front door. It was blessedly warm inside and she made her way to her room, already lost in the haze of her thoughts, all of which centred around Stepan. These did not feature worries over a phantom mistress, but featured the two of them as they'd been tonight, surly and sensual by turn.

Anna turned up the lamp in her room and began to undress. Stepan had been jealous tonight of the captain. There had been a tone to his words when he'd come upon them in the inn yard. He'd not spoken like a brother protecting a sister, but like a man protecting a woman.

What had he said? *'No one in the assembly hall tonight would ever think you were a little girl.'* And then just now in the drive, *'You deserve pearls'*…a young woman's first jewels that marked a debutante's transition into society and out of the schoolroom, a girl no longer. In Kuban, a girl received pearls when she first started putting her hair up for formal occasions, a feminine rite of passage.

Perhaps those words tonight had touched her most of all. Stepan had seen her as a woman, had treated her as a woman, had touched her as a woman. She fumbled with the laces to her pink gown and the dress slid to the floor, leaving her in her chemise. The lamp caught the shadow of her nipples through the fabric, dusky rose in the light. He'd touched her there. Tentatively, she put her hands on her breasts, retracing Stepan's caress. She lifted them, cupping herself, running her thumbs over the still tender peaks, recalling that tonight she had responded to him as a woman responded to a man.

The realisation forced her to examine the other half of the equation as she slipped her cotton nightgown over her head. Tonight, she had seen Stepan as a man. Tonight, they had not been family friends. Gone had been the constraints of couching Stepan in a brotherly role. There'd been nothing brotherly about his behaviour. It had been replaced by something else. It prompted the question—what did tonight mean? It was an echo of the question she'd asked at breakfast. What did it mean to be with him? Who were they to one another if their old roles had been cast away? What new roles might they assume?

Anna-Maria burrowed beneath the warmth of her blankets and blew out her lamp. Those were thoughts for another day because she knew very well that to answer one of those questions would only bring on more. Tonight, it would be enough to relive the discoveries made in the more tender moments: discoveries about herself, about him, about what might lay beyond. Those would be fine thoughts to fall asleep on. Her only regret was that they hadn't had their waltz.

* * *

He should have waltzed with her. Stepan leaned back against the squabs of the carriage, regret and unsatisfied arousal warring for his attentions. If he'd waltzed with her, if he'd gone back inside with her, none of this would have happened. He wouldn't be in a carriage after midnight alone with an erection that wasn't going to resolve itself. For that matter, he wouldn't have been in a carriage with Anna-Maria, his mouth on her mouth, her throat, her neck, her ears, his hands on her breasts, her body pressed to his. Just remembering the heat of those moments was enough to uncomfortably sustain his erection.

He'd had no business kissing her, not after the disaster of kissing her the first time. He'd had no business touching her, but that had held little sway when their bodies had decided to duel. Then the duel had become less a competition and more a co-operation as they pushed each other towards pleasure. He'd like to say he hadn't enjoyed it, that it had all been for her benefit, another lesson of sorts about the consequences of actions. But that would be a lie. He had enjoyed it. He'd savoured the feel of her hands on his face, of her teeth sinking in to his ear, of the swell of her own natural passion. There was so much more he could show her.

No. There would be no more. He could not risk it. Any more and he'd need to announce his intentions—intentions he was not entirely clear on himself. What did his attraction to Anna-Maria mean? Where did it lead? Perhaps the better question was where *could* it lead? She deserved far more than him. He had no family to offer her. He didn't even know if he had love—real love—to offer her. Was he even capable of that? How could he be when he'd never known it himself?

These were sobering thoughts and they did their work subduing his arousal. He had no business pursuing Anna-Maria when all he could offer her was all he'd ever been able to offer a woman—an affair, a few nights, a few months between the sheets with a man capable of giving pleasure, but not much else. Anna-Maria was not meant for a casual lover. She was meant for a husband, one of two things he could never be.

The carriage rolled to a halt at the edge of the bluffs and Stepan got out, grabbing a lantern.

He shaded his eyes and looked around, letting out the signal whistle, the call of a black-headed gull. He knew a moment's worry until Joseph materialised in the dark. 'How did everything go? Is the vodka off?' He put a hand on the boy's thin shoulder, relieved to see him safe.

'Yes.' Joseph was grinning in the darkness.

'And the others, is everyone safe?'

'They're probably halfway to London.' What Joseph meant was that they were as safe as they could be and that was safe enough for now. They were beyond Captain Denning's reach at any rate. Stepan nodded his head in relief. Perhaps this was like the worry a father felt when his child was released into world and he could no longer protect him.

'Good.' Stepan removed his hand from Joseph's shoulder. 'You've done well. Do you need a ride anywhere?' He gestured to the carriage. It was too late for Joseph to be out walking. He realised he wasn't sure where the lad slept these days.

'No.' Joseph shook his head. 'I'll just go back down to the caves and catch a few winks. Me and some of the other boys have blankets and it's comfortable enough.'

They were sleeping down here? Good Lord, he hadn't known. He thought about the cave's damp walls and would have liked to have disagreed with Joseph's claim to comfort. Instead, he made a mental note to make enquiries with local fishermen who might be able to take in a good worker or two in exchange for room and board. He knew too well from his own experience that a young man had his pride. He'd been Joseph's age not that long ago. Joseph and the others wouldn't want charity; they'd want to work for their board. In the meanwhile, he would send down extra blankets and pillows and a hot meal. And he'd make arrangements for Joseph to sleep with the grooms up in the stable. It couldn't be permanent, but it would do for a while. Stepan reached in his pocket for some money. 'Since you're working day and night now to guard our goods, you should have pallets. This should cover it.' He was careful to word his gift in such a way the boys wouldn't look upon it as a handout. 'Let me know if there's anything else the boys need. Clothes, shoes. Anything at all.'

He felt a sense of satisfaction as Joseph tucked the money away with a nod. Perhaps this was also how a father felt when he was able to provide for his child. He would never know. Along with not being a husband, a father was the other thing he'd never be.

Elias Denning slammed the report down on his desk, hard. The *thunk* of paper against wood was not nearly as satisfying as driving his fist into something. An image of Stepan Shevchenko's face loomed briefly in his mind as the perfect fit for his fist. He'd not liked having his interlude with the lovely Anna-Maria Petrova interrupted by a man who treated him as if he were a callow youth brought to heel instead of a military man with real authority, authority more real than Shevchenko's honorific title. Nothing had happened; the lady had been genuinely faint. But perhaps something could have happened after she recovered. He hadn't been above turning the situation to his advantage.

He had not liked Shevchenko from the first. The man thought to call himself a prince... Of what? The man had no country, at least no country that would acknowledge him, from what Denning understood. Here in England, the man was no better than a merchant importer. Denning despised having to cultivate an acquaintance with this foreigner, this *immigrant*. That's what he was, *all* he was, without his title. Denning heard the accent beneath the man's well-spoken English. How dared Shevchenko go about giving himself airs, acting the equal of an Englishman? Where had Russia been at Waterloo? Russia had been burned and bleeding from Napoleon. It had been Englishmen who'd won the day for all of Europe. And now, Shevchenko was here, parading himself among them, forcing good men to acknowledge him and his pretty whore. *Miss* Petrova? He wondered if there was anything of the innocent miss about her. He'd been on the verge of discovering the secrets behind those cognac eyes and lithe body in the inn yard until Shevchenko had intruded.

In other circumstances, he would have dealt with Shevchenko and then screwed the hell out of Miss Petrova for good measure. She would be brilliant bed sport, complicit or otherwise, with a body like that. But the mission required he stand there and nod his apologies. His success here, and his impending promotion, depended on establishing relationships with men like Shevchenko who relied on trade for their livelihood. His mission was proving more impossible the more he learned about it.

Denning eyed the report with distaste, proof of his first failure although no one would blame him for it. A smuggling gang had moved a significant amount of spirits and spice packets the night of the assembly. While he'd been dancing and flirting with the lovely Anna-Maria, the smugglers had gone about their business and on the main roads no less. Of course, that last was speculation. No one had seen them, but the speed at which the goods had reached London seemed to indicate they could not have lingered overlong on muddy back roads and, perhaps on a more interesting note, this excursion had been planned.

This was the part Denning didn't like. He sensed rather strongly that the speed of this run suggested someone had waited purposely for the night of the assembly in order to use the dance as a cover for their movement. That someone had deliberately sought to make a fool out of him in front of the whole town. There were a hundred awful speculations to draw from that assumption. What if the whole town knew? What if everyone had been in on it from the mayor on down? What if everyone who'd shaken his hand and looked him in the eye had actually been laughing behind his back the whole time? Such an insult to a military officer was not to be tolerated.

Shoreham needed to be punished, immediately. Even if his assumptions were incorrect, a swift and strong punishment would not go amiss in setting the right tone. Shoreham needed to understand who was in charge now and it wasn't the mayor. It was him, Captain Elias Denning, and no one would laugh at his expense again.

'Lieutenant!' Denning bellowed, giving his disappointment full vent.

'Yes, sir!' A ruddy-cheeked young man rushed into the room with a stiff salute. That's what Denning liked, a show of prompt respect.

'I need a meeting with my officers called for ten o'clock this morning, then I want to meet with the city's leading merchants and importers at one o'clock to apprise them of certain developments.' That would include Stepan Shevchenko. He would take a little private pleasure in having the upper hand this time as he delivered his edicts. The importers might squirm a bit at the punishment he had to mete out, but it would be over all the sooner if they came forward and informed on those who were skirting the law and stealing their legitimate profits. 'Also, Lieutenant, I'll need a list of every known smuggling gang working out of Shoreham.' It was going to be a busy day. He had a port to blockade, checkpoints along the major roads to set up and a mayor to divest of authority, and he was just getting started.

Chapter Nine

The worst was happening right in front of him and he had to sit at the table and pretend it didn't matter. But it did and not just to him, but to every other man at the table with him. Stepan glanced covertly at each face, all of them wealthy importers that relied on the 'free trade' of the coast for their real money. All of them were pretending, as he was, that Captain Denning's blockade of the Shoreham harbour was of little consequence, that this meeting was informational and that was all.

Stepan shifted in his seat. Of course, Denning wasn't calling it a blockade. A blockade suggested militant action and a warlike atmosphere. Denning was calling it 'floating customs' and dressing up the prospect of excise men boarding boats to 'clear' them and collect payment while they were still at sea, with words like 'efficiency', 'expediency' and 'personalisation'. No one would have to wait on a harried customs officer when they put into port and had other better things to do than paperwork.

Stepan wasn't fooled and he doubted any of the others at the table were either. 'Clearing' was another phrase for searching the boats, for poking bayonets into packaging and dipping them into barrels on the hunt for items that were being smuggled in illegally. 'It will save you time and money, gentlemen.' Denning wrapped up his exposition with a smile that didn't quite reach his eyes. The men responded with smiles of the same. It was all very civilised on the surface. But everyone knew what had really happened. The British military, in the form of Captain Denning, had declared war on Shoreham smuggling.

An example was to be made of them. There were other smuggling communities up and down the Sussex–Kent coast, but Shoreham was one of the most vibrant due to its location to London. If Denning could shut down Shoreham, it would send a strong message to other less well-situated organisations that the risk wasn't worth it. It would also earn Denning a promotion, something that was difficult to come by in times of peace.

Stepan studied the captain afresh. His earlier assumptions over their lunch in the tavern had been spot on. Denning was coldly ambitious. The lack of a war wouldn't stop him. But it had slowed him down. Captain was a middling rank and Denning was thirty, if not slightly older. He'd spent a lot of time as captain. Perhaps too much. The army was for young men. Men didn't stay in the military for life unless they had no better options. Sons of noblemen sold their commissions when it was time to marry and settle down. The men who didn't… Well, that told its own story. Suffice it to say, Captain Denning would be relentless.

'Gentlemen, if there are not any further questions, we have some unpleasant business to move on to.' Denning took a chair at the head of the long table. 'It has come to my attention that the night of the assembly, a shipment of spirits and spices was smuggled through our roads to London without paying the proper duties. This is an insult to each and every one of you who pay your taxes honourably. If you have any knowledge of who was responsible for it, or any knowledge of similar activities, I would be most obliged to hear it.' He was attempting to divide and conquer them. Fortunately, Stepan had not bragged to anyone about his 'side' business. But it did concern him that he did not know if he could trust the gentlemen at the table. Would these men have his back or, as the last one come to town and a foreigner, would they turn against him first? With the *Skorost* at sea and no way to reach her, it was a damnable time to test the hypothesis. The meeting concluded and the room began to empty.

'Your Highness, might I have a word?' Denning stopped him before Stepan could escape.

'Of course. How may I be of service?' It was his courtier's voice, the tone he saved for life in the Kubanian court where every movement and every word was dissected for hidden meaning and intention. The trick was to always appear amenable.

'I would like permission to call on Miss Petrova—your cousin, was it? Forgive me, I am not clear about the connection between you, only that it seems you are the one I should apply to.' Stepan did not miss the deep-seated question beneath the manners. Denning was testing him.

'She is not my cousin. There is no blood relation, but she is like a sister to me.' The words sounded awkward after last night's carriage ride. There'd been nothing sisterly about that. 'Her brother is my best friend. She offered to keep house for me while I am here.'

Denning fingered a quill idly. 'That is very noble of you. I don't have sisters, but I imagine I would appreciate such sentiment in a friend if I did. Do you? Have sisters?'

'I have no one, Captain,' Stepan said tersely. It would be best to let the captain know from the start he was alone, that there was no leverage to be gained in that direction. But he was as uncomfortable with the small talk as he was with the idea of Denning calling on Anna-Maria.

'Except Miss Petrova and her brother.' Denning looked up from his attentions on the quill, his dark eyes sly. 'Perhaps when I call, you and I can speak privately.' It wasn't really a question. 'We have much in common, your Highness. Both of us are men away from home, in a foreign place. We are outsiders.' He gave a self-deprecating smile. 'Perhaps you a bit less than me in that you've been in Shoreham longer. I hear you just leased the Seacrest estate mere weeks ago.'

Stepan wanted nothing in common with this man, but he had to temper his anger and direct it towards the right reasons. This man was his enemy and would be even without the man's interest in Anna-Maria. He could not let jealousy refocus his anger or his priorities. He had to protect the smuggling ring. His largest shipment to date was due to arrive. He was counting on that money for the boys, for the cause. So many were counting on it, not just for the money but for their futures. 'Yes, Seacrest belongs to a friend, Preston Worth, who is in London.'

Stepan was gratified with a flicker of recognition in the captain's eyes. 'Yes, Worth is a civil prevention officer. He was involved in the Cabot Roan situation a couple of years back.' Denning made a tsking noise. 'Too bad how that ended. I would have shot the bastard on sight. A trial was too good for the likes of Roan.' The captain straightened and scooped up his hat, preparing to leave. 'Good day, your Highness. I'll call tomorrow at one. I find Miss Petrova to be quite a singular young lady.'

Stepan had been afraid of that. The last thing he needed was his enemy in his house, a man who would see his enterprise brought down, calling on the woman he…carried a torch for…a woman he had rather intense feelings for, even if he had to keep them hidden most of the time.

He had to be careful with his words there. Naming those feelings made them real, naming made him acknowledge them. He'd best be cautious what he called them. Infatuation and torch-carrying he could handle. After all, to carry a torch for someone implied a certain level of hopelessness, that those feelings were not reciprocated, that the situation was over before it had ever truly begun. Hopelessness in relationships, impossibilities in relationships—he could cope with those. He'd been coping with those all his life. They were standard operating procedure. What wasn't 'standard' was the hopefulness that sparked when he kissed her, how that precious flame burned when her body answered him, the way it pressed against him, wanting more. And by God, he wanted to give her more. But that would only destroy both of them in the end. Anna-Maria was young and impetuous. She might think she wanted more from him, but she didn't really know him, she only thought she did. Once she knew the truth of him, she would regret her decision. He had to prevent that from happening. To that end, he had to make those decisions for both of them.

A man was calling on her, an attractive officer in a red coat with polished brass buttons and a gleaming gorget, and Anna could not find the willpower to concentrate on his conversation. She could, however, summon enough apparent concentration to be aware of even the slightest movement Stepan made. He could shift infinitesimally in his chair and she would notice. How ironic that the one man in the room who didn't want her attention was the only one who could claim it.

Captain Denning was saying something about the Shoreham cliffs and the Ice Age, trying to appear educated, which he might truly be. She didn't know. She *should* know. He'd done his singular best to engage her in conversation since his arrival. He'd brought chocolates and had obviously taken great care with his appearance. He wanted her attention, something Stepan had made very clear he did not. It had been two days since the incident in the carriage and Stepan wanted to pretend it hadn't happened, much the same way he'd wanted to pretend their kiss in Dimitri's sitting room hadn't happened.

Just as he had at Dimitri's, Stepan now chose to make himself absent except for this visit from the captain. He'd been gone each morning when she went downstairs for breakfast and he came home long after dinner each evening. She shouldn't be surprised. This was what Stepan had always done. Only now, he was glowering at the captain as if he could stare the man out of the room. That decided it. If Stepan wanted him to go, she definitely wanted the captain to stay. She'd been wanting a little society, a little excitement, and here Captain Denning was, wanting to give all of that to her.

'Have you seen the rest of the house, Captain? It's quite magnificent. I would be glad to give you a tour,' she offered when the captain had finished his exposition on chalk cliffs. Out of the corner of her eye, she saw a tic start in Stepan's cheek. Well, tic away. If he was going to pretend their hot kisses in a carriage hadn't happened, she would, too. She must flirt where she was wanted.

'A tour would be lovely—starting with the veranda. That view looks breathtaking.' The captain smiled and rose, offering his arm. He made no attempt to invite Stepan and neither did she. The captain held the door open for her and she felt the weight of Stepan's surly stare as she stepped through. It served him right. If he was going to ignore her, she would ignore him.

Only it was much harder to do in practice than it was in theory. By the time they'd finished the tour and the captain reluctantly took his leave, having run out of reasons to stay, Anna had to admit that simply leaving the room had not been enough to banish Stepan. He'd remained a fixture in her thoughts throughout the tour. She might have been justified in her decision to desert him, but Stepan would be angry and she would have to pay.

She didn't have to wait. The front door was barely closed when Stepan laid down his edict through gritted teeth. 'I don't want that man in this house again. Stay away from him. Is that clear?'

Anna whirled to face him. 'I didn't invite him.'

'You're encouraging him. He'll want to come back,' Stepan growled.

'I was polite. I did not encourage him.' Her temper flared.

'The hell you didn't. You offered him a tour of the house.'

'That is a perfectly fine substitute for strolling the gardens when the weather is inclement. In case you haven't noticed, spring hasn't exactly arrived. I could hardly show him the roses that aren't in bloom. The wind off the veranda nearly blew us away as it was. But we couldn't remain in the drawing room with you looking daggers at him.' She paused and regrouped. She'd done nothing wrong. She didn't need to defend herself. She ought to be the one asking the questions. 'Why don't you like Captain Denning? You hardly know him.'

'It's none of your business, Anna-Maria. I just don't want him here and I don't want him around you.'

She crossed her arms. 'You can't have it both ways, Stepan. You can't kiss me senseless one night and then treat me like a little girl the next. It's not fair to me. I've been sheltered and protected too long. I am done with that, unless you give me a very good reason not to be.'

A storm lit Stepan's eyes, turning them a dusky quicksilver. 'This is not about kisses, Anna-Maria.'

She borrowed his words, her own voice low and provocative as she gave a sultry drawl. 'The hell it isn't. You've kissed me twice now and run away both times.' Anna met his gaze with a challenging stare of her own. 'Are you afraid of me, Stepan? Are you afraid of how I make you feel? Because I'm afraid of how *you* make *me* feel: hot and cold, warm at my core, yet my body shivers when you touch me, it begs for more. No one has ever affected me like that. I didn't know people could affect each other that way.' She was out on a limb now, feeling fully exposed, but she wanted to expose him, too, and maybe the best way to draw him out was to draw herself out, as well. Maybe, if he could see he wasn't alone in the confusion of these new and surprising feelings, he would relent.

But Stepan did not relent. 'What you feel is nothing more than youthful infatuation. It is entirely natural and it *will* fade. The other night should not have happened. We were both angry, emotions were high and we misappropriated them. You confused your emotions and I should have stopped you. I did not. I am entirely culpable for what happened next. It will not happen again. As for the captain, I ask that you believe me when I say there are things at work here far beyond your knowledge. Please do not meddle in them. Please do not challenge me on this. If you cannot abide my decisions, I will respectfully ask you to leave.'

Dear heavens. Anna pressed a hand to her stomach, feeling sick. The entrance hall seemed to spin. She'd confessed her very soul to him— an apparently very girlish and immature soul— and he'd ignored her. She had not realised until now how improbable she'd believed such an out-come. Deep down inside, in places where the unequivocal truths of her life lived, she'd never expected such an impersonal response. Stepan, her bulwark, her constancy, had rejected her. Had anything ever hurt more?

It was the hurt that triggered her suspicion once her stomach stopped churning. The reali-sation brought her up short. Stepan would never hurt her. This was an absolute truth she'd stake her life on. Viewed through that lens, had any-thing ever made less sense than what he'd just done? Just said?

Gradually, reason reasserted itself and with it came one burning question. What was he hid-ing? More to the point, what was he *protecting* her from? It must be incredibly dangerous if he was willing to go to these lengths to keep her from it. He was pushing her away with ferocity. Well, she could go to lengths, too. She wouldn't stop until she knew. And when she did know, she would see that he was protected, too. She would see to it that he wasn't alone.

Chapter Ten

It was hard to protect someone who wasn't there. It was also more difficult to learn their secrets. She couldn't very well interrogate Stepan if he was absent for dinner. There was no sign of him later that night either when she'd finally given up and gone to bed. She'd not given up lightly. She'd spent the hours after dinner actively searching for him, but it was as if he'd simply disappeared. What worried her most was that his horse was in the stable and his carriage was in the mews where it belonged.

Nothing was out of place except him and that created all nature of worry. Wherever he had disappeared to, he hadn't driven or ridden there. He'd gone on foot. A hundred horrid scenarios ran through her mind as Anna-Maria made ready for bed. Seacrest was remote, as were most estates outside of town. There was nothing around but vast acreage. In Seacrest's case that vast acreage included the cliffs and the sea.

Stepan had been angry when he'd stormed out of the entrance hall to parts unknown. It had been daylight when he left, but darkness still fell early this time of year. Had he walked too far to get home in the daylight? Had he stumbled in the darkness and fallen? Had he twisted an ankle? Or had he stepped in a rabbit hole and done worse damage, maybe broken something?

It was hard to imagine Stepan a victim of such menial accidents or injuries. He was sure-footed and athletic. His days in Kuban had been spent out of doors doing who-knew-what. Even back then she hadn't really known, she'd been too young to wonder. She remembered him on the journey, though, how nimble he'd been in the mountains when the roads had narrowed to a dangerous path with cliffs on one side and nothing on the other, just a sheer drop into a ribbon of river far below. He and Nikolay had led the horses through, one after another, repeating the hazardous path time and again. Then he'd come for her.

She'd been petrified. Her father and the others had been already safe on the other side where the path widened again. Stepan had taken her hand, looked her in the eye with that solemn silver gaze and said in his low voice, so much like the one he used right before he kissed her, 'Anna-Maria, I need twenty steps from you, that's all it is. Twenty steps to freedom.' He'd tied a length of rope about her waist and the other end to his, connecting them together. 'I will not let you fall.' With nothing more than the certainty of his words, the confidence of his gaze and her steadfast belief that Stepan would keep her on that mountain with nothing but his own weight and the tensile strength of thick Kubanian hemp, she'd crossed the path.

That Stepan would not mistakenly trip into a rabbit hole and be rendered helpless. So where was he? Wherever it was, he'd come back from it and departed again, this time leaving her a note propped at her plate for breakfast. There was relief and disappointment in that. He was safe. All her worry, thankfully, had been for naught. But he was still gone.

Anna-Maria opened the note. It contained a mere two lines written in his bold hand followed by instructions. Her lips twitched. The lines weren't even complete sentences.

Gone to London on business. Back soon. Take Joseph, the new groom, with you if you go out.

Business. She was sick of that word. Stepan used it to excuse a variety of absences. She wished she knew what the business was that seemed to be so all-consuming. She might like a piece of such business, something to keep her occupied day and, apparently, night.

Anna-Maria buttered her toast in thought. The idea of 'business' nagged at her. What did her brother and the rest of them think would occupy her days once the waiting was over? Once she'd gone to London? Did they truly think she'd change her mind about marriage and a husband? She didn't want that, not yet. She wanted to do *something* meaningful. She knew the men were involved in politics and plots up to their eyeballs despite their dedication to family and wives. Their lives hadn't 'ended' with marriage. Why should it be different for her?

Did they think she didn't listen at the dinner table when Dimitri and her father discussed the latest contents of letters that came from Nikolay and the others? She knew Nikolay supported the Union of Salvation, that his father-in-law was attempting to foment a palace rebellion in St Petersburg. She knew that Ruslan had sheltered a woman last August in London, who claimed to be the only surviving member of the royal family after a state coup had seen the summer palace ransacked. Ruslan had gone back to Kuban to see the revolution through. That revolution had freed Anna-Maria and other women like her, entirely. No longer were the archaic marriage laws in place that required her to marry as her family and the Tsar saw fit.

Anna-Maria chewed her toast. She was sincerely jealous of Ruslan being able to see his work come to fruition, to be able to participate in something so meaningful. She was hungry for it. There was plenty of injustice in the world.

She'd seen it on her journey from Kuban, the first time she'd been anywhere other than the annual trek between the family's palace at the lake and their extravagant home in town. It had made her acutely aware of the privilege she'd received by accident of her birth.

To be sure, she'd had her own problems growing up: a father who couldn't stand to look at her and the prospect of a foreign marriage that would take her far from home for ever. But she'd never wanted for anything, for shelter, for clothing, for food. And she had Dimitri. She was not alone, she was not without hope, not like the street waifs in Marseilles who had begged for even the meanest of crumbs and coins from her.

She'd emptied her pockets to them, each of them tearing at her heart, until Stepan had stepped in, gently disengaging little grubby hands from her skirts, dispersing coins from a leather purse and sending them on their way. She would have taken them all with her. 'And done what with them?' Stepan had chuckled. 'I don't think Dimitri's house is big enough for all of them.' She'd merely looked up at him and replied, 'But his heart is.' Stepan had taken her hand and led her back to the ship with a smile. 'And so is yours, my dear girl. Don't worry, there will be poor orphans where we're going, too.'

Only there hadn't been. Anna reached for another slice of toast. Little Westbury was a rather affluent part of Sussex and, even if it hadn't been, it wasn't a city which made it less attractive to those in need of help or work. Of course, she assisted Evie with baskets for tenants and they made blankets and socks for the ladies' charity circle at the church, but those efforts were one step removed. She never knew where her socks went or who her blankets helped.

One thing was certain: she couldn't sit here eating toast all day and wishing things were different. Today, she had a whole house to herself. Maybe if she looked hard enough, she'd discover what Stepan's business was. Some might call it snooping. She preferred to call it exploring. Anna-Maria set aside her napkin and pushed back from the table, ready for her self-assigned adventure. She'd start in the office where Stepan spent most of his time, then the library, then the stables. She had a very long list by the time she settled behind the big desk in the office and opened the first drawer.

By the time she reached the stables, she was losing hope of uncovering anything significant. There had been many disappointments. Desk drawers had been locked or empty and she soon realised the flaw in her plan. This wasn't Stepan's house. Desk drawers were locked because the home's real owner was away. Rooms were devoid of anything connected to Stepan. There were no personal items decorating tables, or books laying half-open where he might have stopped reading. She sat down heavily on a hay bale, dispirited. Her grand idea had come to naught and it was only one o'clock. Even the carriage wasn't Stepan's own, but the spare carriage owned by the Worth family. Stepan's own horse had gone to London with him. Lucky horse.

The only place left to search that might hold any personal items would be Stepan's bedroom. A little tremor ran through her, turning her warm and warmer at the thought. Once, she might have thought nothing about poking through Stepan's private chambers. But now, this new awareness of him intruded, reminding her it was a man's quarters she contemplated invading—a man who had made her feel very much a woman on two separate occasions. Did all kisses make one feel like they wanted to toss caution to the wind? She had nothing to compare them to. If so, she understood more fully now why young girls were counselled against them. Kisses might encourage a girl to seek out even more foolishness.

Goodness knew *she* felt encouraged to want illicit things. When Stepan kissed her, she never wanted it to stop. She wanted to kiss him back, wanted to touch him the way he touched her. She wanted to make him feel like that, too. She closed her eyes and leaned back against the wall, letting her mind conjure up the memories of kissing Stepan. He did enjoy it while they were doing it. It was only afterwards that he got angry. He'd made a little groan in the back of his throat, a hoarse rasp of desire, or so she'd thought. But then, afterwards, he was always so cross, as if he regretted the action. Kissing left him cross and her confused. She preferred not to think about the 'after' part. Anna-Maria sighed and refocused her thoughts. It was far more enjoyable to think about 'during'.

Anna-Maria Petrova was a beautiful woman in general, but especially in this moment. Elias Denning watched her with her head arched back against the wall, her eyes closed, long, dark lashes sweeping her porcelain cheeks. Her skin was so fine, he imagined he could see the blood running beneath it, imagined he could feel the satin of that skin beneath his fingertips. It would bruise easily. He hated to interrupt the interlude. Was she thinking about her Kubanian prince, the one she called by his first name and to whom she showed too much familiarity? Did she cry out his name in the throes of passion? Seeing her in the midst of a pleasant daydream fuelled fantasies of his own. He could make her forget Stepan Shevchenko.

It was clear she hadn't heard him ride up. A gentleman would announce his presence. Denning took a final look and coughed discreetly. Whisky-hued eyes flew open and a becoming blush coloured her cheeks. 'Captain Denning! What an unlooked-for surprise.' She rose and dusted the strands of straw from her skirts. Then her brow knit. 'Did Stepan know you were coming?'

'Did', not 'does'. Elias smiled. Luck was with him today. Shevchenko was not home. He had Shevchenko's pretty woman all to himself. How unwise to leave the hen unguarded when a wolf prowled nearby. How interesting also that these two continually used each other's first names with ease. 'His Highness is not at home?' He tried to look startled by the information.

'No, unfortunately not. He was called away suddenly on business in London.' She was debating what to do with him; he could see the struggle behind those whisky eyes. Another point of interest—what was she hiding or protecting? Why was she wary? Was it because of his earlier misstep at the ball? Or was it something more? Did she not want him to know the prince was gone? He would have to go carefully here and not spook his prey.

Elias smiled, the charming smile he saved for London when there were people to influence and women to bed. 'It's no matter. I came to see you, actually. I enjoyed our talk yesterday and our tour. I had hoped I might reciprocate with a tour my own. I had not expected the weather to be so fine so soon, but since it is, I thought I would brave your sense of hospitality by barging in and ask you to ride with me.' He gestured to the horses. 'You do ride? There's a lovely view of the coast up the headlands a few miles and I have a picnic.' The mention of a ride and picnic brought a spark to her eye, as he'd hoped. A picnic with a handsome officer on a crisp, clear day would get many a girl's blood up and he was confident in his charms.

She smiled, but he divined the internal debate continued. 'Would you give me a minute to change and to make arrangements for a groom to accompany us?'

She'd barely spoken the words when a head popped out of a nearby stall. 'Miss Petrova, I'll have your horse tacked up and I'll be ready to go when you are.' The young groom tugged at his cap respectfully, but Denning detected a hint of distaste in the single-word acknowledgement of his presence: 'Captain.'

Denning smiled benevolently, hiding his ill temper. He'd bet a month's salary the little prick of a groom had been eavesdropping. But he was too pleased at the moment to worry over it. He had his victory twofold. He had the lovely Miss Petrova to himself *and* he understood the grounds on which she'd conceded. Whatever she wanted to hide or protect, she'd decided it was better done by keeping him away from the house.

'Take all the time you need, Miss Petrova.' He deliberately ignored the groom. 'I am in no hurry.' He could afford to be generous. It would take her twenty minutes to change. No woman he knew could get into a riding habit in less. He didn't mind. He'd use those twenty minutes to imagine her doing it. He gave her a polite bow and watched her walk towards the house with a subtle swing of her hips, a movement she was likely unaware of which made it all the more enticing. She was a beauty ripe for passion and ripe for plucking and he meant to make good use of that today.

Shevchenko had left a fetching woman unprotected. He deserved to be punished on the principle alone even if he hadn't been a prince. But since he was, the victory was twice as sweet. Men who hid behind titles and the luck of their birth were no better than the rest of them who'd not been born as lucky and had to earn their way in the world.

He'd surmised early the Kubanian prince had secrets. A prince did not give up his homeland without having a reason. He wanted to know that reason. He also wanted to know why a man who could supposedly settle anywhere had chosen to settle in a borrowed house in a place like Shoreham, which wasn't exactly a social hub. Men who sought obscurity usually had interesting motives for it. Men who sought obscurity while living with a woman who wasn't his sister made that doubly true. If Shevchenko wouldn't tell him those secrets, perhaps Miss Petrova would, even if she meant to keep them hidden. Not all secrets were revealed through words.

He'd ride her across a beautiful stretch of headland, feed her delicacies from his own private stores of food, give her the full sum of his attentions and, when her guard was down and her mind was busy contemplating the heady romance of an officer's courtship, she would tell him everything.

Chapter Eleven

A crisp wind blew across the headlands where they picnicked on a warm quilt, cheese and bread spread between them, a groom from Seacrest a discreet distance away, keeping watch. It should have been idyllic, a young woman's placid courtship fantasy come to life: the picnic, the attractive, solicitous officer, all against the backdrop of the rugged English coastline. It was a veritable painting in the making, yet Anna could not take her ease and enjoy the outing.

She told herself nothing untoward could possibly happen with the groom watching carefully, an escort hand-chosen by Stepan himself. But even after repeating that rationale in her mind like a mantra, Anna could not let down her guard completely. Her reticence was all Stepan's fault.

He wasn't even here and he'd managed to ruin what would have been an enjoyable day under other circumstances. Even more impressive was the fact that Stepan had done it with just four words. *'Stay away from him.'* He hadn't bothered to explain why and she'd allowed those words to be enough for her to worry over being with the captain.

'More cheese?' He sliced a hunk from the wheel and passed it to her on the blade of his knife. 'England is known for its cheese. This is Derby cheese from my home in Derbyshire, as you may have guessed from the name. Each region has a distinct flavour. This one has a port wine taste to it.'

Anna-Maria tried it, wishing she was more aware of the cheese than the blade it came on. She made the requisite compliment. 'It's delicious. Are you a dairyman at heart, Captain?' She tried for a congenial laugh. She *had* to relax. It wasn't fair to judge the man without cause. He'd gone to a good amount of work to arrange all of this.

But you do have cause, her conscience whispered. *Stepan told you so, that should be reason enough.*

And yet, if Stepan had his way, no man would ever look twice at her for fear of Stepan's blade running him through. Anna stiffened her resolve. She had not come to Shoreham simply to replace Dimitri's well-intended tyranny with another's.

'I suppose most of us from Derbyshire are. Cows and cheese are a way of life.' The captain chuckled, his eyes twinkling his unmistakable interest in her.

'Derbyshire sounds bucolic. You must miss it, being away so much.' Anna tried to remember Evie's instructions about conversing with a man. Ah, yes, ask them to talk about themselves. That would be far better than talking about her. 'Tell me about your work, Captain. What brings you to Shoreham?'

The captain grew serious, his gaze intent on her in a way that had nothing to do with personal interest. Anna had the uncomfortable notion he was watching her for a reaction. 'I am here to put a stop to the rampant smuggling up and down the coast. Shoreham is a hotbed of illegal activity,' he explained. 'People will smuggle anything that turns a profit: silk, spirits, spices even.'

'I had no idea,' Anna replied. It was mostly true. Other than what Evie had told her second-hand, she knew nothing about the depth and detail of smuggling. Denning knew she was new to the area; what sort of reaction did he expect her to give?

'Oh, yes,' he expounded. 'The smaller the item, the harder it is to catch because it can be transported in small packages: cloves and cinnamon from Singapore, saffron from the Middle East.' He gave a self-deprecating chuckle. 'I learned that the hard way. Just last week, a shipment of anise and saffron came through illegally, much to my regret, the night of the assembly. It is easy to hide spices from customs officers.'

His voice softened. 'Enough talk of work. What of you, Miss Petrova? You're a woman far from home. There must be a tale there.' His tone implied confidentiality. 'I should very much like to hear it.'

Was this interest or interrogation? Anna had to wonder. Regardless of the captain's intentions, she could not refuse to answer. Anna smiled sweetly and gave a delicate shrug. 'There's not much to tell. We are from Kuban. My brother is Prince Dimitri Petrovich, the famous archaeologist.' She let the import of her brother's title linger between them. 'When he was on a dig in West Sussex to restore a Roman villa a few years ago, he met a girl and simply decided to not come home. He sent for me instead and here I am.' Perhaps the captain would take the brevity of her tale as a sign of maidenly modesty. Any gently bred girl knew better than to talk about herself at great length.

Anna was not so lucky. The captain's pale blue eyes roamed her face. 'Ah, a true romance, then.' He smiled, perhaps to disarm her as he asked his next question. 'That explains your brother, but what of the others, Miss Petrova? You did not come alone. More bread?'

She took the bread and more cheese to buy time for her answer. 'I could hardly make the journey alone. They came as my guard. It is a good opportunity for them to see a piece of the world.'

'You are loyal, Miss Petrova. It is an admirable quality, but you needn't stand on pretence with me. I've heard rumour the princes were exiled. It's safe to say they came because they had no other choice.'

Anna stiffened. Nikolay and Illarion had been exiled, but Ruslan and Stepan had not. They'd come out of affection for their friends. The English could not seem to grasp the depths of Russian friendship and the loyalty that went with it. Friendships were for life. 'If you know so much already, you needn't have asked me.'

'I did not mean to offend' the captain was quick to apologise. 'I merely sought to know you better. I confess a certain curiosity where Prince Shevchenko is concerned. What is his relationship with you? Or is the relationship merely on your brother's behalf?' He glanced away, dissembling. Anna fought back a wry smile. That was a very good question these days. She felt herself soften towards the captain at last, touched by his subtle addressing of the delicate question. 'I suppose what I'm really asking and making a hash of, Miss Petrova, is what is your attachment to the prince? Is there any impediment to my interest? I should not like to importune you with unwanted intentions.'

He shrugged. 'I am a man who has struggled for every scrap of luxury and status he possesses. Those things have not come easily to me, so in my mind they are not things one would give up, yet Prince Shevchenko has. I find it difficult to imagine sacrificing those worldly goods to come to England. It seems almost preposterous and illogical *unless…*' Here, he stopped to slant her a knowing gaze. 'Unless there was something, or someone, a man coveted more than riches?'

The suggestion struck her rather strongly. Was he implying Stepan had left Kuban for her? That he'd stayed in England specifically for her? Those were powerful thoughts. She could not afford to contemplate them at the moment, however. Anna shrugged, dismissing the captain's enquiry with a vague response. 'I think you read too much into it. They are all good friends and loyal to one another.'

Something flickered in the captain's eyes. 'Then might I hope to see you again?' Whatever the captain's motives for today's outing were, there was an overt request for courtship that must be dealt with. How could she possibly agree to it? If she did, he would call again and she would be in direct violation of Stepan's command. More than that she'd be in direct conflict with her own feelings. Was she the sort of woman who kissed one man and allowed herself to be courted by another, even if the man who'd done the kissing had asked nothing of her? But how could she refuse the captain? And on what grounds? It was an impossible situation.

Anna looked at her hands. 'I am flattered by your attention, Captain. Truly, I am. But I am to make my debut in London in the spring. My brother has hopes for me.' She fluttered her lashes. 'Even if I wish it could be different, Captain, I am not at leisure to decide where to place my affections at present.' Evie would be proud of her. It was a skilful refusal.

'I see.' The captain stiffened and she immediately felt bad. Perhaps her wariness had been for nothing, after all. He was simply a man trying to court a girl and she'd rejected him. He rose, signalling the end of the picnic and Anna felt even worse. She'd spent the picnic imagining this was all a grand plot of the captain's to expose some other grand plot of Stepan's—neither of which she had any inkling existed—and perhaps neither of which *truly* existed, all because Stepan had told her to stay away from the captain.

He met her eyes with admirable courage, she thought, considering she'd just rejected him. 'Despite the outcome, I've had a delightful time today, Miss Petrova. You are a fascinating young woman. I think you and I might have much in common if we'd had the chance to know one another better.'

His gallantry broke her reticence. She was not so hard-hearted as all that. She had to offer him something. 'Please, Captain, don't feel that we cannot be friends.'

'I appreciate your sensitivity, Miss Petrova.' He smiled congenially and held out his hand. 'In that case, would you walk with me before we go? I want to take in the view.'

The view *was* spectacular *and* windy out on the edge of the headlands. Anna put a hand to her hat as the breeze pulled at it, her skirts pressed against her legs. 'A man could see for miles from here!' she exclaimed, taking in the rugged beauty of the deserted coastline with its empty beaches. 'I think it is rivalled only by the view off Seacrest's veranda.'

'That's exactly what I was thinking.' The captain gave her a sideways glance. A cold frisson went down her spine. Anna had the impression she'd just given something away. But what?

Chapter Twelve

What had she given away? Anna could not shake the sensation. She brooded on it long after the captain had gone. She kept thinking about his reference to the spices during their picnic. The saffron, *shafran* in Russian, had got her attention, but it was the anise, *anis*, that had kept it. The two spices were rolling around in her thoughts long after Captain Denning had taken his leave. Both were grown throughout various regions of Europe, but southern Russia was known for its saffron and Russian anise was preferred by connoisseurs because of the quality of its oil.

Anna-Maria ate her dinner in the library near the fire, not wanting to spend another meal at the long dining table alone. The spices *could* have come from anywhere: China, Italy, Portugal, Turkey, and any number of destinations in the southern Mediterranean. But had they? And who had brought them? Not Stepan. He was *not* smuggling, not stoic, strait-laced Stepan who regretted the slight misdemeanour of kissing her.

Besides, hadn't his own ship put into port and hadn't he paid duties on the goods? That paperwork had kept him out of the house for days. If Stepan had imported spices, he had done so legally and paid for them. What worried her most was that clearly someone *else* had brought the spices in illegally. She didn't want Stepan blamed simply because he was a foreigner with Mediterranean and Russian connections.

Of course, her rational self recognised that her fears were putting the cart before the horse, as the saying went. But those who counselled such practice had the luxury of patience. They had not lived in Kuban. They had not seen powerful families brought low because of one well-placed whisper. They had not seen a Tsar witch-hunt his own supporters out of fear for his crown.

Anna-Maria pushed her plate away, not hungry any more. She had been fourteen when the persecutions had started—old enough to know what was going on, but naïve enough to think it had naught to do with her. She'd not paid attention when the first noble disappeared or the second. She'd believed the stories of their unfortunate accidents—one on a hunting expedition and another at his estate cleaning a firearm. She'd heard Dimitri and the others talk in hushed tones about the changing climate of Kuban, about the new levels of tyranny executed by Tsar Peter. But she had not thought they affected her family or her friends. The greatest fear in her life had been Dimitri going away. Even the thoughts of her upcoming marriage had seemed far off. When one was fourteen, eighteen seemed a lifetime away. Anything might happen between then and now.

And it had. Anna-Maria stared into the fire and tugged the sheep's-wool blanket more securely about her legs as she remembered. Illarion had begun writing poetry—inflammatory poetry, not his usual love sonnets or odes to nature that the Tsar adored so much. Illarion's 'friend' Katya, a court beauty, had married a high-profile general in the army, a man named Ustinov. She'd committed suicide. That was when Nikolay had begun speaking out, too, adding his voice to Illarion's. Stepan came to call more often in those tumultuous days, looking stern as he checked in on her in Dimitri's absence. He and Ruslan would exchange worried looks over her head. Shortly afterwards, they'd banned Nikolay and Illarion from calling at the house for some reason she didn't understand until later—to protect her.

Then came the horrible dawn when Stepan had come to the door, arguing with her father. She'd watched from the alcove at the top of the stairs, seventeen and gangly, dressed in a nightshift with a blanket thrown over her shoulders. Nikolay had been arrested; he was wounded and perhaps dying. Stepan had brandished a letter from Dimitri with instructions. 'I am to bring you and Anna-Maria to London. It is what Dimitri wants. Your son is not coming back,' Stepan had said firmly. He was the only one who could take that tone with her father. Her father had argued he would not leave his country as his wife's grave was here. He could not leave her. Stepan had looked up the stairs and seen her. 'Give me Anna-Maria and you may stay with your own foolishness, but you cannot condemn your daughter to the same fate. You know what will happen to her with Dimitri gone.' Her father did not relent. Stepan's last words had been for her alone. 'We have three days. Gather what you can, Anna-Maria, gems, jewellery, any money you have, sturdy clothes and boots for travel. Be ready when I come.'

Her blood had thrilled at his strong words, at the thought of adventure. More, though, it had thrilled at what Stepan was asking her to do: to defy her father, to embrace her own freedom. In the end, her father had come with them. The lure to see his son again had proved too strong to resist. The thrill of adventure had been short-lived. There had been no joy in seeing Nikolay injured and barely conscious, hands tied to the pommel of his saddle so that he wouldn't fall off. She'd learned that night she'd been naïve to think she and her family were immune from witch-hunts. Watching Nikolay struggle to live, she'd vowed she'd never be taken unawares again.

So here she was, sitting before the fire and imagining the worst possible outcome from the captain's visit. What had he come for today?

Just her, as his overtures suggested? Or had he thought to investigate Stepan? Perhaps she should let him and then he would be forced to exonerate Stepan. The captain would find nothing aboard the ship or at Seacrest, a home that belonged to a civil prevention officer. The idea that Stepan was smuggling was laughable. That he was doing it out of Preston Worth's house was downright hilarious.

Or was it? The fire and her memories were raising all nature of ghosts tonight. Little things started to emerge that had escaped her attention earlier. Paperwork had kept Stepan busy when the *Lady Frances* had put in, *except* for the one day when it hadn't. Add to that, Stepan had been absent from Dimitri's for weeks before the *Lady Frances* had arrived. Where had he been *then*? What things had Stepan being referring to when he'd said this was about more than kisses? Why didn't he want the captain here at Seacrest?

She was not entirely naïve on that account. She understood part of the reason Stepan didn't want the captain here had to do with her. Whatever his other reasons, the fact remained that Stepan *had* kissed her. Twice. And the second time there had been far more than kissing. The second time couldn't be brushed off as a much-needed lesson in deportment. The captain had asked to court her. Any girl would have been pleased with his attentions, but she'd not hesitated in her gentle refusal for the simple reason that the captain did not inspire in her the feelings Stepan raised.

There was a certain twisted irony in that choice. The captain had been well mannered while Stepan had raged at her: Stepan, who was by turns strict and surprisingly tender; Stepan, who stormed off hardly bothering to tell her where he was going or why. And yet, it was Stepan she clung to, Stepan whom she would champion, apparently without question. Because there was no question. He was her rock, her moral compass. He knew right and he did right. He championed the needy and protected the weak. Stepan was all that was noble. Whatever she knew or didn't know about him, she knew that at least.

It occurred to Anna-Maria befriending the captain might come in use, however, if he suspected Stepan of any illegal behaviour. One could never have too many friends, as the old fairy tale went. Friends had saved Nikolay and Illarion back in Kuban when others had been happy to let them suffer as long as it kept the Tsar from looking their way. A plan came to her. Tomorrow, she would go into Shoreham and make amends with the captain. If she could protect Stepan in this small way, then she would do it. Her friendship, and whatever else might lie between them, demanded no less.

His friendship with Anna-Maria demanded more from him than what he'd given. The thought was as unshakeable from Stepan's mind as the mud of the road was from his horse's hooves. Early spring, or late winter, depending on how one looked at it, was an awful time to travel. He'd had no choice, though. One of the returning tub men had brought word the merchants in London were nervous about the situation in Shoreham. They wanted to meet with him, wanted to have his personal assurance that supply would not be cut off and that his goods could get through.

Stepan had gone. He could argue business required it of him, but in truth his temper had required it more. He'd needed to cool off and he'd needed distance from Anna-Maria. He'd needed time to think rationally, something he wasn't doing well with her nearby day and night, tempting and torturing him by turn. Anna-Maria felt it, too, only she was willing to explore it whereas he sought to resist it. For that reason, he'd come to the only logical conclusion he could. He had to send Anna-Maria home. He would tell her today and send her back to Dimitri where they would both be safe.

'Hoy, sir! Halt in the name of the King!' Two soldiers were positioned at a makeshift stop in the centre of the road. It looked more like the cross-rail jumps Nikolay had in his riding arena than a substantial barricade, but it was enough to stop a wagon and a rider would be forced to jump it, something that would not appeal in the mud.

Stepan pulled up his horse. 'Good day.' His tone was jovial, but his eyes were busy assessing. It had only been five days. Captain Denning worked fast. He wondered how many other roads were blocked. He shouldn't be surprised. Denning had warned them all at the meeting.

'State your purpose,' one soldier requested. He was not much older than Joseph, Stepan thought.

'I am returning home after business in London.' Courtesy and compliance went a long way and Stepan was happy to supply them both up to a point.

'Do you have papers? A pass?' The other, slightly older, put in with grave seriousness.

Stepan gave a friendly smile, but inside he was registering alarm. This was far more intense than he'd anticipated. 'I left before there was any such requirement.' He feared they were quickly reaching that point where he would not be able to comply. 'As you can see, I am no threat. There is just my horse and myself. You may search my saddlebags.' He winked. 'Although, for future reference, smugglers are usually interested in getting things out of Shoreham, not into it.' The younger one smiled at the jest and gave a nervous laugh. The other one did not see the humour. Stepan wished he had.

They did search his saddlebags, shaking the contents on to the muddy road only to discover nothing more than a shaving kit and a few apples. He was glad the present he'd brought for

Anna-Maria as a peace offering was safe in his coat pocket. They let him pass and Stepan nodded his thanks. The two young men were only doing their duty, but the incident reminded him far too much of the Kuban he'd left and a certain fear took up residence in the pit of his stomach.

Stepan urged his horse forward. The logical part of him knew the fear was irrational. Captain Denning was no Tsar Peter. Denning didn't have a country at his disposal. But one did not need to be a Tsar to instill fear and fear was a powerful motivator: fear *of* one's neighbour, fear *for* one's family, fear *about* the future and what might take place. Fear caused friends to turn against friends, to see to one's own protection instead of the protection of others. He'd seen it happen.

He was already seeing signs of it as he jogged his horse through the surprisingly quiet, empty streets of Shoreham. Well, *mostly* empty. The soldiers were out, patrolling the streets while shopkeepers stood behind empty counters with no customers to help. Denning was smart. Stepan had to give him credit for that. The man had wasted no time in recognising he wouldn't succeed by going after the smugglers alone. He had to go after the whole town. Otherwise, the town would protect the smugglers. Now, however, there was a personal cost to each shopkeeper: no business meant no income. Stepan tapped a hand against his leg as he thought. Would the town recognise there'd be no business either if there was nothing *to* sell? Smuggled goods made up a significant portion of the items on the shelves—goods no one could afford to buy if merchants had to pay full price to purchase them.

A commotion up ahead grabbed his attention. A shopkeeper was dragged into the street between two soldiers, a third drove a blow into the man's stomach. A fourth took a club and swung it into the shop window, the sound of shattering glass overriding the man's struggles as he bore blow after blow. They would render him senseless at this rate.

'Stop!' Stepan swung off his horse, running forward before thought caught up with reason. He grabbed the collar of one soldier, pulling him off the man, and went for another, yelling all the while. Hands grabbed at him, restraining him.

One soldier recognised him. 'Prince Shevchenko!' That brought the brawling to a halt with more effectiveness. Men picked themselves off the ground, dusting their clothing and looking around for leadership. What did one do when a prince was scuffling in one's midst? Did one obey the prince or a twenty-year-old lieutenant?

Stepan stepped in front of the beaten man, not wasting the opportunity provided by uncertainty. 'On what grounds have you destroyed this man's property? On whose authority have you beaten him?' People were peeking through windows and coming to doors now in curiosity.

The lieutenant stepped forward, eyes narrowed, a sly smile on his thin lips. Stepan knew his type immediately. Ambitious and selfish. 'Captain Denning gives the orders around here, not you, your Highness.' The last was said with deliberate sarcasm, pointing out that Stepan had no real authority except that which his personality commanded.

Stepan chose to overlook the insult. 'And where might I find the captain?'

Again the smirk. 'On your ship, your Highness. He is going through your books and I believe your guest, Miss Petrova, is with him.'

Stay calm, Stepan counselled himself. It was what he did best. He stayed calm in the eye of the storm. It had been his calmness that had seen Nikolay freed. It had been his calm that had won the argument with Dimitri's father to evacuate to London. It had been his calm that had helped Anna-Maria over that narrow cliff in the mountains. But today, that calm was sorely taxed. He wanted to punch someone, starting with the lieutenant and his arrogant smirk. With luck, he'd get to punch the captain.

He nodded his thanks as if the lieutenant had not insulted him and walked back slowly to his horse. He swung up and headed towards the docks, at a walk, as if he had all the time in the world, as if he was not concerned about Captain Denning boarding his ship and perusing his accounts, which he wasn't, or that he wasn't in the least bothered by the revelation that Anna-

Maria was with the captain. That worried him far more than the captain being aboard his ship. There was nothing Denning would find aboard the *Lady Frances*. But Anna-Maria was a different story. What was she doing there? Was she there of her own accord? Had the captain learned something? Was he using her as bait to get to him?

It was the last that Stepan feared. When a man acted alone, he had nothing to lose which he hadn't already come to grips with losing. But when a man had someone he cared about... Well, that was the most powerful leverage of all. Stepan tethered his horse at the gangplank of the ship and went up, straight to the captain's quarters, brushing by his ship's captain, Rustinov, with a curt nod. He opened the door, the sound of it heralding his entrance.

Two heads swivelled in his direction, one from the window with wide eyes and a hesitant smile, the other from behind the desk with hard eyes and a frown. One looked happy to see him, relieved. The other looked...

'Disappointed?' Stepan said coolly, drawing

all of Captain Denning's attention. He strode forward and planted his hands on the desk in front of the other man. 'Can't find what you're looking for?'

Denning met his hard gaze. 'Not yet.'

Chapter Thirteen

'Not *ever*,' Stepan corrected without hesitation. 'The books for the *Lady Frances* are in order and there are receipts for the goods imported just last week.' It was easy to speak with conviction. Each word in those sentences was true. 'All duties have been paid, as you can *plainly* see.' He didn't want the captain to find a reason to search further. Not that there was anything to find. The other books had been removed from his office and safely tucked away elsewhere. But what he did *not* want to happen was a repeat of what he'd seen in the street: windows smashed, the wilful destruction of property and perhaps the attempt to wilfully harm his person. If they came for him, he *would* fight.

Perhaps Anna-Maria sensed it, as well, as he

and the captain stared one another down. She came forward from the window with purpose. 'Stepan, this is the new protocol,' she explained with one of her light touches on his sleeve. 'Captain Denning is reviewing everyone's books.' She flashed Denning a smile Stepan did not like at all, especially when the captain's stern expression seemed to soften.

Stepan looked past Anna-Maria. 'The new protocol? Then, I assume you have a warrant for this invasion of private property?'

'*I* am the warrant, your Highness.' Denning rose from behind the desk, but Stepan was willing to challenge the quality of that authority.

'I find it suspect that you could not wait until I returned, so that I might assist you with your questions, but instead you had to search when there was only Miss Petrova on hand, who knows nothing of my business interests. Is that your "new protocol", Captain? Preying on lone women? Smashing merchants' windows and beating helpless, unarmed men senseless in the streets? One would think you were looking to make examples of some very specific targets; unarmed men and foreigners simply trying to make a new life. Be careful it doesn't make you appear to be a bully, Captain. No one likes a bully, not even the army. They won't promote you for it.'

Anna-Maria's hand on his sleeve tightened. 'Stepan, I volunteered. I had no idea when you'd be back, but I knew you had nothing to hide. I offered up the books to Captain Denning in hopes of being a peaceful example.' Her brown eyes searched his, pleading silently for co-operation and for caution. He saw a hundred stories in those eyes. She was thinking of Kuban, of how it had been at the end when the Tsar's tyranny had targeted them at last; she was thinking of Nikolay, bloody and broken, of Illarion in chains, of Ruslan's father dying in prison because he would not recant, of her own father nearly imprisoned for Dimitri's broken betrothal to an eastern Pasha's daughter. Only the intervention of her cousin, Yulian, and his willingness to marry in Dimitri's stead had stopped it. Now Stepan saw her fear for him in her gaze. She understood how vulnerable they were as outsiders. They were easy targets. No one would stand up for them.

No, Stepan corrected mentally. Not they. He.

He was an easy target. No one would stand up for *him*, no one of any merit. Joseph and the land crew would, but they were adolescent boys and they could offer nothing that wouldn't incriminate the larger business beneath the Seacrest cliffs. He was in this alone. It was safest for everyone. At least that's what he used to think. The captain looked at Anna-Maria in such a way that had Stepan rapidly rethinking the premise.

'Miss Petrova has the right of it,' Denning said with a hint of what might have been warmness to his tone. 'She did volunteer, your Highness. I am most appreciative of her efforts.' Denning rubbed his hands together in a manner that suggested a forthcoming confession. 'I am afraid you are right, however. I am looking to make an example of you, a good example. If everyone sees how co-operative you are, I hope they will follow suit and we can avoid further nasty business.'

He couldn't win. Cold fingers spread in his stomach. He saw the captain's play clearly. There was no scenario here in which he was not used as bait. Either he resisted and became a target for the captain to bring down, Denning knowing that no one was likely to stick their necks out for a man they barely knew and, in fact, would likely sacrifice to save their own skin; *or* he cooperated with the captain and earned the townspeople's distrust that way. In either case, the captain was culling him from the herd and Anna-Maria had fed right into the strategy in her attempts to do good, to protect him. Well, Denning would find he'd not chosen an ailing bull moose to bring down.

'Since all is in order, Captain, I think your work here is done.' Stepan shut the ledger and held the captain's gaze with serious intent. 'I'll see you out.' He wanted to get Anna-Maria home. He was more convinced than ever that his decision to send her back to Dimitri was the best choice. Then he had to meet with Joseph, even if it meant bringing his crew chief to the house. But needs must when the devil drove and the devil was driving hard. He had Anna-Maria, his boys and his business to protect.

The devil drove him all the way home, Anna-Maria behind him on the saddle, her arms wrapped tight about his waist, her touch a constant reminder of everything that lay unresolved and at risk. His trip to London was supposed to have provided him with distance and objectivity when it came to his feelings. But at one fell glance, all that objectivity had crumbled. Seeing her today had sent a bolt of primal possession through him.

He hadn't liked that she'd been with the captain, that she smiled at him and he smiled at her as if there was something between them. Dear Lord, he'd only been gone four days and it felt as if the world had turned upside down: checkpoints on the roads, military officers imposing their own sense of law and Anna-Maria consorting with the very cream of that evil crop. It was a nightmare of the past come to life in the present.

At the house, Stepan helped her down with gruff instructions. 'Wait for me inside; we need to talk.'

'Yes, *we* do.' Anna-Maria met his eyes with her own unwavering gaze and equal grimness. This was not the petulant sauciness of a young girl in a temper. This was the voice of a woman speaking and it left him feeling somewhat chastised as if he was the one who'd done something wrong.

Stepan quickly sent word to Joseph and returned to the house. He found Anna-Maria in the library, standing before the long windows overlooking the ocean, her shoulders squared, her back straight as she took in the view. Outside, heavy clouds were gathering. There would be rain and worse by dark, not the most ideal circumstances for moving goods. Joseph would have a difficult time. It wouldn't have been necessary if Anna-Maria hadn't meddled. 'I told you to stay away from him.'

Anna-Maria turned from the windows, a storm of her own flashing in her eyes. 'You did not tell me when you were coming back. I had to manage on my own as best I could. Co-operation seemed most prudent.'

'It plays into Denning's hand!' Stepan explained, crossing the room in swift, purposeful strides. This was not a discussion he wanted to have at a distance. Who knew what the servants might hear and what they'd do with it. The last thing he needed was his borrowed servants sending word to Preston Worth about illegal activity in his own home.

He gripped Anna-Maria's arms. 'You should not have meddled.'

'Meddled? Is that what you call it?' Her eyes weren't the colour of whisky any longer, but of hard agate, the kind one finds at the bottom of rushing streams. 'You were gone and I had the captain up here wanting to take me on picnics and out for rides.' Stepan heard the recrimination in her words. He'd left her unprotected. Oh, not in the physical sense. Joseph had been on special assignment to look after her and Mrs Batten and the other servants had offered protection aplenty of that sort. But his lack of explanation had left her vulnerable, unable to fully understand the danger presented by the captain. 'He asked permission to court me and I didn't know what to say.'

His gut twisted. 'Is there something between you and him?' Jealousy had him by the short hairs. Those smiles from the afternoon haunted him. Had they meant something more than play-acting? At the time, he'd not assumed they meant anything of a romantic nature. Perhaps he'd been wrong. He could not lose her, not to a man who was trying to bring him down.

She gave a wry smile. 'Only you, Stepan. *You* are between us. I was trying to protect you! Why do you think I couldn't decide how to answer? I wanted to do what was best for you. I thought if I were friends with the captain, it might—'

He broke in, unable to stomach the image. 'I don't need you to protect me. I don't need you to flirt with him.' This was why it was best to work alone, to be alone. There was no collateral damage.

'No, you obstinate man, *you* listen to *me* this once.' Her voice dropped to a hush and she stepped even closer, her hands gripping his lapels. 'While we were out, I asked him about his work. He told me he was here to ferret out smugglers *and* he mentioned there had been a cargo of spices smuggled in. *Shafran* and *anis*, Stepan. Spices from the Middle East, from Turkey and the lowlands of the Caucuses. From *our* part of the world.' She shook him a bit in her intensity. 'The captain is a smart man. It's a simple connection to make. There's only one Russian importer in Shoreham, Stepan. It would be easy to pin that blame on you.' Outside, lightning flashed over the water. The storm was moving in fast.

Anna-Maria's words came in a rush now. 'But I knew you hadn't done it. It *couldn't* have been you. The *Lady Frances* was in port and you'd spent days doing the paperwork. What better way to exonerate you than to volunteer your books? You have nothing to hide. You are not a smuggler.' Except that he was. Except that he had everything to hide. The *Lady Frances* was only a very elaborate decoy for the reality of his business. And now, Anna-Maria had brought a viper into his nest.

Her grip relaxed on his lapels, her argument made. 'Whatever the captain might be doing, my choice was still the best option.'

That was his Anna-Maria, headstrong and stubborn. Heaven help the man who crossed her. Right now, that man was him. She was glorious in her siege, like a Valkyrie of the north. But his pride as a man could not allow her to stand in his defence any more than his pride could allow him to declare his feelings, or to act upon his feelings in the most passionate of ways. He had nothing to offer her and everything to lose by doing so, including her.

Stepan unfastened her hands from his clothing, willing to offer an olive branch. 'You did the best you could. However, there were no best options,' he said firmly. 'The captain is a dangerous man, no matter how solicitous he seems towards you at the moment. It could be that he is using you to get to me as much as you believe you are keeping him from me. I won't have it, Anna-Maria, which is why I am sending you back to Little Westbury so that you will be safe until this tyranny of Captain Denning's is ended.'

Her eyes flared, two whisky-lit flames in the gathering dusk. Lord, she had the most beautiful eyes. It was almost worth courting her anger to see them flash. 'So that I will be safe? Or is it that you will be safe from me? You won't have to protect me, won't have to worry over me, you won't have to take me dancing and watch me waltz with other men.'

'I've told you before, this is not about kisses. I don't expect you to understand, Anna-Maria. I am trying to make a new life here.' A life that could not include her for multiple reasons, her safety for one.

'You're not building a new life. You don't have a new home like Nikolay or Dimitri. They've put down roots in their communities. You've put down nothing. You move around like a nomad, in and out of rented homes. You won't even come up to London for my debut. You're isolating yourself,' she challenged, stripping him to the bone with such shocking clarity, he was speechless. 'You refuse to let me or anyone into the corners of your life. There is only you and your precious business, whatever that may be.'

Good Lord, the woman was exasperating! Stepan turned away and pushed a hand through his hair. 'I am trying to protect you,' he growled. He'd left town for four days and look what had happened!

'And I am trying to protect *you*. That's what's really bothering you.' Anna-Maria was as relentless as the brewing storm. 'Only a man can protect? Can a woman not protect her family?'

When had she grown up? This was not the child Anna-Maria. He'd known that physically for some time. But these were the words of a woman's mind, a woman who thought about the world and understood its dynamics. These were not the thoughts of a simpering miss who was nothing more than a blank slate to write on. These were the thoughts of a woman who knew her own mind and, more frighteningly, knew his. Thunder rolled in a great booming clap. He hadn't time for this. Joseph would be waiting downstairs for orders.

'I have things to see to. Pack your things, Anna-Maria. You will leave in the morning.' God willing. Who knew what the storm would do to the roads? He'd cross that bridge when he came to it and hope it wasn't washed out.

Anna-Maria crept down the servants' stairs, careful not to be seen, although it was a good time of day for sneaking. The servants were all in the kitchen preparing the evening meal and the relentless Mrs Batten was spending the night in town with her sister, thank goodness, or she'd already have the trunks out. But Anna was determined to go nowhere until she had answers. If Stepan would not *give* answers to her, she would find them for herself.

At the very least, she wanted to know where he went and what this business of his was. At the most, she wanted him to admit their kisses meant something, even if they left him confused. That would make two of them. None the less, she'd chosen him over the captain the moment Denning had mentioned the Russian spices. With every smile, with every flirtatious overture she'd given the captain, she'd reiterated that choice. She would do whatever she could to protect Stepan, just in case he needed protecting. He'd not thanked her for it. Perhaps this was what unrequited love felt like—the continual practice of unacknowledged selfless deeds.

Anna stepped out of the servants' stair and into the main hallway, quietly shutting the door behind her. She was certain Stepan had come this way. His office was down this hall. She tiptoed towards the sliver of light peeking beneath the office door. Someone was inside. She pressed an ear to the door, catching the murmur of low, male voices, one of them Stepan's.

'I need you to move the distillation equipment and the rest of the goods. Get them out to the alternate location further down the coast, or, if you can't travel tonight, get them deeper into the caves where no one is likely to look. I expect when Denning realises smugglers don't keep open accounts of activity in their offices, he will start searching properties.'

Dear Lord. Anna was reeling with the implications. She nearly missed the rest.

'Joseph, he knows about the spices. If he starts to search properties, he will come here first. The only thing that might stay him is the grand irony of coming to a prevention officer's home to find smuggled goods.'

Joseph. The new groom who was apparently not a groom.

No wonder he'd been so keen to accompany her on the picnic. 'And Miss Petrova's smile,' came a cheeky response that was cut short. She could imagine the sharp look that remark must have earned him.

'I will not send her to beg, is that understood?'

'Yes, milord. If that will be all, I'll get the boys right on it.' Joseph sounded chastised and penitent. She felt a moment's sympathy with him. She knew what it was like to be on the receiving end of Stepan's scolding tongue. But a moment was all she had to spare. Her mind was overwhelmed *and* she had to hide. She was in no state to face Stepan now. Anna darted to the curtains framing the long hall window. It was hardly original, but it had to do.

She stayed behind the bulky folds for a while, long after Stepan's footsteps had passed. She let her mind catch up with the information. This was a horrible turn of fate. Stepan was a smuggler. Not only that, he was *the* smuggler she'd tried to protect him from.

Stepan, a smuggler. A criminal. A lawbreaker.

She clutched at the heavy fabric of the curtains, sitting down hard on the ledge of the window. It couldn't be true. Not her noble Stepan, her moral compass, the man she counted on to know right and to do right. Wasn't this the very argument she'd just made with herself? And in one revelation, that image, that belief was destroyed. Emptiness swamped her at the loss.

She could not comprehend it. Why had a prince of Kuban lowered himself to the status of a common criminal, a man who could be hung? Why would he risk himself so recklessly and without cause? He didn't need the money. Didn't he know they all counted on him, that they couldn't do without him? *She* couldn't do without him.

What would her life be like without her north star? Fearful tears threatened as she imagined a life stretching before her without Stepan's strength always on the periphery, waiting to come to her aid, his presence constant and steady when all else was at sea—what would life be like even without his chiding and his grimness? They were as much a part of him as the other. And his touch, that touch that made her burn. What would her life be like without ever knowing that heat again? Knowing that she had jeopardised Stepan with her choices?

The rest of it hit her hard. She put a hand to her stomach, trying to calm the twin tides of panic. In her attempt to protect Stepan, she'd invited his worst enemy to look at his ledgers, a man who could see him hanged or transported. Based on Denning's actions to date, he'd not hesitate to hang Stepan as a show of force. She had unwittingly put him at risk. Her brother would never forgive her if something happened to Stepan.

Her brother. What would her brother do if he knew Stepan was smuggling? Dimitri would confront him. Dimitri would ask why, he would seek explanation. She would do the same, then; she would plead with him to stop before it was too late. There was still time. It was the one thought that calmed her. Denning would have to catch him first. Whatever Stepan had done, it wasn't in the ledgers. There was no paper trail. Second, he had a few weapons in his arsenal: irony and a smile, if he'd let her use it. First, she'd have to convince him to let her stay and she'd have to get him to confess. She needed a plan and there was little time to lose.

Anna stepped out from behind the curtains and hurried to the kitchens to inform the cook, 'Please have dinner brought to the library tonight.' Tonight, she would beard this Kubanian lion in his den and force him to see her as a woman who was equal to him—and whatever burdens he might carry—by any method possible. Tonight, there could be no holds barred. Too much was at stake.

Chapter Fourteen

'What is all this, Anna?' Stepan's question brought her out of the chair by the fire with a start. Lost in thought, she hadn't heard him come in. She'd planned to challenge him immediately upon his arrival in the library, but hearing the suspicion in his voice as he took in the food laid out on a low table between the chairs and the firelit intimacy of the room, she decided on a different tack.

Anna rose and gave a soft shrug of her shoulders. 'Dining rooms aren't for stormy nights.' There'd been enough challenges between them and those challenges usually ended in fights that resulted in Stepan creating distance between them. That was not the conclusion she was looking for tonight. She wanted to draw him close, not drive him away. They teetered on a knife-edge of no return. If she drove him away now, she would never get him back.

Anna gestured to the food. 'Come, sit with me and eat. You must be tired and hungry after travelling today.' And after so much more which she couldn't say out loud.

After coming home to see checkpoints set up along the roads, after brawling in the streets of Shoreham to save a merchant, after coming home to confront Captain Denning, after quarrelling with me, after meeting secretly with a fellow smuggler who might at this very moment be moving your stolen goods to a new location.

Stepan's day had been busy indeed, full of shocks and instant decisions. Hardly the kind of day one expected from the staid man who was set on being oh-so-proper that he bordered on boring. But she knew better now. That man was a façade, an incomplete image of who he really was.

Anna studied the strong, austere profile across from her, a dichotomy of its own, she realised, the long, sharp nose, the high Slavic cheekbones she'd seen so many times. It was a face saved from harshness by the hint of softness at its mouth. At first look, Stepan's mouth matched the rest of him—hard-set and given to grimness. If he'd been a military man, he would have been a demanding officer. But if one looked closely enough, the softness, and the kindness, were there, too. That same humanity was in his quicksilver eyes when they weren't storming. It was his mouth and his eyes that gave him his handsomeness, just as his nose and his cheekbones gave him his strength, his stoicism.

But he was not boring. Anna filled a plate with cheese and cold meat. Stepan had fooled them all with the act. Anyone in London who thought him a bore didn't know the half of it. Anyone who thought him too proper hadn't kissed him, or eavesdropped behind closed doors. She had, though. A frisson of awareness uncoiled down her spine, spreading warmth in its wake. She'd turned over the rock and seen what was underneath: a secret life full of danger and stormy passion. This was a man young girls should run from, but despite it all, she wanted to run to him. She wanted to be part of this other world he lived in.

Stepan opened the wine and poured each of them a glass. 'Are you packed?'

'No.' Anna gave a soft smile, watching his face. 'I've decided to stay, after all.' She said it as if the decision was hers to make.

Stepan's hand tightened about his wine glass. 'I think it is best if you go. We've already discussed this.'

'I couldn't possibly leave a friend in need.' Anna held his eyes over the rim of her glass as she sipped her wine. 'It's one of the lessons I learned from you and Dimitri and the others.' She had him there. Loyalty and devotion were paramount to Stepan.

His eyes glittered dangerously. 'You've already handled Captain Denning. What makes you think I am "in need"?'

Since I learned you were committing a hanging offence against the Crown. Anna wanted to rage like the storm outside. But a fight would give him what he wanted—something to wedge between them, something to send her away with. Anna set down her wine. It was time to move in for the kill, calmly, of course. 'Since I learned you are a smuggler.' She picked up her glass again, watching Stepan's face go blank. 'I heard you talking in your office today. I know all about your double life and now I want to know why.'

'You were eavesdropping.'
She knew.
She knew the one secret he wanted to keep from her. The significance of that hit him like a blow to the stomach. How could he keep her safe if she knew? Thank goodness she hadn't known *before* Denning had commandeered his books.

'Eavesdropping? Really, Stepan? I don't think that's the bigger crime here.' She was cool tonight. Gone was the raging princess who would have scolded and yelled. In her place was a temptation of a woman who sat before the fire, with her hair down and wine on her lips. She licked those lips now before speaking. 'When were you going to tell me? Does Dimitri know?'

'Never and no. Dimitri is not to know. You cannot tell him, Anna-Maria. You must promise me,' Stepan answered, trying to turn the point to his advantage. 'You understand why I need you to go now. If Denning thinks you know something, you become a liability to me and leverage to him. He could use you against me.' Surely that argument would hold sway with her. One's own personal safety was usually a powerful motivator.

But Anna-Maria crossed her legs confidently. She had an answer for that, too. 'Denning is another reason I need to stay. I can manage him with a smile, a little flirting.'

'No!' Stepan's fist came down on the arm of his chair. 'You will not toy with him. It is far too risky. He is a dangerous man, Anna. Do you have any idea what he could do to you and no one could stop him?' He did not want to imagine Anna subjected to any kind of torture designed to break him.

Her eyes flared, the cool mien she'd worn starting to slip. This was the Anna-Maria he knew. 'I am from Kuban, Stepan. I know *exactly* what absolute power can do. Do you think I haven't thought of it with the roadblocks and the sea barricades? It's like the past has come to the present. What about you? Do you know what he can do to *you*?'

That was when he saw it—the caring, the concern that surpassed a young girl's infatuation and superseded the physical tenets of desire. Physical desire he might have dealt with. Infatuation he could have overcome with time and eventual disillusionment. But love? That thing he knew nothing about. But the Petrovichs did. Dimitri and Anna-Maria were capable of it. He'd seen it a thousand times. Love was the Petrovichs' most powerful weapon. It was what made them dangerous to a man who'd sworn to be alone.

A litany formed in his mind, a silent warning to Anna-Maria. He could never be enough for her. *Do not fall in love with me. I am not worth it. Even if I could protect you, I will still disappoint you.* He would carry the mantra with him like a mental shield.

'I know very well the price for smuggling *if* one is caught.'

'Why do you risk it, then?' The quiet question took the conversation in an entirely different direction. This was no longer about her involvement, but his. 'You don't need the money, Stepan.' She would not be pawned off with a simple answer.

'Because it is a fight against injustice.' Would she understand? He searched her gaze, wanting to find validation, suddenly realising how much he was counting on that. Would she see him as nothing but a criminal or would she see the nobility in this choice; how could he *not* choose this path while others suffered? 'It gives meaning to my life and purpose to my days. I am needed.'

She held his eyes for a long time in thoughtful silence. Then she reached for his hand. 'I know what it is to want to be needed.' She was quiet before she spoke again. 'But we need you, too, Stepan. *I* need you. Alive—not a martyr to a cause.'

'Do you think I can't make a difference?' Stepan challenged. 'That one man's sacrifice cannot change the outcome? You didn't think so in Marseilles when you emptied your purse for the urchins.'

'That was different. I couldn't hang for it. I sacrificed nothing, not even money. Those coins meant little to me. I had more.'

'I don't mean to be caught.' Certainly not by the likes of Captain Denning—a man who saw this as a mission that served his personal gain without thinking what his success would cost the coastal economy. If Denning succeeded, people would suffer. More children like Joseph and the others would go hungry.

'What of you, Stepan? Do you think the prospect of what Denning could do to you does not fill *me* with a certain amount of dread? I'd rather take my chances flirting with him than see you at the gallows,' Anna-Maria pressed.

'And *I'd* rather take my chances outsmarting him than see you imprisoned and raped in the name of one man's justice.' Or one man's revenge, if he tweaked the man's nose too much.

He rose from his chair and knelt before her, clasping her hands where they lay in her lap. He looked into her face, letting his eyes plead with hers. Her hair fell over her shoulders. She'd worn it down tonight and it gave her the look of both Madonna and Magdalene at once, a temptation come to life.

'Why can I not worry for you? Why can I not fight for you as you fight for others?' she challenged softly. Did she understand how provocative she looked? Good Lord, she was burning him alive with those eyes, with those words and those wine-stained lips, the touch of her hands in his.

His hands clenched over hers. 'Because you're mine, damn it, *you're mine*,' he growled fiercely, knowing the fight was lost, not because he couldn't resist her—he'd been resisting for a while now—but because he didn't want to any more. He did not want to resist while lightning flashed on the waves and rain pelted the long glass windows. He wanted to give in, to take comfort and pleasure before the roar of the fire, in her arms.

'Show me, then, Stepan. Make me yours.' Fire lit her eyes with desire's flame. There was nothing of the Madonna about her now as he breathed in the lavender scent of her, his body tightening in want, his mind temporarily overriding all the objections that formed his resistance, replacing them with maybes and what ifs. What if in this room they could be Anna-Maria the woman and Stepan the man? What if they could suspend their common history and ties? Suspend the choices he'd made that put him beyond her reach? Maybe then it would be possible to discover who they might be together.

Stepan rose up, his mouth inches from hers. 'I want you, Anna-Maria, but there can be no future in it.' He heard the hoarseness in his own voice. Did she hear it, too? Did she understand what it meant? What wanting entailed when it moved from the emotional realm to the physical?

'But there can be tonight, Stepan.'

His mouth sealed hers in a kiss, full-bodied and open-mouthed, as he took the invitation. His hands gripped her thighs through the fabric of her skirts. He gave a moan of appreciation, the sound a connoisseur might make upon tasting some perfectly prepared delicacy. His senses were on high alert as he tasted her anew: the wine on her tongue, the clench of her hands in his hair signalling the intensity of her own hunger, the smell of her—lavender and the faintest hint of female arousal—the sound of her need a breathy panting at his ear.

'Stepan.' His name was a gasp on her lips and it spoke a thousand messages: that they had passed the stage of experimenting mouths, that kissing was no longer enough, no longer able to satisfy the craving they raised in one another. His hands slipped beneath her skirts, sliding up silk-stockinged legs. 'Take them off.' She breathed her command against his neck and he complied, his fingers skimming the high, tender skin of her thigh, working the garter and then rolling down the silk on first one leg and then the other. Stockings discarded, his hands pushed back her skirts, his mouth following in their wake with a trail of kisses over the curve of one calf, over the inner skin of one thigh until he reached the secret place between her legs. He was aware of her as he knelt between her thighs, the scent of her in his nostrils, the wetness of her teasing his fingers.

'Part for me,' he whispered the invitation at her core, letting his breath play over her damp curls. She did and he kissed the tender crease of her thighs in reward, feeling her body tense, hearing her breath catch. He licked at her seam then, tasting her, teasing her as he sought the hidden nub within her folds.

Her hands gripped his hair, seeking an anchor, her legs widened and her pleasure became his pleasure. They were joined together in this act, the most intimate pleasure he could afford to give her, and the most she could afford to receive. Wanting had not destroyed his sense of reason entirely. They could have this and perhaps survive it, although that seemed in question at the moment. His heart was pounding as she arched into him, pressing her core to his mouth, to his tongue, pushing him, pushing herself to the precipice of release where they might soar. Above him, Anna cried out, an incoherent series of sobs, her body starting to thrash and strain against him—wanting freedom, wanting release, wanting *him*. And then, when it seemed she would burst, she shattered against his hand, his mouth. With a final cry she slipped from the chair and into his arms, her body boneless.

He held her in his arms, their bodies stretched before the fire, as she recovered. This was a new sweetness, to hold her, to know that he alone had brought her to this state, at her invitation. His arm tightened around her in realisation and in possession. How long could he have her? How long would it take her to realise his flaw—and that it went far deeper than smuggling—that he knew plenty of pleasure, but nothing of love? He pushed the idea away, refusing to let such thoughts cloud the moment. Here and now, he was enough.

Her hand rested over his heart where it still pounded from his own exertions and he felt her smile where her head lay against his chest. 'There was pleasure for you?' she asked softly, a reminder that while she was indeed fire and passion, she was innocent, too.

'Yes. To offer another pleasure is a pleasure for the giver, as well.'

'But it is not all. There can be more.' The hand over his heart moved lower. He stalled it in a gentle grip. She would find a full erection there if he allowed it and he could not. He'd already allowed too much.

'There is more,' he acceded. 'But not tonight.' Perhaps not ever, he silently chided himself. Most likely not ever. To say perhaps created the hope that the possibility of wedding her, of bedding her, existed. Wedding her was the only way the latter could happen for him. He would not take her to his bed without the sanctity of marriage. She was not like the widows of the Kubanian court. She was pure diamond, full of light. He would not sully that nor would he limit that light by claiming it and taking away her choices. Anna-Maria was the light and she was meant for so much more than his darkness.

Darkness always swallowed light, much as cool water overcame hot. He'd learned that from his father. No matter what efforts he'd made to make his father love him, *want* him, the darkness had won. As a result, it lived in him now, the curse, perhaps, of the Shevchenko men who seemed doomed to destroy those around them. He could only hope to contain it, to keep it from tainting her. He would not let his darkness devour Anna.

He returned her hand to his chest and released it. She sighed reluctantly at the loss. 'Tell me about smuggling, Stepan. Tell me about your cause.'

Stepan recognised a flanking motion when he saw one. He would have to grant her these questions. If she could not have him one way, she would have him another. 'Because I must fight injustice where I find it.' He felt more than saw the pucker of her brow and settled her closer against him as he explained. 'Freedom comes in many forms, as does tyranny. Taxing decides who can participate in the economy and how. Only the rich can afford to import and pay taxes on those cargos. And for what? To fill a king's pockets for his own luxury. Enslavement has multiple guises, Anna, labour is just the most obvious. Economic enslavement is more subtle.'

'As is marriage,' Anna commented with a wry edge to her sleepy voice. 'But a man does not hang for *that*.'

'No, he does not,' Stepan whispered, doubly glad he had limited their foray into pleasure of the revocable kind, the kind that did no damage. He'd left her untouched in all the ways that mattered to society. She still had her choices before her. She could walk away from him.

'I think of it sometimes,' she whispered quietly, her hand playing on his chest. 'If I had married the Pasha's son, I'd be living in Turkey, part of a man's harem, at his beck and call, my own will of no import to him.'

There was a catch to her voice. Stepan hurried to ease it. 'It cannot happen now. The laws are abolished and you are a continent away.' He did not like to think of her in that foreign arrangement. Polygamy was not for her, its concept of marriage and love so very different than hers. It would have destroyed her.

'No, but it could have if no one had fought for me. If Dimitri had not offered himself, if Yulian had not been willing, if you hadn't come for me against my father's objections.' She was drawing circles around his nipple. 'I will never forget that night. You were so fierce, standing up to my father. I would have walked out of the house with you right then, in nothing but my nightgown.'

Stepan chuckled softly. 'You would have been cold.'

'I doubt it. You would not have allowed it.'

'Hmmm.' He liked the feel of her hand on him, her touch light as it skimmed his chest, and he wondered, 'Is that why you resist marriage? Because you think of him? Of what it would have been like in the Pasha's household?'

'Perhaps.' Her hand stilled on his chest. 'Or maybe I resist because I know little of marriage, polygamous or otherwise. What I do know hardly recommends itself. It tore my father apart. Love hurts.'

'True enough. And yet Dimitri has embraced it, to the good, I think. It's a pleasure to see him with Evie. Their happiness is obvious.' He was torturing himself going down this path.

'Yes. I wonder, though, can we all be Dimitri?' she argued, testing his hypothesis with her cynicism.

'Nikolay and Illarion think so. Ruslan, too.' Stepan couldn't help but crack that nut open with her here before the fire. 'I did not peg you for a cynic, Anna.'

'A realist.' She sighed against him. 'Marriage is different for a woman. She gives her all to it whether she chooses to or not. There is no equality in marriage. Equality is freedom, as you've so adequately advocated tonight. Why should marital equality be any different than economic equality? Why should only certain people have access to it?'

She shifted, her body warm. 'Love can be both empowering and disempowering, a double-edged sword.'

'Indeed,' Stepan murmured. He'd worried about taking her innocence only to find it was quite gone and had been for some time. And yet the light in her still remained. Despite her cynicism, she'd found a way to defeat the darkness.

He envied her that. It intensified his desire for her, his desire to possess her, to fight for her. The woman nestled against his shoulder held his heart and his secrets, and tonight they'd made another secret. No one could ever guess what had happened in this room any more than anyone could ever guess he was a smuggler. Those secrets were dangerous in their own ways and she possessed them both.

Outside, the storm raged, battering the windows. There was no question of sending her away now, storm or not. He should feel guilty over what he'd done. But not yet. There would be plenty of time for guilt later and it *would* come, Stepan was sure of it. Tonight he'd broken promises to himself and betrayed a friend's trust whether that friend knew it or not, all for the selfish fantasy of having Anna-Maria, of pretending for a short while that he knew how to love.

Chapter Fifteen

He needed penetration—something more than putting up roadblocks and sea blockades. Those were external, passive measures. They could not *expose*. He needed someone on the inside, a rat, a mole, or an unsuspecting innocent. It was the one thought in Elias Denning's mind as he listened to his lieutenants run through their weekly reports, all of them with a singular theme: after two weeks of laying siege to Shoreham, their efforts had caught *nothing*.

It was not enough to smash windows and beat shopkeepers, to seize importers' ledgers and ransack warehouses full of legitimately acquired goods. He needed to catch someone red-handed and that was not going to happen no matter how many roadblocks he set up until he broke Shoreham's complicity. As long as the good citizens of Shoreham thought to protect each other, that complicity would stand.

Denning leaned back in his chair, hands laced over the flat of his stomach, and looked each of his officers in the eye. 'Gentlemen, can you tell me what each of your reports have in common?' he said benignly. He would unleash the full force of his dissatisfaction on them soon, but he'd let them walk into the trap first.

One lieutenant drew himself up smartly, taking the bait. 'They all indicate there has not been a smuggling attempt since our methods have been put in place, Captain.'

Denning came forward over the table, ready to wipe the pride from the lieutenant's face as he roared, 'That means absolutely *nothing*! Do you know why it means nothing? Because we have *no* proof.' Without tangible evidence, who knew what some enterprising soul might have smuggled out of town in plain sight or who was still running illegal goods along the back roads of Sussex?

He'd discovered successful smuggling was far more about relationships and trust than it was about fast horses and secret pathways. With collaboration, one could smuggle in plain sight. There was nothing he loved better than a good mystery and the thrill of pitting his mind against the unknown. It was like a knot that, when unravelled, revealed truth at its core. Shoreham-by-Sea was proving to be such a knot, although the unravelling was not going as smoothly as Denning had hoped.

He braced both his hands on the table and fixed his men with a dark stare. 'What we need is to find a weak link and expose it. That link is not a thing or an action, it's a "who". We need to find a tattler. Use whatever leverage you have to.' His men exchanged looks and he knew what they were thinking. Force hadn't worked well so far. They'd smashed windows and beaten merchants and still submission hadn't come. No one had talked and the damnable thing was, everyone knew who the captain was looking for and Denning knew they knew that he knew they knew. But no one said a thing.

The theory was that eventually a merchant would tire of shelves full of goods customers couldn't afford to buy and would come forward, or a smuggler would tire of empty pockets and would make a reckless run. 'Shoreham as a collective isn't desperate enough. Not yet. But perhaps there is an individual who is desperate and, if so, I want that individual found. Turn your attention to the poor, the most needy and the most vulnerable.' He recognised now that it had been folly to pursue the wealthy importers. They might be fully participating in the smuggling and catching them might be the quickest route to bringing down the whole operation, but they were also the most well protected. They had money and resources. The poor tub man who smuggled to augment his piddling wages as a fisherman didn't have those protections. It was not as flashy to net 'Jones the common fisherman' as it was to bring down a wealthy importer, but it would be a start.

Denning gave instructions to continue searching the coastline for hidden coves and caves and dismissed the officers. He had his own work to do. His men might indeed turn up a much-needed weak link in the chain and give him a legitimate fish on the line. But if not, he needed a private contingency. If he wanted a promotion he had to show that if one could not catch a real smuggler, one could always fabricate one.

Denning paced the length of his field office, thoughts forming and coalescing into a strategy. If he chose the right victim to frame, no one would gainsay him. He had the authority of the military and English law behind him, and others would be more concerned for their own hides than that of their neighbour, as long as he chose the right one.

Stepan Shevchenko came to mind quite readily for several reasons. He was an outsider and a foreigner, someone Shoreham might be less likely to protect if given the right inducements, especially if there was nothing to protect. Shoreham could give him Shevchenko if they weren't protecting anyone in his network—especially if there wasn't one—or if there were any struggling tub men to protect, or products the community was counting on, the cost in betraying Shevchenko would be minimal.

Denning smirked. The more he thought about it, the more he liked it. Framing someone for smuggling might actually work better than catching the real thing. Shevchenko was exactly the 'big fish' he hoped to net. He'd prefer catching a wealthy importer who ostensibly sat atop his own smuggling network. Denning knew he was spinning fictions at this point. Shevchenko's books had turned up nothing of note and his ship had been…well, to put it bluntly, 'shipshape'. But Shoreham could afford to give him up.

There were other reasons to go after Shevchenko, as well. The haughty 'prince' had tried to interfere with his work. He had not hesitated to call off the soldiers in the street. That sort of man might decide to rally the people against him. The last thing he needed was for the smugglers to organise any more than they already were. Right now, he understood fear was driving them underground and forcing them to keep to themselves. But if someone were to unite them, they would have power. He wouldn't be able to stop them, then. Shevchenko had already made him look foolish on more than one occasion: the inn yard the night of the ball, during his visit to Seacrest, on board the *Lady Frances*. The list was mounting.

He would not tolerate an upstart, self-styled royal from a place he'd never heard of before

last year to get the jump on him—profession-
ally *or* personally. There was the issue of Miss
Petrova between them, as well. When Elias Denning wanted a woman, he took her regardless of
what previous claims might have been made.
Few women complained and few men resisted.
It was seldom in either of their better interests
to do otherwise. It was time Stepan Shevchenko
learned that lesson as the unfortunate provincial
Governor in Barbados had learned. That man
he'd generously let watch. Denning smiled in
remembrance. The more powerful the man, the
more he liked to bring them down. It was time
for another visit to Seacrest.

It was past time to go down to breakfast. Anna-
Maria had been putting it off. If she waited long
enough, she might come up with an answer to
her question: The morning after, how did a girl
face the man who'd given her pleasure? Evie's
lessons had not covered such a topic. Then again,
Evie's lessons hadn't covered what had happened
last night. More than one rule had been broken. Stepan might have pleasured her, but she'd
started it and that hadn't been covered in Evie's

lessons either. Debutantes didn't invite men to seduce them. Anna-Maria approached the stairs with uncharacteristic tentativeness. Maybe Stepan would already be gone for the day.

What a ninny she was! She'd finally got what she wanted. She'd broken his staunch self-control—she had seen what lay beyond when they set aside their prescribed roles. She'd had the full force of his attentions and now she wanted him to be gone? That wasn't quite true. She wanted the awkwardness to be gone. She wished she were sophisticated like his other lovers in Kuban, worldly women of the court who knew just how to behave in any given situation.

The breakfast room was deserted when she reached it. She didn't know if she should be relieved or not. She didn't have to face him, but at the same time she *wanted* to face him, wanted to see in his eyes what she'd seen last night: the passion, the pleasure, the desire, all for her. Just her. She wanted it again, only this time, *she* wanted to pleasure *him*. Could she make him shatter against her hand as he had her? The possibility made her face go warm as she fixed her eggs—her hand on Stepan, stroking him, holding the hardness of him. They were bold thoughts for a girl raised in sheltered circumstances. Did other girls think such things? Want such things? If they did, did they *claim* them? She would claim them, tonight if possible. She smiled to herself as she ate. Simply being here was a victory in itself. Stepan had not sent her away, after all. Proof of what a girl could do when she set her mind to it. What it all meant, she had no idea. She would take it day by day.

'Have I caught you at a guilty pleasure?'

She looked up startled, her mind not registering what her ears had heard. She'd been expecting Stepan. She still was. She blinked, not believing her eyes. It was not Stepan who stood before her, but Captain Denning, dressed in his impeccable uniform and holding flowers. He smiled and swept her a bow. This was bad. Flowers were bad. Actually, they were good, technically. Evie's lessons *had* covered this. Only she didn't want flowers from Captain Denning. 'Captain, what a surprise.' Behind his shoulder the butler looked upset, indicating the captain had overridden protocol and charged forward without permission.

She glanced at the little clock on a side table. The captain had violated protocol in another way, too. She might have been late for breakfast, but she hadn't been that late. 'The flowers are lovely. I'll send for a vase right away.' She nodded to the butler, who hurried away. With luck, he would return with more than a vase. Then she offered the captain a coy smile. 'Isn't it a bit early for a social call?'

'It would be, except that this not a social call, Miss Petrova. May I sit?' Captain Denning smiled, too, and helped himself to the chair across from her, another breach of good etiquette. A gentleman never sat until invited. She'd not taken him as an ill-bred man on previous occasions. She could only infer these oversights were intentional. What she couldn't divine was the reason for flaunting convention. Was it meant as an insult? If so, she wasn't sure what she'd done to earn the comment, or was it meant to be a show of authority? Did he mean to suggest he was above the law or that he made his own rules? The butler returned with a vase and took the bouquet to the sideboard before discreetly withdrawing. Either Stepan was nowhere to be found, or the butler hadn't thought to look.

'A business call with flowers, Captain?' she questioned with another dimpling smile that hid her growing trepidation over his unorthodox presence. After what she'd learned last night, she could no longer believe he was here for her alone. 'I don't know if I should be flattered or confused.' She gave a breathy laugh. 'If it's business you've come to discuss, I am afraid Prince Shevchenko isn't available at the moment.' She didn't want to admit she didn't know where he was. She was acutely aware that without Stepan's presence, she and the captain were the only two people in the house aside from the servants—Mrs Batten was still down at her sister's. Too bad. Anna would have liked to see Mrs Batten giving the captain a dressing-down for his early call.

'I have business that is better done with you. I need a woman's opinion.' Captain Denning helped himself to toast and tea. 'I have been thinking about the spices I mentioned at our picnic. Do you recall the saffron and the anise?' She tried to keep her expression neutral, but he smiled, suggesting she'd not been successful. 'I thought you might. You would know them better than me, I think. They are from the south of Russia, from your home, I believe.' He settled a napkin in his lap, making himself at home. 'Or they can be. I understand they are grown there. Can you tell me about them?'

'I am not an herbalist.' Anna-Maria hesitated. What was he getting at? Was he probing for information or was he merely issuing a warning?

'Come, Miss Petrova, no need to be shy,' Captain Denning pushed. 'Saffron is expensive. It is the purvey of wealthy women such as yourself. I do not forget you're a princess.' He flattered her shamelessly. 'Surely, you know what it is used for? How the women get it?'

'Some use it for hair dye. I imagine they get it at an apothecary. It's not illegal.' Anna-Maria set down her fork, challenging the captain.

'It is illegal when a tax is not paid on it coming into the country.'

It was time to go on the offensive. She fixed the captain with a hard stare. 'Are you insinuating that I have something to do with illegal saffron?' The claim was meant to make him appear ridiculous in his speculations. He remained woefully unperturbed.

'Not you, my lady. But perhaps Prince Shevchenko knows something about it? After all, the herb is Russian and he is Russian. The spice was imported recently and he was the last with a ship to arrive heralding from that part of the world. If he, *or* you, could help me solve the riddle, I would be grateful.'

She shook her head and rose, signalling the conversation was done. He rose with her. 'I am afraid we have no help to give you, as you should already have been aware. You saw no record of saffron or anise in the *Lady Frances*'s ledgers. It did not come from the prince's ship. Now, if you would excuse me? I have things to do this morning.' She intended to leave the room. If he could break rules, so could she, but he had the door to his back and he easily blocked her passage with a hand at her arm, his body filling her only exit.

'Do not think to fob me off with a smile and a haughty air, Miss Petrova.' His grip was hard, his eyes cold. 'I thought you and I were becoming friends. We danced, we rode together, we picnicked. Then I come here today asking for a little friendly help and you all but throw me out.'

She tugged at her arm, but he did not let her go.

'Let me be clear, I am here hunting smugglers. I *will* find them, Miss Petrova. I will bring them and their accomplices to justice. Do you know what justice is for a smuggler? It is hanging. It's a most unpleasant way to die. The neck snaps, the bowels go. Hopefully one is dead before that happens, but it's not a guarantee. The neck does not always break cleanly. They are painful, those last few moments.'

Bile rose in Anna-Maria's throat, but she would not look away from him, she would not blink. It was what he wanted. He wanted fear from her as he backed her to the wall, his grip on her arm too strong to break. She made contact with the wall none too gently. 'I have nothing to be afraid of, Captain. If you've come here to threaten me or to frighten me, you have failed.' It took all her courage to say that and a great deal of bravado. She wasn't certain she didn't have anything to be afraid of. What had Stepan done? Yesterday she would have fearlessly defied the captain with a certainty knowing that Stepan had no hand in the crimes of Shoreham. Today she knew better.

'You're a lovely young woman and possibly a naïve one.' The captain's eyes dropped to her lips, but it brought on none of the sensations Stepan's gaze did. 'I would be inclined to overlook any complicity on your part due to your own innocence.'

'In exchange for what, Captain?' Anna-Maria parried. The man was the basest of animals if he thought she'd betray Stepan for the sake of her own protection. If he believed that, he didn't understand the depths of Kubanian friendship.

'For your gratefulness.' His eyes lingered on her breasts and her mouth, leaving no mistake as to what he defined as gratefulness.

'I have nothing to offer you,' she replied staunchly. Whatever favour she might have briefly shone on the captain out of courtesy for his rank was rudely erased in these moments. He'd showed himself to be a wolf in sheep's clothing. For the first time, she saw the true danger of him. It was not in his rank, or in his assigned duty, but in his manner. Here was a man willing to prey on those he perceived as weak and vulnerable.

'If you change your mind, you know where to find me. No excuses, Miss Petrova. Now, I think a down payment on that gratefulness is in order and I'll be on my way.' Without warning, his mouth claimed hers, hard and bruising, his body trapping her to the wall. She struggled, pushing at him with her hands, but he was strong, far too strong for her. His tongue invaded her mouth and she bit down, hard, tasting blood. He reared back in shocked surprise, a hand swiping at his mouth and coming away red. 'You little bitch!' He raised his hand to strike her.

Chapter Sixteen

Anna-Maria braced herself for the blow, but it never fell. 'Step away from her!' Stepan roared through the doorway, seizing the captain's arm and pinning it behind him. 'How dare you lay hands on a princess of Kuban, you filthy cur?'

'You are assaulting an officer of the King!' Denning wasn't to be outdone. He got a leg behind Stepan's, effectively tripping him. The two men went down, crashing into the breakfast table. China clattered, silverware jumped as they brawled on the floor, fists pummelling. Denning might have more experience in dirty fighting, but Stepan was more prepared.

She wasn't sure that was the right word. Perhaps premeditated was more apt. Denning hadn't been expecting strong resistance when he'd kissed her. The men rolled towards her and Anna leapt out of the way, taking refuge by the window. She had never seen Stepan like this, fury unleashed. It was one thing knowing a man could fight. It was another to see it. It was both impressive and frightening.

She stifled a scream as Denning bit down on Stepan's hand, earning a half second of distraction. Stepan retaliated, finally able to get on top of him. Straddling the captain, he landed a bout-ending facer to Denning's jaw. He dragged the stunned officer to his feet, manhandling him towards the door.

'I wasn't aware forcing oneself on a woman was the King's law. What an uncivilised country this must be,' Stepan spat. He shoved Denning into the care of two waiting footmen. 'The captain was just leaving. Please make sure he does.'

Anna-Maria sank into a chair, her courage leaving her now that the fighting was over. But Stepan was still bristling. 'Are you all right?' He was beside her, kneeling at her chair, searching her face as he took her hands.

'I am fine. He was just…rough. He didn't harm me.' She lowered her voice. Her own hurts and fears could wait. She searched his face. 'If he catches you, he *will* hang you,' she whispered. 'And it will be my fault. He will not forgive you for this latest insult.' This morning had been about more than smuggling. It had been a blow to Denning's masculine pride.

Stepan gave her a hard stare. 'He'd have to catch me first.' The mysterious something crackled to life between them, flickering in his eyes, and she knew he saw it in hers, recalling the power of last night, rekindling the need to have that power, that pleasure again.

'I do not find that at all humorous.' She wanted to be in his arms, wanted to assure herself that he was here and whole.

'Good. It was not meant to be.' His eyes glittered with danger and sensuality, drawing her in all the while pushing her away. 'As this morning so aptly demonstrated, smuggling is a perilous business.'

His words did not reassure her. For the first time, it hit her with full force what she'd walked into the middle of. This was a deadly game of cat and mouse with complex layers. On the surface, this was about smuggling, about bringing lawbreakers to justice. Those lawbreakers were different depending on whose side you were on. To Stepan, this was a battle against injustice. But beneath that surface lay another dark competition between two men for a woman. *For her.*

'I want you to know why I stopped last night, Anna.' Stepan's grip on her hands tightened, his voice low. 'I would not have, if I thought I could offer you anything at all.'

He would have made love to her on the rug before the fire. The very image sent a primal shiver of desire skittering down her spine. Even in the light of day, the words conjured up a heat low in her belly. Leave it to Stepan to declare himself in the most unorthodox of ways. Whenever she imagined the moment, they were wrapped in one another's arms in the lingering remnants of a kiss or something more, not sitting in the middle of the breakfast room, his knuckles raw and bleeding.

Perhaps that, coupled with the intensity of her own desire, accounted for her own unorthodox response. 'You don't have to be a smuggler, Stepan.' She whispered the words, knowing already the request bordered on blasphemous.

'You can stop now. Denning can't catch someone who doesn't exist. We could be together and you would be safe.' She wanted those things above all else. She stood and reached for him, her arms seeking to go about his neck. She would show him…

'No, Anna. Although you'd tempt the devil himself.' He disengaged her arms and stepped back, his dark gaze shuttered. He'd closed her out. Again. The realisation pierced her deep at the core of her soul. He *wanted* to be alone. Not just temporarily, not just physically, but always and *in* all ways. He was alone in this room right now even though she stood before him.

'Don't shut me out.' She ground out the words with terse force. 'Don't tell me you don't want me. You've already admitted as much. And I want you.' She would fight for him right now with words, with kisses, and the servants be damned.

Something flickered behind that shuttered gaze. 'You don't know what you want, Anna. In London you will have choices, so many different types of men and lifestyles to choose from. Dimitri has hopes for you. You cannot possibly decide until you see what is on offer. You've been nowhere; you've seen nothing.'

'I've seen *you*. Whatever else there is to see is unimportant,' she said simply. Once, she would have railed at his words. Today, she was steady, her course unfazed. 'This is not about Dimitri. This is about us, Stepan, and what we can be. That is our choice alone.'

He pushed a hand through his hair, pulling it loose from its leather tie. 'I cannot risk you, Anna-Maria. No matter what I want, I have to give you up.'

A more superficial woman would believe he was choosing his cause over her. That woman would see this as rejection. A devilish stab of jealousy would gouge her over the realisation if she let it. But Anna knew better. She saw it as protection, as the sum of who he was: a man who was noble and good, who put the needs of others above his own. She held his silver gaze. Gingerly she reached for his scraped hand. 'You don't have to choose, Stepan. It doesn't have to be me or your cause. I only meant to imply you had a choice to walk away if you wanted.'

She wet her lips. 'If you won't walk away from

it, then I'll walk towards it.' She could not do otherwise. Her choice had been made long ago, she could see that now, and come what might, heaven or hell, she would not back away from it. 'I choose you, just as I chose you over my father's refusal to leave in Kuban, just as I chose you over my fear on that ledge in the mountains. I have always chosen you. I always will.'

'It's not only that, Anna. I can offer you nothing.'

She shook her head. 'You and I understand that term quite differently. Let me be the judge of what you offer. It has always been more than enough for me.'

Something palpable passed between them at her words and she knew in her bones this was a moment that would change everything. It would change *them* and it would change what lay between them. Stepan nodded slowly, accepting her complicity. He gave her his hand, warm and strong. 'Then come with me. I have something to show you.'

She went without question, letting her silence be proof of her trust, her belief in him. He led her down a staircase secreted behind the panels in the study to the caverns below Seacrest, the sound of the surf growing louder as they descended. Stepan spoke little on the stairs, only referring to the hidden passageway, saying, 'In case you ever need it.' She could imagine the reasons why she'd need to know: in case she ever needed to escape, or needed to hide herself, or needed to warn him. There were too many reasons, dangerous reasons that reminded her how precarious their situation was, of the danger she'd committed herself to. It did occur to her that this was one last strategy of Stepan's to warn her away despite her brave speech.

At the bottom, Stepan stood aside with a flourish of his hand. 'My workshop.' Workshop was far too modest of a term. The cavern spread before her was filled with adolescent boys working at various tasks: sorting through trunks, taking inventory and stacking casks. This wasn't a workshop, but an underground factory. They could be as loud as they liked, any sound they made was muffled by waves and stone.

She was careful with her face, aware that Stepan watched her take it all in. 'So this is where it all happens? What do you do exactly?' She studied the casks. 'I thought they'd be bigger.'

Stepan laughed. 'I'll give you a tour. We start with distilling. The vodka comes unmixed at full strength, which could kill a man if he drank it. This way, we can import as much product as possible in the smallest cask possible.' He arched an eyebrow at her unspoken query. 'Smaller things are easier to hide.' He pointed to a large tub in the corner. 'We mix the undiluted vodka with enough water to make it potable and then we fill up half ankers with the final product and ship it out.' He held up a set of half ankers. 'The men who carry them are called tub men. They simply walk to London or to a waiting wagon with these.'

'Walk? You expect me to believe they just walk right out with these over their shoulders?' The simplicity of such an arrangement seemed at odds with the danger it presented.

Stepan shrugged. 'Well, the bat men go with them as guards if need be. It's hard to protect oneself while wearing a cask.'

'I'm overwhelmed. This is impressive.' She shot Stepan a look. They circled the cavern and she saw the obvious—the spice trunks Denning was after, the silks, finer than anything any London draper could lay claim to, the Turkish carpets. She saw the less obvious, too—all the young men it took to run this enterprise of Stepan's. He was keeping several families in food and shoes.

'This reminds me of Aladdin's cave from the fairy tales.'

'This is only the back cave. There's another one further up, closer to the beach where we unload. It's vacant right now while Denning's at large,' Stepan explained as they walked among the crew. He stopped and spoke with the boys at intervals, smiling and complimenting them, shaking hands and slapping shoulders.

He introduced each of them by name. There was Timothy from London, who'd been working in a brothel doing odd errands in the middle of the night to pay for his board; Malcolm and Matthew, two brothers who'd swept floors in a gaming hall and slept in the alleyway behind it; there was Irish, who didn't know his real name, who was younger and thinner than the others, but fiercely loyal to Stepan. 'Found me in the rubbish, milord did, when I was six and my parents threw me away,' he boasted. 'Now, I'm his lookout because I'm small and no one can see me.' When he was six? That meant he couldn't be more than eight now. Anna felt a piece of her heart break.

Stepan ruffled the boy's ginger hair. 'He's right. Irish is the best.' There were others to meet: the local lads who were fourteen and fifteen and trying to earn a wage for their families, some of them without a father at home and younger siblings to feed. With each one, the affection between them and Stepan was genuine and it touched her to see Stepan in such a setting. This was a man born to lead. He simply couldn't help it.

Stepan's mouth was close to her ear when he spoke. 'Do you see why I can't walk away? While there is still injustice, while there is still need, while these boys and others like them need a champion, I must fight as best I can.'

'This is your Marseilles.' She gave him a soft look. 'I've always seen, Stepan.' It wasn't enough to simply give these boys jobs. He could do that well enough with the legitimate end of his shipping business, but it wouldn't solve the larger problem. The economic injustices would still exist. He could help far more people this way directly and indirectly. Ruslan had his revolution and Stepan had his.

She recognised Joseph and he winked as they passed. 'Show her the good stuff, milord, it's behind the curtain.'

Stepan led her into an alcove where two trunks stood open, carefully packed with ells of silk. Stepan reached inside the wrappings and pulled out a length of ice-blue fabric. 'This is some of the best silk in the world.'

Anna fingered it appreciatively and then smiled as their hands brushed, sending a tingle up her arm. 'Freedom feels beautiful,' she whispered. 'Thank you for showing me.' The gift of bringing her here was an extraordinary show of trust. She was overwhelmed.

She let her eyes hold his, let him know she saw everything that he'd done for these boys, that she understood his fight, that she knew it could be no other way for him and, because of that, it could be no other way for her. 'You've a good heart, Stepan.' She moved into him, wanting to draw him to her. She was so hungry for him. She'd never felt closer to him than she did in these moments. He'd exposed himself utterly in bringing her here, stripped himself bare. He had entrusted her with his life, with the lives of the boys who worked for him and all those who counted on him.

'Don't, Anna. If you kiss me now, I will be lost.'

'I want to be lost, lost in your world, lost with you. That's what coming down here is all about,' she insisted, moving towards him again. Why did he continue to resist when the battle was won?

'I should send you home where you will be safe.' He was still trying out the old argument. Did he think seeing all of this would change her mind? If anything, it had only intensified her commitment.

'But you don't want to,' she argued softly, watching the truth of it play in his eyes. His desire was rising.

'No, God help me and Dimitri forgive me, I don't.' Stepan's voice was a fierce whisper. 'Anna, I gave up any future I might have had when I chose this. But I will not take your future from you.'

The fire between them stuttered. There was something new in his tone. This was not the old argument about her Season in London. This was not about smuggling, but something new, something more.

'I don't want to go back.' In any way. Not back to Dimitri, not back to the innocence she'd had yesterday. She met his gaze. 'I thought I had made that clear upstairs.' His hand drifted down the curve of her cheek, raising the hairs on her arms in a delicious thrill.

'I need you to be safe,' he murmured, perhaps one last attempt to dissuade her. 'Not just from Denning's retribution.' She searched his face, not understanding. 'I need you to be safe from me.'

She gave a soft smile. 'I am safe enough with you, I always have been.' She licked her lips in a delicate gesture, watching his eyes go dark, this time with desire.

'You don't know me, not like you think you do.' He moved closer to her, letting their hips brush against one another. 'This is a dangerous game.'

'We've played dangerous games before,' she reminded him. 'Leaving Kuban was a dangerous game. We might have been hunted.' Their foreheads pressed together, his head bent to hers, his hands at her hips.

'No,' he corrected. 'I don't mean smuggling or exile. I mean *this*.' He made a small gesture with his hand in the tiny space between them. 'Us. *This* is dangerous. We've never played with us before. There is no coming back from it, only going forward. I promised myself I wouldn't...'

'Shh.' Anna pressed a finger to his lips. 'There's been no coming back since you've told me. We are in *this* together. We cannot control Denning, we cannot control what happens tomorrow, only what happens now, only what happens between us. All you have to do is choose me, Stepan.'

'I've always chosen you, even when I didn't want to, even when I knew I shouldn't.'

He kissed her then, long and slow, in the private chamber with the thundering pulse of the waves in the background, the curtain shutting out the world, shutting out all thought and all time. This room was a world of its own, a place where they were safe, where nothing could reach them, not Denning, not London, not her brother, not their pasts, a place where they might be together as Anna and Stepan. It seemed right that the place was a magical cave filled with silk beside the sea.

Stepan's mouth found the sensitive spot at the base of her neck. 'Should we go upstairs?' His breath was coming faster now. 'There is only the trunk and the sand.'

She didn't care. She breathed the only word that came to her. 'Either.' All that mattered were Stepan's hands on her, his mouth on her. She wanted her hands on him, too, wanted to feel the hard maleness of him. She reached for him and this time he did not deny her. She felt the length of him, the heat of him through his trousers, proof of his intentions and his readiness. There would be no going back indeed. His hand cupped her breast, his thumb running over its tip, bringing the familiar pleasure and her body thrilled to it, her knees buckling with the intensity and the anticipation of more to come.

Stepan lifted her then with a hoarse instruction. 'Put your legs about my waist.' He bore her to the cavern wall, balancing her carefully as his hand worked his trousers open. 'This will be far better than either the trunk or the sand.' He kissed her hard and her desire ratcheted. She gripped him tight between her legs, her skirts falling back. The cold air of the sea hit her bare skin, an erotic contrast to Stepan's warm hand at her core, that hand stroking and readying her until she could feel her slickness on his fingers, and her own pleasure rising. His phallus pressed against her thigh, priming her for his entrance, reminding her of his length and power.

She gasped her invitation in a low moan. 'Stepan, please.' She didn't know what it was she wanted, or sought, only that she wanted as she'd never wanted before and, whatever it was, he alone could provide it.

Anna felt the push of him as he entered, felt herself stretch and give as he sought compliance. She gave a mewl of protest as he withdrew, feeling empty without him. 'Shhh, Anna,' he murmured against her hair. 'I'll be back. We must go slow this first time.'

Slow would be the death of her. With each foray he gained ground and with each foray the anticipation in her grew until she thought she'd burst from it. One last time and he was in, fully sheathed. He kissed her then, his body starting to move in a new rhythm, his hips against hers inviting her to join him, his mouth swallowing her moans as her hands fisted in his coat and her pleasure grew. She did not care that the rock was hard at her back, or that too many clothes still separated them. She cared only that he was inside her and that they were together, moving as one towards an unseen cliff where ecstatic madness awaited.

He gave a hard thrust that wrenched a cry from her. They were nearly at that cliff. She felt the change in his body, as it was gathering for a final effort, a final thrust and then they fractured against the cavern wall, his dark head buried against her shoulder, his own shoulders heaving beneath her hands. So entwined were they it was hard to tell where one of them began and the other ended. Anna stroked his hair, a soft, secret smile on her lips. Perhaps that had always been the case. Perhaps this was no different. Ah, but, no—this was different. It was unlike anything she'd ever known. The exquisite violence of shattering was followed by peace, like the thunderous crash of waves against the shore leaving behind a placid foam.

'What are you thinking?' Stepan whispered.

'I want this peace for ever. I want to stay like this for ever.'

He chuckled. 'You're a greedy girl.'

She sighed, sleepy and unbothered by the argument. 'Tell me you don't want this. Just us, the waves and peace.'

'Perhaps I can tempt you with a bath?' Stepan shifted. He was leaving her, as he must. The practicalities of their situation came to her. How long did she expect him to bear her weight?

'A bath sounds nice.' She unwrapped her legs and he set her down gently.

'All you have to do is climb the stairs.'

Right now the long staircase seemed impossible, so boneless did she feel. She laughed softly. 'There's always a catch.'

Stepan pressed a soft kiss to her lips. 'It will be worth it, I promise.'

Chapter Seventeen

Stepan did not disappoint. Anna sank into the bath's steamy depths and closed her eyes. She let the hot water soothe her tender parts. As baths went, she would long remember this one—the deep, hot water in the exquisite white-porcelain slipper tub, soft, thick towels laid out beside it, and carefully carved cakes of French milled soap scented with lavender. This was a luxury nonpareil to have such a bath at her disposal; the high slipper back of the tub made for comfortable lounging and the tub's long body made it possible to stretch out.

She'd not had such an extravagance since she'd left Kuban. Between the fine crystal and this elegant tub, Preston Worth knew how to live. But she had little thought to spare for the elusive

Preston Worth and his luxuries. Her thoughts were firmly centred on Stepan. How could they not be when her body carried the echo of the afternoon with it? She sponged her breasts with a washcloth, feeling the tender throb of them where Stepan had cupped them, where his thumbs had run over her nipples beneath the fabric. The ache of her breasts matched the ache between her legs, an ache that carried pleasantness along with soreness. Anna arched her neck and sighed, letting her mind recall every moment in the cavern's alcove.

'May I join you?' Stepan's quiet baritone cut through her daydreams.

Her eyes flew open and her body sank further beneath the bubbles. How silly of her to be modest *now*. She'd had her legs wrapped around him and his phallus deep within her just an hour ago and suddenly she was concerned about a little bare skin? She studied Stepan. He was still fully dressed and he must be cold. She'd been more chilled than she thought when she'd got into the tub. 'You're wearing rather a lot for bathing.'

'So I am.' Stepan's grey eyes teased. His fingers worked the length of his cravat free, his waistcoat and then his shirt until he stood before her bare chested. She forgot her own nudity—his was much more interesting. The musculature of his torso was carved into well-defined ridges, each set leading the eye downward to the flat plane of his stomach cradled between the defined jut of hip bones. Those hip bones disappeared beneath the snug fit of his trousers—a fit that did little to hide, but much to enhance, the maleness within.

Her gaze focused on the heavy bulge in his trousers, perhaps because she was curious to *see* with her eyes what her hand and her body had already felt. Stepan met her gaze, his own eyes hot and knowing as his hands undid the fastenings of his trousers. He pushed them off until he stood before her naked and entirely exposed, every glorious, male inch of him.

He reached up to the thong that held back his hair and pulled it, letting his dark hair fall loose. It barely skimmed his shoulders, not nearly as long as it had been in Kuban, but it was long enough to frame the sharp lines of his face. It gave him the primal look of a Cossack and her breath caught at the sheer beauty of him. 'I had not imagined…' she murmured, awestruck.

Stepan gave her an utterly seductive smile, bearing her frank appraisal unabashedly. 'How could you have?' They both knew he was the first naked man she had seen, that hers were the eyes of both the virgin and the vixen. Gently bred Kubanian girls did not look upon any bare male skin after the age of twelve. Nothing could have prepared her for the sight of him, a sight that was supposed to be reserved for a girl's wedding night. Anna thought this was something far better.

Stepan stepped into the tub, sliding his big body down behind her, his long legs wrapping about her. This was going to be no ordinary bath. This was to be an introduction to further intimacy, further proof of their togetherness. She leaned her head back against his chest, his hands cupping her breasts in the most natural of gestures, as if those hands belonged on her. He nuzzled her neck, placing slow kisses along her throat. This was a new kind of intimacy and she revelled in it, this feeling of being naked together, skin against skin in the tub, hands and mouths languidly exploring with no pressure to rush. She felt the muscled ridges of him against her spine, the hardness against her buttocks, but there was no hurry. That would come later.

He was hard against her, his sex rigid and aroused by her nearness. Later, he counselled himself. Now was for touching, for talking. He wanted to show her intimacy could be more than sex.

Anna trailed a hand through the water, her voice quiet. 'Do you miss Kuban, Stepan? Do you think about it?' She stretched her neck back to look at him upside down and he was nearly undone by the gaze in her eyes, so soft and so trusting, so giving.

He answered honestly. 'I think about it sometimes. I miss images of the place: the winters, the snows, the howl of wolves at night. Those are only moments. I don't miss the reality of Kuban, not court life, not the politics, always manoeuvring. Perhaps it's different now because of the revolution, but I don't want to go back. What would I go back to? I have no one there, just empty houses. There's no one waiting for me, no one caring one way or the other.' Because everyone who mattered to him was here.

Stepan took the washcloth and drew it down her body, delighting in the goosebumps it raised on her skin despite the water's heat. 'Do *you* miss it, Anna?' It had not occurred to him that she might.

'No. Everyone I love is here.' He envied the ease with which she spoke of her feelings. 'But leaving Kuban didn't solve my problems as I thought it would—' She broke off. 'I don't know who I am here. I feel as if everyone expects me to be a copy of Princess Anna-Maria, a girl who waited for people to make decisions for her, about her. But I can't be that any more—maybe I never was. Maybe you're lucky, Stepan. You have no one. There aren't any expectations for you. You can't disappoint anyone,' she hypothesised out loud. 'Can I tell you a secret? I used to think you were the luckiest child ever having palaces to yourself and money to spend.'

Stepan didn't laugh. 'Don't ever think I was lucky, Anna.'

'Was it bad, Stepan?' she whispered.

Bad? Beyond bad, but how could she know?

Certainly, she knew the facts of his upbringing. He'd been the Orphan Prince. Every family at court had known that. But she would not know what that meant. She'd been too young. He supposed it had looked like heaven to a girl who'd been unwanted and unloved by a father who blamed her for his wife's death.

'You didn't know my father. He was dead before you were born. Even when my father was alive, he was not interested in me.' Stepan started soaping her again; the feel of her body beneath his hands helped him relax and made it easier to talk. He never spoke of his past, but here in the tub, with her and nothing else around them, he found he wanted to tell her. She deserved to know the sort of man he was. 'My father liked reckless living in whatever form he could find. I remember he rode a horse into the main hall one night on a dare. I was six and I was terrified. The horse was a huge stallion and when it reared up, I screamed. My father was furious. He scolded me and sent me to bed, called me a coward and the next day he set me on a horse of my own and insisted I have riding lessons. I was terrified of that, too. Other boys my age had ponies, but my father insisted no son of his was going to ride a pony. It was the one time he took an interest in me. It wasn't pleasant.'

'I can't imagine you being afraid to ride. By the time I knew you, you were glued to a saddle and fearless.' Anna laughed softly.

'Shall I tell *you* a secret, now?' He had his mouth at her ear, her body pressed to his as close as two people could get. 'I was relieved when he died. I was nine and I could stop living in fear of him coming home. Before I went to school, I spent my childhood at the Shevchenko summer palace, away from the city, out of his sight, but every so often, he'd come crashing in. He never stayed for long, but those were awful weeks. I practised staying out of sight. I'd leave the house early in the mornings and stay out until dark, just roaming, anything to be alone, to be safe.'

'It sounds like a hard way to grow up,' she said softly.

'It was the only solution available. I wanted to protect myself, but I wanted to protect others, too. I was a danger to them. My father knew I would do for others what I wouldn't do for myself. I couldn't bear to see someone else suffer on my behalf.' His hand stilled, the memories coming evil and swift. He held them back. He would not pollute the light of her with his darkness.

'Tell me,' she urged and the piece of him that wanted someone to know him body *and* soul pushed against his caution.

'He would use the tenants' children against me. Whenever he wanted me to do something I disliked, or whenever I disappointed him, he would whip them instead of me and he'd make me watch. No one wanted to be my friend, as you can imagine.' Until Dimitri. Oh, how he'd craved that friendship. Would she see now how much her brother meant to him?

'I was very unpopular in my father's village. But that was all to the good. I decided it was better for everyone involved if I did not love, so that any affection I might hold for another could not be used against me. And I decided it was better to be alone, so that no one would suffer for me.' He didn't talk to anyone like this, not even Dimitri.

'I learned the lesson so well I wasn't even sad when he died. I remember the day my nurse told me he was dead. He'd been dead for three days before any of his friends thought to send word to his son. I just stood there, hearing the words. I was simply relieved.'

She sighed. 'Thank you for telling me. That explains so much.'

Stepan tensed. Did she see the monster in him now? The monster who couldn't love? Who didn't know love? A monster who'd been created out of necessity? Would she give him pity now? He wanted that the least.

'If there's anyone who knows love, it is you, Stepan. Love for those boys in the caves, for your fellow man, for your friends,' she said fiercely, her whisper an absolution of his past, a hopeful benediction of what the future could be. For a precious moment, her light was holding his darkness at bay, but he could not let her believe the lie she'd spun for herself. He was no hero. Her light would simply not allow her to see the truth.

Stepan shifted his body sending the water sloshing, and finished his story. 'Even though I was relieved when he died, it didn't solve the loneliness. The emptiness had already taken root. I had learned my lessons too well, as had those around me. His death freed me, but it did not lift the curse. I was raised in palaces by servants who had no real affection for me for the most part. What does a ten-year-old boy want with money, palaces and vaults full of jewels? They meant nothing to me. I wanted friends, I wanted a father who played on the lawn and wrestled—one like Nikolay's and like yours.'

He wrung out the washcloth, sending a rivulet of warm water down the valley between her breasts. He felt her shift in protest of his words. 'He was different before you were born. I am sorry you didn't know that man,' he said solemnly. 'But it's not too late for you and for him. There is love in him. You can see it in his grief. But in the end, he gave everything for Dimitri and for you. He wanted a better life for you *both*.'

'He hates me,' Anna said staunchly. 'When he looks at me...'

'He sees her,' Stepan concluded. 'He sees love and he resists it because it hurts and he can't get past that, and you fight him.' He set aside the washcloth. Enough sermonising. What did he know about love? And here he was telling Anna about *her* father.

'Some day, when I have children, I will love them,' Anna said with sudden fierceness. The words caught him by surprise. He feared being a father, feared repeating his father's mistakes. But not her, not his brave Anna-Maria. Even though her own father had been less than a good parent to her, it didn't occur to her to worry over repeating those mistakes. He sponged her back, the water starting to cool. They would have to get out soon.

'You will make a splendid mother.' And she would. Anna-Maria feared nothing. The forbidden image of her with a child at her skirts, another in her arms, came again, spearing him with its white heat, so strong he had to get out of the tub for fear he'd ravish her right there. They hadn't made it to a bed for her first time, but he was determined they have a bed for her second.

Stepan wrapped a towel about his hips and held one out to her. 'Allow me to play the lady's maid.'

She rose from the water like a Venus and a fantasy rocketed through his mind of kneeling before her, her body dripping wet as he put his mouth to the sweet juncture between her thighs, and a thousand other wild dreams.

'What are you thinking?' She smiled coyly as if she could guess. Maybe she could?

'I'm thinking if I give in to my fantasies of licking you dry we'll never make it to the bed.' His voice was a hoarse rasp. 'You're beautiful, Anna.'

She blushed. She had none of his savoir faire when it came to standing nude before a lover. It was a poignant, humbling reminder of who she was and what she'd given him today—her trust along with her maidenhead. He kissed her then, murmuring the words, 'You honour me.' And then more practically, 'We'll have to tell Dimitri. I must ask him and your father for their permission.' Would they hate him for this? Would they see his love for Anna as a betrayal of his love for them?

'It's a little late to be asking for permission.' Anna laughed and wrapped her arms about him. 'What do you think they'll say about us?'

'Why do you worry over it? My father loves you like a son and Dimitri loves you like a brother. I think they would be pleased. Surprised,' she confessed, 'but pleased. There's no reason they wouldn't be. You are a noble man, an honest man and a good man who has proved his loyalty to the House of Petrovich threefold.' She kissed him. 'You doubt your own worth too much, Stepan. You see barriers where there are none. Now, I believe we were headed to bed?'

He lifted her then and carried her to the bed, his body tense with wanting as he made a seduction out of drying first one long leg and then the other, then the flat of her belly and her full, firm breasts. 'Can you take me again, Anna, so soon?' He moved between her legs and they opened for him as she strained upwards, reaching to kiss him.

'Always, Stepan.' Her hands were in his damp hair, holding him to her, her mouth on his. He would never tire of her kisses, of her touch, of her body against his. He entered her with a tender thrust, revelling in the arch of her back as she rose up to meet him. Discomfort or not, his Anna was intrepid, never backing down. She moaned beneath him as he surged and retreated, surged and retreated again and again. Her hips met his as the rhythm built between them, exquisite and powerful. God, he wanted to live in these moments for ever, in her light. But his body drove them relentlessly towards conclusion, towards one last burst of bliss as he spent, his head against her shoulder, her hand in his hair, her name on his lips in a hoarse cry.

Here in her arms, he was whole. He wasn't alone any more and it scared him senseless even as he wallowed in the joy of it. How long could such completion, such *peace*, last? Now that he'd tasted heaven, how could he ever return to earth? Which provoked the most dangerous question of all: what would it take to make this last? Could he afford it? Could *she*? What would it cost to make Anna his for ever? It was a lovely question to fall asleep on. He would settle the particulars with her in the morning.

Chapter Eighteen

Elias Denning collapsed his spyglass with a satisfying *thunk* and turned to the skinny, dark-haired boy struggling beside him on the bluffs. 'Is that the ship you were signalling?' It was barely dawn and the ship was still far out, just a speck on the early morning horizon. 'Why would you need to signal the boat at this distance?' Denning mused out loud although he had a fair idea: to turn it back before it ran into the 'floating customs offices' that patrolled closer to the harbour.

'I'm not tellin' you anything,' the boy said in angry defiance. Denning looked him up and down; the lad was nearly a young man, maybe sixteen, with an alarming maturity in his eyes that said he understood the world and how it worked.

'You don't have to. I know you. You are the groom from Seacrest.' Denning let him mull over that little bit of information. He'd recognised the boy right away. 'Joseph, was it? I think that's what Miss Petrova called you.' The boy might have made a fine officer if the opportunity had presented itself. He had the bearing for it. But the opportunity wouldn't come, not for a boy from the streets. He was simply beneath the army. Denning nodded to the two corporals holding the boy. 'Bring him back to the barracks and we'll see how he feels about talking later.'

'What about the ship, Captain?'

'Not much we can do while they're out of range.' Denning tapped his fingers against his thigh. 'Let's wait for them to make a move.' If the ship belonged to Shevchenko, the move would come soon. It was too much of a coincidence that there was saffron travelling to London from Shoreham and Shevchenko's groom was signalling ships off the Seacrest headlands. Justice was coming. He just had to wait for it. How convenient it would be if the man he thought to frame as a smuggler turned out to actually be one. Finally, something was going right.

'We have time,' Denning told his men. 'That ship won't make a move until tonight when it's dark. We'll send men back to keep an eye on it, though. Whatever move it makes, it won't make it without us knowing.' He reached into the boy's pocket and retrieved the mirror. 'Corporal, you may want this.' It was possible he would be able to lure the ship in with a few flashes of false security. He gripped the boy by the collar and hauled him forward. 'You can watch me eat breakfast and then decide how hungry you are.'

'I won't be hungry enough,' the boy spat with admirable fire. Denning laughed. He would enjoy breaking this stubborn youth. He didn't even realise how much he already knew. Getting the boy to talk would just be confirmation of what he already guessed. Today was going to be a good day, it might even be the day he brought Stepan Shevchenko down.

'That's all right, laddie. After breakfast, I have someone I'd like you to meet.' The boy would soon learn his place. Street smarts were no match for military discipline, or military punishment. Denning was too intent on his plans as he led his captive away to notice the slight form of a boy hidden in the tall grasses of the bluff, curled up like a ginger-haired rabbit. When he'd gone, the boy crept away from his hiding place and ran.

'Milord! Milord! I must see milord! Please, it's an emergency!'

The panicked cries woke Stepan out of a sound sleep. Beside him, Anna stirred, warm and feminine in his arms, but there was no time to savour the delight of that, or act on any of his plans from the night before. His body was on full alert at the sense of urgency. Only the boys from his land crew called him 'milord'.

He tossed back the covers and strode to the hallway, pulling a shirt over his head as he went. The voice sounded young and it was coming from the bottom of the stairs where a boy struggled with a half dressed footman.

The boy looked up and saw him. 'Milord!'

'Let him be,' Stepan directed the footman. It was Irish and Stepan's heart pounded. 'What has happened?' He came down the stairs, ignoring the footman's wide-eyed stare at his undress.

'Joseph. Soldiers. The ship.' The words tumbled out fast and incoherent in the boy's fright.

Stepan knelt by Irish, putting his hands on the boy's arms to steady him, to support him. The boy's teeth chattered from fright, excitement and cold. Wherever he had been, he was damp and chilled. 'Come into the study where you can warm.' To the footman, he gave a barrage of orders: 'Stoke up the fire, bring tea and something hot to eat. Porridge if you have it.'

'Now, tell me everything,' he said to Irish once he was settled and his shaking was under control.

'I was on night watch and I picked up a ship close to dawn. We thought nothing of it. We had no ships scheduled to arrive, but we checked it out anyway.' The boy's eyes went wide. 'It was the *Skorost*, milord. The ship's early. Joseph went out with me to signal it, to warn it off, but we weren't the only ones watching the headlands. The captain's men came upon us. Joseph took the mirror and shoved me in the grass to hide. He didn't tell anyone I was there.' The boy finished his report. 'I wanted to fight them, milord, but Joseph said it wasn't allowed, I was to stay hidden no matter what.'

Stepan gave a half-smile. 'You did right. Who would have told me if you'd been taken, too?' His mind was reeling, trying to assimilate the information and what it all meant. The *Skorost* was early! Joseph taken! And Denning knew or was very close to knowing the *Skorost* was his. The captain would not overlook the coincidence.

He'd not expected the ship until next week. This presented something of a problem, but not as large a problem as Joseph being taken. His land chief had taken an enormous risk in going out to signal the ship. Joseph had known the headlands were being watched. Yet Stepan knew the boy's loyalty to him required him to try to save the ship.

What did he do now? Did he try to get out to the *Skorost*? Did he rush into town and attempt to free Joseph before Denning could pry any information out of him?

'What will happen to Joseph, milord?'

He knew all too well what would happen to Joseph. Denning could be cruel. The memory of the man's hands on Anna was still fresh in

Stepan's mind. A man who showed no restraint with a gentlewoman would show no restraint with a boy. His youth would not protect him. Stepan knew Joseph—the boy would resist, which would push Denning further. That decided it. He would go to town. He dismissed Irish with orders. 'I will send word about how to handle the ship. Tell the others not to worry. I will get Joseph.'

'How will you do that?' a soft voice questioned him from the door as Irish left. Anna stood there, her hair loose at her shoulders, a dressing gown belted at her waist. She held out a banyan to him.

She looked beautiful, tousled from loving and sleep, and Stepan's heart gave a painful twist. This was the cost of having Anna for ever: subjecting her to danger at dawn and midnight escapades. As long as they were together, his secrets were her secrets. Even if she did not participate any further in his enterprise, her knowledge was enough to condemn her. He doubted Anna would leave it at that. It would be her argument to invite more danger. As long as she was here, as long as she was already condemned, she might as well go all the way—in for a penny, in for a pound. That was an argument he couldn't allow her to win.

Having her beside him made her an accomplice whether she chose to be one or not. It was why he'd kept Dimitri and the others at arm's length. Ruslan probably guessed, but he was in France where English law could not hurt him. Dimitri and Nikolay had lives here, lives that could be ruined if they knew and he was caught. Ignorance protected them just as it had once protected Anna.

His conscience mocked him. *You wanted to know what it would cost to keep Anna with you? Well, now you know. It will cost her life and it will cost your honour. You've deflowered your best friend's sister, you've exposed her to your smuggling ring and she's been assaulted by a British officer. With you, she's forced to live a double life: the life of a smuggler's lady in Shoreham and a noblewoman's life in London. She will be forced to wear two faces just as you do and she will never be able to stop.*

Just as he would never be able to stop.

When he'd chosen to smuggle, to be a free

trader in protest of the economic injustices of taxation, he'd committed a crime that could never be erased. It would always have to remain hidden. Stepan had never felt the enormity of that decision as he felt it now. It would define the rest of his life, what and who he could have. That included Anna.

She came to him, concern creasing her brow. She touched his cheek. 'What are you thinking? Let me help.' Her body was warm, the heat of the bed still on her skin. She smelled of the scents of last night's bath. Even with danger pressing, his body roused. He wanted nothing more than to take her back to bed and shut out the world. He wanted the impossible. He put his hands on her arms, gripping her through the silk of her robe, and swallowed hard.

This was his penance, to have her only once. To have one night against all the other nights that would come. His foolish hopes of last night were just that—foolish hopes. He'd been weak and had allowed himself to buy into illusions. 'Anna, I need you to leave. I need you to go home to Dimitri and forget all of this; forget about the cavern and what you saw there, forget the hidden staircase and the boys, and the ships.'

'I can no more do that than you can simply decide to stop smuggling.'

'No, I will send the ship away. You will be safe.' Perhaps Anna had been right yesterday when she'd whispered her temptations. Perhaps it was time to give up his principles, give up the fight, after all. The costs were mounting along with the risks.

Anna's gaze hardened. 'If you send the ship away, Denning wins. Tyranny wins. He is enforcing an unjust law and an unjust practice that favours the rich, just as you said. If you send the *Skorost* away, it solves nothing. Neither does sending *me* away.' Her gaze did not waver. 'The alcove, your kisses, the bath, and last night? They cannot be erased any more than my feelings or yours can.'

He heard the temper simmering beneath her words. She was angry with him. His voice was low and stern. 'Go to London, Anna, and find a powerful husband who can protect you far better than I can.' It cut at his heart to order her away, to *give* her away, but what choice did he have if he wanted her safe?

'You took my virginity,' she argued. 'There is nothing for me to offer a London gentleman now.'

You took my heart, he wanted to reply, but it would give her too much ammunition. If she thought he prevaricated, they would both be lost.

'You are beautiful, Anna. There will be a man willing to overlook such a thing.' He was betting on that. Regret was coming hard and fast now. He should not have taken her to bed, he should not have given in. The least he could do now was atone for that by sending her to safety.

'You are sending me away so you can do something foolish,' Anna pressed on.

'I am sending you away so I don't have to worry about you. How can I think about my ship and my men if I am thinking about you?' She would be an enormous distraction. Already, fears for her ran through his mind.

'I can take care of myself. I thought we'd decided I wasn't a little girl any more.'

'What if Denning comes here and threatens you again? What if he wants you to reveal the caverns?' That was his real fear, that his cause would claim the woman he loved.

'I will not tell him anything.' He could see she was insulted, but she didn't understand the lengths Denning would go to.

'He won't ask nicely, Anna. What happens when he puts a knife to your throat? What if you give in?' The boys would be betrayed. They would hang or face transportation. He saw Anna pale at the implication. He lowered his voice, his own fear causing it to crack. 'And good God, Anna, what happens if you *don't*? Do you think I want to come home and find you dead with your throat slit?' It was an impossible dilemma.

'What about me? What happens when *you* simply ride into town to free Joseph and Denning arrests you instead? Or worse, you trade yourself for him because there's no other way. Am I supposed to sit at home in Little Westbury, not knowing what's become of you? I am to be safe, but you are not?' Her hands gripped the folds of his shirt. 'I love you, Stepan Shevchenko, and when I went to bed with you, I did so knowing full well what you are and what you do. You can't expect me not to be a part of that, to be a part of your life.'

His heart broke a little bit more. 'Anna, I don't want you to be part of that life. If anything happened to you...' This was what happened when one had people who cared for them, who said words like 'I love you'. He would have to force her away.

Anna moved past him to stand in front of the fire, taking up a station in the room. Her posture made it clear she would not be dismissed. Her eyes flashed. 'First of all, you need me to help you with Denning. Second of all, we need a better plan than you riding into town for Joseph.'

He did need her. His right hand was in Denning's clutches. Despite the tightness in his chest at the mention of 'we', Stepan smiled. 'I'm way ahead of you there.'

It would be his most daring escapade yet, but sometimes the most daring were the most successful. He would take a dinghy out the *Skorost* and he would personally sail the boat into Shoreham harbour. The boat had already been sighted. It made no sense to wave the boat off. Such an action would be tantamount to admitting guilt, promoting the idea the ship had something to hide. He would unload that boat in the harbour under the captain's very eyes. And he'd pray that the converted barrels with their secret compartments would escape detection.

'What are you going to do?' Anna fixed him with a long stare, a smile of her own playing at her lips.

'I'm not going to ride into town. I'm going to sail in.'

Anna's smile widened as she moved into his arms, her arms slipping around his waist. 'Perfect. And I'm going with you.'

This time, he didn't protest, another consequence of what also happened when people said 'I love you'. They started to believe in the impossible—that love would triumph over fear and danger. Today, Stepan hoped they were right. Everything depended on it.

Chapter Nineteen

The sea was exhilarating! Anna kicked off her shoes and scaled the ropes and helped furl the sails, laughingly taking instructions from Stepan's crew when she made mistakes. That afternoon, as they worked to make the ship ready for Stepan's great bluff, she might have been one of them in a pair of boy's trousers and her bare feet, her hair tied back in leather strip. She hurried up and down the ropes, rolled casks and swabbed decks, all with equal enthusiasm. Stepan had stopped forbidding her on the ropes after the third time.

Anna shaded her eyes with her hand and looked about the deck for Stepan. He'd been everywhere this afternoon: above decks, below decks, in the rigging. His captain had politely ceded sole leadership of the ship to him and the men had responded, understanding time was of the essence. The sails had been furled and the anchor dropped. The *Skorost* was going nowhere until all was ready. Anna quartered the ship's deck with her gaze—this time she found him at the wheel deep in discussion with the captain. Everything was nearly ready, then.

Anna walked to the bow of the ship and leaned on the rail, the exhilaration of the day mellowing as she looked out over the water. The afternoon was cooling, shadows starting to fall, the sun a little lower in the sky than it had been. Behind her, a cry went up from the men to unfurl the sails and the anchor chains began to groan. They would be underway and the dangerous work would begin.

A thrum of excitement surged in her blood at the thought. This was what life would be like with Stepan: a continuous bout of adventure and risk, a life full of purpose, fighting for others. It was also what love would be like with Stepan: a constant, gentle tug of war between his need to protect her and her need to be part of his world. The latter was what he needed, too, whether he realised it yet or not. He'd let her come today because he needed her. Not only because she could manage Denning in a way he could not, but simply because he needed *her*—her beside him, *them* together.

Stepan was counting on her; his very *life* and the lives of his crew and his land crew were depending on her tonight. The thought ought to scare her, but it didn't. The challenge of it excited her, it made her fingers tingle and her pulse race with the sense of purpose she'd longed for. The ship began to move, the wind lifting her hair and filling her face with its gusty breath.

Oh! She liked this! Anna closed her eyes and spread her arms wide to feel the power of the wind fully against her body. This was what freedom felt like—wind and sun against her face, a ship cutting through the water beneath her feet. A ship could go anywhere, at any time. A ship was not tied to the land or a place. She let the wildness take her, let the fantasy rise in her mind. What if they just sailed away?

She was wicked for thinking such things when there were more pressing concerns: Joseph, the cargo, outwitting Denning. Those things should take precedence in her mind, but there would be time tonight for all that. Right now, she wanted to give herself to the wind and the sea.

Arms encircled her and drew her against the hard warmth of a body. She smiled and murmured his name, 'Stepan.' Her lover. What a delicious thought that was. Oh, how just the suggestion of it could make her burn. 'You never told me you knew how to sail.' He'd been a revelation today in his breeches and rolled-up shirtsleeves, coats discarded, the wind battling the leather strip for his hair. This was the real Stepan. There was nothing of the stoic about him today as he bellowed orders. Watching him haul casks, muscles flexing beneath his shirt, had been intoxicating.

The real Stepan was a daring smuggler; a man who seduced her with a smile; a man who said he wanted her with his eyes, with a touch; a man who would brawl in his dining room for her. She liked that man far better than the stoic version. More than liked. She *loved* that man, flaws and all.

'He doesn't know how to love, he doesn't know what a family is.'

Dimitri's warning came back to her from across the years. She smiled to herself. She knew now that wasn't entirely true. Stepan had always known how to love, he was just afraid to. She could change that. 'I should be angry that you kept all of this to yourself. It's wonderful. I can only imagine what the stars look like at sea. I think I like sailing.'

Stepan chuckled, low and warm at her ear, his arms hugging her close. 'You should sail through an autumn squall before you say that.'

She was too content to argue. These precious moments were the calm before the storm. 'Maybe I should.' Already, wildness was seeping into her contentment. 'Why don't we just sail away, Stepan? We could go to America or to the Caribbean. There's plenty of adventure for us there. Say we'll go tonight, after we get Joseph and the cargo is safe.' A thrill of adventure ran through her. 'We could do it. The moment Denning is off the ship and we are free to hoist anchor.' She could stand here all day with the wind in her face and Stepan at her back. This was all she really needed. How interesting to discover that with the right man, marriage could be freedom, that freedom and marriage were not mutually exclusive of one another.

'Leave it *all*?' he murmured of the practicalities. She knew he was thinking of the money, the wealth in his bank account at Coutts on the Strand, the jewels in the strongbox there, the clothes at Seacrest, all their things.

'You have this boat and this crew. We can bring Irish and anyone who wants to come. We can send word for them to meet us somewhere.' Out of caution, Stepan had ordered the land crew to scatter. No one was to be near the caves today in case Denning decided to invade.

'You have it all planned out.' Stepan laughed. 'I'm to support all of them with no funds?'

'You will build another fortune,' Anna said simply, believing it completely. She could see it now. He could be a trader, a merchant, even a smuggler if he preferred, anywhere in the world. He'd built a fortune here, he could do it again somewhere, anywhere. It didn't matter to her. 'You've always been able to do anything, even the impossible.' She realised it was true. He'd freed Nikolay, he'd got them all out of Kuban. Those were impossible things. Making a new life was nothing to a man like him. He'd already done it once.

'You would leave your brother? Leave the others?' That was the stoic Stepan talking now. She would banish that man if she could, except that it was a part of him as much as the adventurer. To lose that part would be to lose part of who he was.

'We'll find other causes. I am sure there's injustice in the Caribbean or America, too.' She laughed softly. 'And perhaps the others are wise enough to look after themselves for a bit.'

A chuckle rumbled in his chest. 'Nikolay? Wise enough? Hardly.' Anna heard the resignation in that chuckle. She squeezed his hand in support and empathy. It was time for him to let go of the past and grab the future with both hands. He'd delivered his friends out of danger, he'd stood by them as they found new lives and loves. It was his turn now.

She turned in his arms, facing him, her hands in his hair. 'Break away for me, Stepan,' she murmured and in that moment she swore a private vow that she would be enough for him. She would be enough to break his self-imposed chains. She reached up and kissed him softly on the mouth and she felt his arms close around her. It wouldn't be much longer now before the game began. The excise boats were growing closer and the sky was fading. The energy of the bright March afternoon had given way to the quiet of twilight. She breathed him in; the salt on his skin, the wind in his hair all testaments to the wildness alive in him, as assuredly as the hints of soap and cologne on his shirt anchored him to civilisation. This was her man: the Smuggler Prince.

The cry went up from the crow's nest that the customs ship was approaching actively now that it was clear the *Skorost* intended to put in to the harbour. 'It's time.' Anna licked her lips, slowly stepping away from Stepan's warm embrace.

Stepan's hand curled around hers, his voice quiet. She half expected him to protest her assistance one more time. Instead, he said simply, 'I'll help you dress—' and then because he couldn't help himself '—if you're sure? I can have you set ashore.'

She pressed a finger to his lips. 'I am sure, Stepan. My place is with you, always.'

Everything was laid out in the captain's quarters, Stepan's clothes and her dress, or rather Beatrice Worth's dress—a grand red-silk confection cut daringly low. Stepan had instructed her to bring it when they'd left Seacrest. It would be her job to keep Captain Denning at the table tonight long enough for the cargo to be unloaded right under his nose while he and his men ate and drank.

A soft lamp lit the captain's quarters as she poured water into a basin for washing, aware of Stepan's eyes on her. She made to pull her borrowed boy's shirt over her head, only to feel Stepan's hands on hers, the familiar words at her ear. 'Allow me.'

He stripped the shirt over her head, his phallus already hard. Anna had been a fine sight today, strutting about the decks barefoot in those just-a-bit-too-tight trousers, snug through the hips—a solid reminder that the figure beneath was not a boy's. 'I was proud of you today.' He dipped the cloth in the water and wrung it out before sponging one arm and then the other, mimicking his actions from another bath not so long ago when the water had been warmer, the soap more French and a tub present. 'You took to those ropes like you were born to them.'

He gently bathed her breasts, watching her pink nipples stiffen from his touch, from the cold. He wanted to kiss those breasts, wanted to hold them in the palms of his hands until they were warm again. But there was no time. Denning would be upon them soon. The bastard had been watching them all day, waiting to pounce. Stepan had made him pay for that. He and the crew had made a long, slow show of doing repairs from the storm, just outside Denning's reach.

'Come, let me play the lady's maid.' Stepan led her to the bunk where her garments were laid out. He knelt before her, working the trousers over her hips and down. God, she was beautiful; those full breasts, her narrow waist and the rounded flare of her hips. He gripped those hips and pressed a kiss to her navel, murmuring a promise. 'When this over, I will take you to bed for days on end.'

'I shall look forward to it.' Her hand drifted through his hair. They were both pretending the future was assured. They were making plans and promises as if tonight was a *fait accompli*, when nothing could be further from the truth. Tonight was life or death. Freedom or imprisonment and it all hinged on the point of a knife. One false move and the future would come crashing down.

He looked at up her with a smile and held up a silk stocking. 'Give me your foot.' He dressed her then, with all the care a lover might *undress* his beloved. He rolled up her stockings, remembering with aching clarity the night he'd rolled them down. He slipped a chemise over her head, tightened her stays and at last slid the red silk into place.

He must be crazy to do this, to allow her to help him, to risk her. It wasn't too late. He could stop it now. He could send one of the boys back in a rowboat with her. She could be safe at Seacrest. But, no, he reminded himself. There was no guarantee Seacrest was safe. If Joseph broke, the soldiers could come at any time to search the premises and they would not be polite. She was risking her neck whether she was here with him or at Seacrest. Perhaps that was selfish logic fuelling his rationale to keep her near. Still, he'd prefer she be beside him, where he could fight for her, die for her if need be. And she deserved her revenge on Denning. The man had assaulted her. She had a right to claim retribution.

'Would you like help with your hair?' He stepped back from her, from his Anna, a lump in his throat. If she was truly safer *with* him, why did he feel like he was sending her to her execution?

'I can do it.' She smiled at him confidently. 'You need to change, as well.'

He did. He changed in silence while Anna put up her hair and fastened two small ear-bobs. She spied him struggling with his cravat. She put in a final pin and came to him, deftly tying a knot on the first try. 'There, you're ready.' She gave him a radiant smile. 'Just in time; I think I hear Denning.' The volume on deck was increasing.

'One last thing.' Stepan reached into the pocket of his evening coat and pulled out a pouch. 'You'll need these.' He poured a short strand of pearls into his hand. 'You should have had them before. I got them after the assembly, after I realised.'

Her eyes glistened as she took in the pearls. She licked her lips. 'After you realised what, Stepan?' How like his Anna to press him about something personal with soldiers waiting to search his ship.

'That you weren't a little girl any more, Anna. As pretty as that crystal heart was, it was a girl's charm, not woman's jewellery.'

'Will you put them on?'

He let his hands linger at her neck as he fastened them. 'You look lovely tonight.' Too lovely. It would captivate Denning and the others, which was the whole point. But still, the fact remained the dress was obscenely low. His voice was hoarse. He'd have to remedy that before he met Denning. He cleared his throat. 'Are you ready?'

She gave a wicked smile that heated his groin. 'Almost.' Her hand was soft on his arm. 'Tell me we'll go tonight, when all of this is done.'

His eyes dropped to her lips. There was no limit to what he'd do for this woman. He'd fight for her, he'd die for her, he'd lie to her if it got them through this night. 'We'll go tonight,' he whispered, slipping out the door and on to the deck, ready to play the consummate business-man sailing his ship into port as if it were a nor-mal everyday occurrence.

Elias Denning stepped aboard the *Skorost* with confidence. Tonight, Stepan Shevchenko was not getting away from him. It was a fore-gone conclusion. The boy in custody hadn't bro-ken, but his friend had, the thin one who clerked at Shevchenko's warehouse. The boy from the bluffs had nothing to show but a bloody back and a death sentence. He'd have done better to have given in from the start and at least saved himself. Shevchenko was doomed regardless, but the boy had been blindly loyal and now he'd hang for it unless Elias felt benevolent. Just how benevolent would depend on how well things went tonight. He checked his watch with a smirk. Right about now, soldiers would be ransacking the Seacrest caverns and gathering proof.

Shevchenko approached, looking disgust-ingly immaculate. 'Captain, to what do we owe the pleasure of your presence? Surely you don't come out to greet every incoming ship?' It was not a warm greeting. Shevchenko wasn't going to pretend they were friends.

'Your Highness, I come out occasionally when there's a ship of interest. I had no idea it was yours,' Denning lied smoothly. 'It lay off the coast so long today it concerned us. We thought it might be in need of assistance. Of course, you're familiar with the new protocols until we get the smuggling situation under control.'

'Yes, I have the manifests right here.' Shevchenko handed over the lists of the cargo being transported.

Denning nodded to the lieutenant with him. 'Go down into the hold and check the cargo. Make sure it matches the manifests while we sail into port.'

'Why don't you and I accompany him?' Stepan gestured to the hold, showing no sign of concern. The man was far too confident for Denning's taste. But it was early in the game yet and Denning was no fool.

A half hour later, all the casks had been accounted for. His men had tapped on every inch of the hold's floor and hull's walls, listening for secret bottoms and hiding places to no avail. They'd opened casks of wine and dipped in sticks testing the depth of the casks only to have the sticks measure appropriately. It was a common ploy to have cask contain a false bottom with wine on top but brandy on the bottom. That didn't seem to be the case here.

'As soon as you have the totals, I'll pay the duty on the wine.' Shevchenko gave a cold smile.

'Of course.' If there were spirits, or silk, or more spices aboard this ship, there was no sign of it.

The ship bumped gently into the moorings, signalling their arrival at the docks. Denning was running out of time. He had to keep the cargo on the ship. Once it touched land, it was out of his jurisdiction. A warehouse was private property. He'd need a warrant to get in there—not that it had stopped him before, it just made for more explanations to his superiors.

'Would you care to stay for supper, Captain?' Shevchenko ushered him upstairs to the decks. 'You can taste some of the wine. We have a delicious supper planned in celebration of the *Skorost*'s arrival.'

'We?'

'Yes, Miss Petrova is with me. Please say you'll stay.'

'Then, I can hardly refuse.' The offer was so odd he was forced to satisfy his curiosity. Perhaps Shevchenko was counting on it. There was game afoot and if he left, he'd miss it. It could hardly go badly for him. Shevchenko didn't know it yet, but he held all the cards: the boy, the confession and, soon, the content of the caverns under Seacrest. By the end of the evening, Shevchenko would be in chains. This would be the prince's last meal as a free man and Miss Petrova would be at his mercy without her protector. What might she be willing to do to save her prince? It seemed just deserts were on the menu tonight and he was ready to feast.

Chapter Twenty

'More wine?' Anna signalled for another bottle to be opened—the ninth since she and Stepan, Denning and his four lieutenants had sat down for supper—the second since Stepan had left the table to 'check on a few things'. Only the second? It seemed like he'd been gone an eternity. She could imagine him in her mind, down in the hold, directing the silent removal of casks and trunks with their covert interiors. Silence was the key to success.

Nine bottles gone and it wasn't nearly enough. She wanted the men drunk, drunk enough to swagger home, the cargo momentarily forgotten, drunk enough to not hear the men moving cargo on the decks outside these doors. In that regard, it had gone well so far. The louder they could be in here, the more it would help, though. The wine was supposed to encourage that. But the men all seemed to be terribly well mannered and decent, more was the shame.

'No more for me.' One young lieutenant waved away Irish with the bottle. Another looked like he was going to follow suit. That was no good. The men must drink.

Anna rose to her feet, rescuing the bottle from the boy. She put on her charming smile, the one that showed off her dimple. 'What is this, Lieutenant? No more wine? Say it isn't so!' She poured him a full glass, refusing to take no for an answer. She bent low as she did so, giving the blushing young man a look at her cleavage. Sober excise officers were not on the menu tonight.

'And you, Lieutenant? Your glass is shockingly empty!' She moved from man to man, trailing her hand over shoulders, collars, resting her hand on sleeves, smiling coyly as she poured, bending, laughing, touching as she went, drawing blushes, and eventually bolder, lingering glances. She swept up a fiddle. 'Do any of you play?' She smiled warmly until one of them cracked.

'I do, ma'am,' a stout, ruddy-cheeked soldier offered.

'Oh, fabulous!' she exclaimed. 'I want to dance.' She pulled up the man nearest to her. 'You'll dance with me, won't you?' She didn't wait for a response. She drew the young man into the empty space beside the table, putting a hand on his shoulder. She slanted a coy smile at the fiddler. 'A polka, if you please?' Within two stanzas she had the room clapping along with the dance, within four she had the men on their feet.

She winded one officer after another, taking turns with each of the gentlemen. 'Captain, I believe it is your turn.' It was hard to keep a smile on her face, more difficult still to take his hand and allow him to touch her body, but she could give none of her repulsion away. She must dance with Denning as she'd danced with his men. She had to keep them laughing, keep them drinking, keep them dancing until they forgot Stepan was absent, until they forgot about the cargo, until they remembered only that they'd had a spectacular night.

'I think champagne is in order!' she called over her shoulder to Irish as Denning turned her in a tight circle.

'My, my, Miss Petrova, you do know how to throw to party,' Denning murmured. 'One has to wonder at your motives?' His breath was close to her ear. 'After all, I was beginning to think you didn't like me.'

'Do you not like to celebrate?' she teased, flirting outrageously.

'Not usually with my enemies.' He gave a cold smile. 'Did you think I had forgotten, Miss Petrova? That your prince brawled with me for touching you? That he nearly broke my jaw?'

'I believe he had just cause. You were threatening me, as I recall.' Anna smiled, feeling as if that very smile was pasted to her face.

'Persuading, my dear.' His grip at her waist tightened and she was drawn up hard against his body, a reminder that the captain was a strong man. She would be no match for his physical strength should it come to that. Surely, with four other men present, the captain wouldn't be able to get away with hurting her. But she'd feel better if Stepan came back. Where was Stepan?

'Tonight, it is my turn to persuade.' She met his gaze fearlessly. 'I will prove to you once and for all that Stepan Shevchenko is no smuggler. What sort of smuggler sails his ship into port and lays offshore in plain slight, fixing broken masts?'

'For your sake, I hope you're right, Miss Petrova. My men will do their duty and uphold the law, even if the outlaw is wearing a very enticing red gown and free with her wine.'

She tossed her head back and gave a wide smile. Anyone watching them would suspect nothing. 'It was not illegal to dine and dance *or* drink the last time I checked. I've done nothing wrong, Captain.'

'Not yet. You're a very good actress, Miss Petrova. You may have missed your calling.'

'Share her, Captain, you've had her long enough!' a lieutenant called out good-naturedly. The wine was starting to take effect. Good. She swung out of the captain's arms, reaching for the lieutenant.

She might have kept them dancing all night if it hadn't been for the champagne. Denning took possession of the bottle when it came and he uncorked the bottle with a resounding pop that cut through the fiddle and the dancing, both which stopped in sudden silence. It was an unfortunate coincidence that, in the silence, a loud thud hit the deck.

Denning's eyes narrowed, the frothing bottle forgotten. With one hand he drew a pistol and issued orders. 'Men, to the decks! Two of you down below, two of you above! Go!' The cabin cleared with organised alacrity, trademark of the British army.

'Aren't you needed with your men?' Anna asked, feeling conspicuous, although it was probably better if she kept him here. The other officers were young, perhaps impressionable and perhaps too drunk to understand whatever it was they might see. They could be subdued before they drew their weapons or thought to fire them if it came to that. But that didn't mean she was safe in here, alone with him.

'What do you think my men might find?' He eyed her coldly, filling two glasses with the iced champagne. 'Untaxed casks of spirits?' He handed her a glass, his body close enough to press her back against the edge of the table.

'Why would you think they'd find anything when you failed to find *something*?' Anna couldn't resist the goad. 'The only goods on this ship are the ones you've seen and the ones Stepan has paid the duty on. He is an honest, upstanding…'

Denning slammed a hand down on the table, the goblets jumping. It took all her willpower not to jump, too. 'What do you take me for, Miss Petrova? Do you think for one minute that you're fooling me? Stepan Shevchenko is no more an honest business man than you are an innocent miss. He is a high-class smuggler and you, *Miss* Petrova, are his whore.'

Anna went still. 'You have no proof of any of that. Those are the delusions of your own mind. You're jealous that I prefer Prince Shevchenko to you, that is all.' She desperately wanted a weapon. She could break a glass…she could attempt palming a butter knife with its blunt edge. But neither of those would do much against the captain.

Denning pressed against her, crushing her red skirts against his trousers. 'I have something better than proof. I have two boys in my custody, one of whom confessed to a smuggling operation being run beneath the cliffs of Seacrest, the very home where Shevchenko lives.' Her immediate thoughts were for Joseph. Had he confessed? What had Denning done to coerce him? But the second boy? Who would that be? Was Denning lying, trying to frighten her? Her mind tried to sift through the information and separate fact from fiction.

'I am not bluffing, Miss Petrova. I can see you're weighing the odds, wondering if I tell the truth. I have the clerk from Shevchenko's warehouse, in case you're wondering. He's a far weaker specimen than Shevchenko's crew chief.' He caught her chin between his thumb and forefinger, forcing her to look at him. 'I've always admired your skin, Miss Petrova. I would hate to see it ruined. Have you ever seen ruined skin? Say after a flogging? Bloody nasty, it is, and it never heals well. Scars for a lifetime.' He turned her face left and then right. 'Same with knife-cuts. Scars for ever, especially if the cut is deep enough.'

'You seem to make a habit of telling me grisly

tales, Captain,' Anna replied coolly. 'For the record, I don't find it appealing.'

His hand closed over the base of her throat, his thumb covering the pulse note there. She fought back her panic with logic. He was not going to strangle her. She was too valuable to him for a while longer. 'It's not meant to be appealing, it's meant to be instructive. It's very difficult to watch another suffer, especially when the other is a friend or a loved one—at least young Abernathy would agree with that. He didn't last long once we started in on Raleigh. Seems Abernathy was quite fond of his friend. I only got ten good lashes in. Apparently Abernathy was willing to do anything to save Raleigh, even sell out Prince Shevchenko.' His eyes gave her a narrow caress as he studied her throat. 'Too bad his confession was too late. In the selling out of the prince, Abernathy incriminated Raleigh, too.'

'They are children!' Anna argued, although they were only a few years younger than she was.

'They are criminals, Miss Petrova. I had no choice but to indict Raleigh.' His thumb massaged her neck. 'I might, however, be willing to commute his sentence.' He smiled. 'The question is, what would *you* do?' He gave a cold chuckle that sent a shiver through her. 'I see you are already considering it, already desperate to save the boy. Very well. I will name my price. I don't think you'll find it too onerous. Likely you've already done this before.'

Anna swallowed, steeling herself. She could do whatever it took to keep him in this room, to keep him away from Stepan and whatever was going on outside this door.

'I've had an obsessive fascination with your mouth ever since I met you, Anna. May I call you Anna? Miss Petrova seems too formal at this juncture.' His eyes glittered and she watched in horror as his hand slipped to the fall of his trousers. Dear heavens, he couldn't mean for her to do *that*?

'On your knees, Anna.'

His hands pressed down on her shoulders, forcing her to comply, forcing her to face his engorged phallus at eye level, angry and red.

'Let me be very explicit here. I want your mouth on me, my dear.' His hands twisted in her hair, jerking her head up one last time. 'Tongue, lips, a little teeth, if you please, and remember—Joseph Raleigh's life is on the line. If I like it, I'll save Joseph Raleigh from the noose and you can justify your sin by knowing he'll live the rest of his life in Australia. Not a bad trade for a few minutes of your time.' He let go of her hair.

This was nothing like the intimacies she wanted to share with Stepan because it wasn't intimate, it was naked aggression. It was power and possession, control and force. It was meant to bend others to one's will at the expense of their own. It was everything Stepan had stood against in Kuban and here. She'd be damned if she'd betray his cause by giving in. The act itself wasn't a betrayal, it was merely the product of coercion, of having no choice. But giving in to what it represented—*that* was betrayal. Anna went back on her heels, a fiery glare in her eyes. 'No, I don't think so.'

'What did you say?'

'I said no.' It was hard enough to say once, let alone twice, when a boy's life hung in the balance but she had to claim her own power. If she gave in now there would be no stopping his domination or her decline. He would know her price then. She struggled to rise, hampered by his nearness and her skirts.

He shoved her down again. 'I would be very certain about my decision before I stood up, if I were you. A boy will die for your pride.'

'I am.' She glared her defiance as he pulled her to her feet, the cabin door flying open and glancing off the wall from force. Denning gripped her firmly against him, making her a prisoner to his body as men dragged Stepan into the room between them, bloody, beaten and, worst of all, limp. Her breath caught in undisguised horror.

'What do you think of your defiance now?' Denning whispered at her ear in triumphant glee. 'Your champion bleeds like any other man.'

Dear Lord, what had happened? Something had gone terribly wrong. She felt anger mix with terror. 'What have you done?'

'My job, Miss Petrova. Nothing more.'

She jerked away from Denning and ran to Stepan, aware that her freedom to do so was only because Denning allowed it, a taste perhaps of what he'd allow her if she allowed him other tastes.

'Anna,' Stepan croaked as she stroked back the

hair from his forehead to reveal another purpling bruise. His beautiful face was swollen. He'd taken a blow to one eye, another to his jaw, his lip was split, the knuckles of his hand bloodied. From the look of the two soldiers holding him, he'd not gone easily.

'Stepan, I'm here.' She wished for some water, for a rag to wipe his face. She didn't dare ask for them for fear Denning would exact a price. She sent up a silent apology to Beatrice Worth and ripped a length of silk from her skirts. She could at least bind his hand.

'Oh, I do not think you've earned the right to play nurse.' Denning tugged her away. 'You need to earn those favours, Miss Petrova, futile though they may be. No sense doctoring a dead man.'

'He is a prince of the kingdom of Kuban, you cannot…' The enormity of the situation began to dawn on her in full.

'He is a foreigner, a prince of nothing to me.' Denning smiled cruelly. 'He has no power here, but I do and you'd best start appealing to it.'

In that moment, her principles and Stepan's causes seemed insignificant. She had only a single thought now. How could she save Stepan and the boys? She used the one weapon left at her disposal. She licked her lips, her hand dropping to the low bodice of her gown in invitation. 'Whatever you want, my mouth, my body, they are yours, just give me the prince.'

No. No. Anna would not barter herself to his enemy, not for the cause, not for Joseph, not for him. Stepan shook himself, trying to clear his head, trying to rally his strength. All four of them had come at him. He'd bested two of them, but the other two had weapons and he'd been no match for two armed soldiers after already facing two others. The odds had definitely not been even, not with four men working against him in tandem and now Anna needed him, but his strength was spent. He could barely rise, let alone fight three more men.

Stepan levered himself against one of the soldiers, getting to one knee. He had to at least rise, had to stand and face Denning. He could still bargain. 'Wait, Denning. Bargain with me instead.' His voice cracked.

'What do you have to offer me?' Denning grinned, revelling in his helplessness.

'The vodka. I will tell you where it is, if you let her go.'

'So there *is* vodka?' Denning at least looked intrigued.

'You can't find it without me.' Stepan wished his head would clear. He wanted to think better. He didn't dare look at Anna. That would destroy him entirely. He'd failed her tonight. He'd brought her into danger and every fear had been realised. This was what happened when one allowed emotion to interfere. His men were gone. He'd forced the crew to abandon ship instead of fight. He did not want them taken, as well. It was bad enough Joseph was imprisoned and Anna was in the hands of his enemy. Only his cargo was free at the moment.

Denning held out his hands in an expansive, accepting gesture. 'Fair enough, I can't find it without you. Maybe it doesn't matter.' Denning gave a laugh. 'I was just telling Miss Petrova about your clerk, Oliver Abernathy's confession. I don't need your confession, as well.'

'Without proof you have nothing to substantiate the brutality you've conducted tonight,' Stepan argued hoarsely, overriding the hurt that lurched in him. His clerk had faltered and, in doing so, the boy had failed them all. That was his fault, too. Oliver had never been cut out for high risks. He should not have been put in that situation. It was one more stone to settle on the scales against him.

'You need more than words, Denning. A boy will say anything under duress. I can give you more.' He would give Denning all of it to save Anna.

'No, Stepan!' Anna cried.

Denning strode towards him until they stood toe to toe. 'You know you give me your own death warrant.'

'Yes. Put her on a horse, and an hour after she's left town, I will tell you where the vodka is.' He would take a small, perverse pleasure in pointing out the spirit had been beneath Denning's nose the whole time.

Chapter Twenty-One

Stepan studied Denning through one good eye and the swollen slit of another. He didn't need two good eyes to see the offer was tempting for the captain. The man had come up dry for his efforts too long and the promotion he coveted was waning. 'It's a good offer. You won't get one better.'

Denning licked his lips. 'Lieutenant,' he barked, his gaze not leaving Stepan's. 'Take Miss Petrova to the livery and fetch her a horse. See her on her way and report back to the barracks with the exact time she departed.' He gestured to the officer. 'I need a pair of irons. We have a dangerous criminal to transport.'

'You can't do this!' Anna argued, wrestling with the poor lieutenant, who found it awkward to be confronted with laying hands on a woman. Stepan didn't envy the lieutenant. Anna struggled towards him, reaching for him, but Stepan held himself apart from her. He would not make it easy for her to touch him. He would break if she did. He needed all of his stoic reserve now. This was his penance for flying too close to the sun, for believing love could be for him.

'Let me say goodbye!' Anna sobbed. 'Please, one minute is all.'

'Use two hands if you need to, Lieutenant, but get her out of here!' Denning barked impatiently. 'She's a spitfire, she won't break if you handle her.'

'Let me see him, you bastard!' Anna spat in Denning's face. Stepan would have laughed if it hadn't hurt his lips. He would remember this, his last glimpse of Anna, defiant and fighting, and most important, *safe*. He'd bought her freedom with his life. The price was well worth it.

'That's Captain Bastard to you, Miss Petrova. Call me anything you like. They are only names.' Denning wiped his cheek.

'Stepan!' She appealed to him as the guard hauled her past. He risked one final look at her, letting his eyes lock on her, letting his mind imprint this last picture of her hair falling down, the scarlet of her gown matching her own ferocity, her whisky eyes flashing. There was fight and fury in his Anna and no quitting. He would carry the image with him to the gallows and it would sustain him.

The lieutenant clapped the irons over his hands and led him off. He did not resist: not in the wagon for the short trip to the barracks, not when they shoved him in a dark cell and locked the door. There was no reason to. Compliance bought her safety and her freedom. Resistance could ruin it all. The last thing he wanted was for Denning to renege and bring her back when he was behind bars with nothing left to barter for her. They'd both be at Denning's mercy then.

He'd seen a taste of what that mercy would look like tonight when they'd dragged him into the cabin. There'd been a horrible moment of seeing Denning draw Anna to him, her body a shield, and the glimpse of Denning's trousers already down. The moment had lasted only a second but it was long enough to make Stepan wonder if Denning had wanted him to see it, wanted him to know Anna was entirely at his mercy and he was impotent to stop it. That was the moment he'd decided to trade himself for Anna. If Anna stayed, Denning would have her.

That tragedy had been averted, no need to dwell on what had not come to pass. Instead, he kept his thoughts firmly fixed on Anna: how she'd felt against him last night, soft and feminine; how she'd moved beneath him on the soft bed, her little moans catching in her throat as she took her pleasure, their bodies still damp from the bath; and when the cell grew cold and he shivered, he thought of that bath. Was it really only last night that he'd known such exquisite peace? Embraced such impossible possibility, that he could love this woman and she could love him and they might manage to make a life together?

'Tell me we'll go tonight. I am sure they have injustice in America.'

He could almost hear her laugh as she said it. He should have kept sailing. They could have sold the cargo in the Caribbean...

'On your feet, Shevchenko.' Denning's key rattled in the lock. The fantasies would have to be delayed. 'Your hour is up.' Stepan struggled to his feet and smiled, content in knowing that Anna-Maria was nearly to Little Westbury and the safety of Dimitri's home. He could see the oft-travelled road in his mind, winding north and west away from Shoreham.

Anna flew down the road on a horse the colour of moonlight, her heart in her throat, tears drying on her cheeks. A thousand what ifs assailed her. What if she hadn't ordered the champagne? What if Denning hadn't popped the cork? What if she'd kept the men dancing? Would anyone have heard the cask drop? Would the cargo be safely stowed in the warehouse and Denning foiled? Would Stepan have come back to the table, immaculate and blameless? She didn't know, just as she didn't know precisely what had happened on deck, why the fighting had started, what had the dropped cask triggered that had resulted in violence.

Whatever it was, the game must have been up, or Stepan would not have tipped his hand with brawling. He had been outnumbered, which boded ill. Knowing Stepan, he had chosen to fight to secure the crew's' escape. She knew very little, only that Denning had Stepan and, very shortly, Denning would have Stepan's confession and the right to execute him all because the foolish man had traded himself for her. The thought made her stomach clench, Denning's vivid description of what the execution would look like coming hard and fast to mind. Anna leaned over the horse and vomited on to the road. Stepan dead. She swayed, dizzy with the thought of it. She had to get herself together. She had to make Stepan's sacrifice worthwhile.

There'd been no choice. He was doomed, he might as well have made his last free act worthwhile, to use himself while he still had value to barter. Even amid her tears, she knew that much was true. For her to stay meant utter defeat. With both of them taken, there'd have been no hope. As long she was free, though... That idea sparked deep inside her. Had Stepan set her free to go for help?

But who? And where would help of the kind she needed come from? She needed a man who outranked military captains, a man who could pardon criminals and overturn sentences, a man who was above the law if he chose. She knew men like that in Kuban, men who could help, but not here, and because of that, Stepan would die. The tears started anew and she shivered in the night. She'd never felt so alone since they'd left Kuban. She was nothing here.

She reined in the horse at the fork in the road, staring dumbly at the crude sign illuminated by the moonlight. A turn north-east would take her to London, a turn north-west would take her home to Dimitri—her brother and her rock. He would solve this. She'd run to him with every trouble she'd ever faced in life and he'd patiently untangled each trouble with her. He'd even stood between her and the arranged marriage to the Pasha's son, offering himself instead in marriage to the man's daughter.

To the north-west lay the certainty that Dimitri would stand in the breach for her and for his old friend again if she asked. Stepan had rescued his family for him and he would return the favour as best he could. Dimitri was a willing warrior, but in her gut, Anna knew this time her brother wouldn't be enough. Neither could she ask it of him. He was a husband now and a father. This was not Kuban. Dimitri was not a prince here with power, as Denning had so cruelly pointed out tonight. Dimitri would be an obstructer of justice, a man who could be thrown in jail.

Anna gathered her courage and turned the horse to the north-east, to London. She would follow the road and pick up the River Darent on its winding course to the Thames. She didn't know exactly where London was, only that the Darent fed the Thames and that London was a half-day's ride, or in this case a half-night's ride *if* she didn't blow the horse, ride him into a pothole, or any other myriad crises that could befall a rider in the dark.

Anna considered it. She'd need more than half a night. Travel in the dark was slower. It had been just past nine o'clock when she'd left. She would make London by sunrise, she *would* find Preston Worth and she would drag him back to Shoreham if she had to. He was the one person she knew in this new world who could make a difference. She could have him back in Shoreham by the afternoon. Surely, that would be soon enough. Surely, Denning couldn't just hang Stepan. There had to be a trial, some kind of procedure to follow. She kicked the horse, managing a trot while the moon was high. She would have enough time, she had to. She loved Stepan. She couldn't lose him now.

'Anna-Maria! What are you doing here? My dear girl, what has happened to you?' Beatrice Worth took one look at the red gown and wrapped an arm about her, ushering her inside the wide entrance hall of Worth House.

'Wait.' Anna's teeth chattered. 'My horse,' She made a tired gesture to where the mud-splattered animal stood with a street urchin.

'Your horse?' Beatrice's eyes widened. She called for a footman who sped down the steps to take care of it. 'Where did you ride from?' Beatrice was dressed for the morning and smells of breakfast wafted from somewhere deep inside the house. It had taken longer than Anna'd hoped to find the Worths and London had been far more vast than she'd imagined.

'From Shoreham—something terrible has happened.' She was starting to shake, her legs too rubbery to hold her. She clutched at Beatrice and began to fall, the night, the cold, the journey, her emotions taking their toll. Then a solid force was there beside Beatrice, scooping her up in strong arms, calling for blankets and tea. She let herself collapse for just a moment. She'd found Preston Worth. Her task was half-complete. Now all she had to do was persuade him to intervene.

Beatrice pressed a cup of tea into her hand and settled a blanket at her shoulders, both of them patient as she told her story. 'I am sorry about your house,' she concluded, wondering if she'd made the right choice after all. Preston Worth was a prevention officer. He might decide Stepan had gotten what he deserved for smuggling, friend of the family or not. 'I'm sorry about your dress, too,' she added, looking nervously at Beatrice.

Beatrice grasped her hands. 'Don't worry about such a silly thing. You've been incredibly brave.' Too bad it wasn't Beatrice she had to persuade, Anna thought. Beatrice had been so welcoming, so concerned, even now with the truth laid out between them. But Preston remained silent.

'He's smuggling vodka and spices?' Preston clarified. 'Out of the caves beneath my estate?'

'Yes.' There was no way to evade the truth. She debated saying more, pleading Stepan's case one more time, but she stayed silent. Worth struck her as a man who gave his decisions great thought. She had to be patient and give him the time to think.

'I've never liked Denning the few times I've met him for work,' he said at last. 'To give that man free rein is to invite disaster. I wouldn't want anyone at his mercy, especially not children.' He shook his head. 'But the smuggling...'

Anna knew what he was thinking. How did he reconcile going against a man who was on the same side? He was a prevention officer. Beatrice broke in, quietly, respectfully, with a powerful opinion. 'This isn't about arms deals and wars, and the sort of men you chase down, Preston, men like Cabot Roan. This is about local people trying to survive in an economy that doesn't favour them. You've said yourself that there needs to be a better way. Until there is, decent men are at the mercy of unjust laws.'

Preston looked at his wife and Anna felt something intangible move between them, a great understanding known only to them. 'Bea, Stepan broke the law.'

Beatrice nodded. 'An unjust law and Denning is subverting the law. What do you think Denning's justice will accomplish? Peace? A restoration of order? Nothing was ever out of order until he came.'

'Please—' Anna could remain silent no longer '—I love him.' And love it seemed was of a higher order for Preston Worth than laws and justice.

Preston rose, decision emanating from every pore. 'If Denning is indeed circumventing the law in his practices, we might stand a chance.' He gave Anna a sharp look. 'We bring only a paper sword to this fight, you have to understand that. But I will try.' To Beatrice he said, 'We have to go right away. I'll call for horses and the carriage. Have Matthew and whatever you need for the journey ready in an hour.'

'I can ride.' Anna-Maria tried to rise from the sofa, but her legs wouldn't hold even as relief swamped her. Preston would help.

Preston fixed her with a stern, scolding stare. 'No, you can't. But you can ride in the carriage with Bea and my son. Meanwhile, we have troops to rally. I'll send a note to Nikolay Bak-lanov asking for his assistance and a rider with a note to your brother and the others in Little Westbury: Liam and Jonathan.' He smiled, his eyes softening a little. 'We'll bring our own army with us: a soldier, a diplomat, a knight of the realm and a prince or two. An impressive coterie. Denning will think twice about calling our bluff.'

Beatrice put her arm around Anna. 'We'll do all we can. The Worth name is powerful. You love him. I can see it in your face.'

'With all my heart.' Anna felt her lip tremble, her body giving way to exhaustion. 'It just hurts so bad.'

'I know, my dear girl, I know.' Beatrice held her close and Anna prayed the Worth name would be powerful enough to stop the hang-man's noose.

Chapter Twenty-Two

The sun came up slowly, fingers of daylight playing around the small window set high in the cell. Stepan had always associated daylight with hope. But not today. Every moment the cell grew brighter, hope faded, not that there had ever been any or that he'd wanted there to be any. He would face this day not with hope or with despair, but somewhere in between; with resignation. This was what he deserved for reaching too high, for hoping to claim love when he'd known better. The recriminations he'd heaped on himself in the night did not go away in the light of day, they merely reasserted themselves, gnawing at his conscience.

Stepan lifted his face to the shards of light and closed his eyes, taking himself miles from dampness and shackles to a room with pink-chintz chairs and white curtains pulled back from a window, a dark-haired woman asleep in a soft bed, hair spread on a pillow. He could see Anna waking, safe and warm. The sad ache in his heart relaxed as he let the vision take him. He put himself into the picture. He would rise from the chair and go to her. He would lie down beside her and tuck her up against him, his arm wrapped about her, resting possessively low on her abdomen. He would breathe her in and she would murmur his name. He would take her from behind then in a languorous joining.

'Are you dreaming about her, about your girl, milord?' Joseph's quiet voice interrupted the fantasy from the one cot. Denning had brought the boys in late last night. For collateral, Stepan thought.

He opened his eyes slowly, reluctant to come back to reality. 'How do you feel this morning?' Joseph had been barely able to walk last night.

Joseph gave a wan smile. 'I am sore.' He shivered. 'And cold.'

Stepan had worried about that fever and festering from the lashes. 'I will try to get a blanket for you.' How he would do that, he had no idea. He sat down next to the boy, attempting to share his warmth until then, not that he had much warmth of his own to offer.

'Do you think your girl will bring help?' Joseph asked.

'No,' was all Stepan said and the two sat in silence. This was the dilemma he'd grappled with through the long night. Did he hope Anna would get help? Or did he hope she went home and accepted fate? He'd not set Anna free for her to risk herself. Images of Anna riding in the dark had kept him awake last night. He imagined her falling off the horse, the horse hurting himself in a hole, Anna lost and at the mercy of highwaymen.

Joseph gave a disappointed sigh beside him. 'I thought she loved you, milord.'

'She does,' Stepan replied. It was because she loved him that she would not try such a dangerous stunt. She would go home to Dimitri and keep herself safe. In time her heart would heal and she would find someone else to love. His would never heal, but that hardly mattered. His 'never' would be far shorter than hers.

And yet his hope had not wanted to die so easily. He'd had to bludgeon it to death with blows of cruel reality. 'Even if she went for help, Joseph, who would she find? Who would come?' Those questions had been the death knell for his hopes. He'd spent hours in the night systematically using the sharp edge of that reality to slash through his short list of friends.

No one would come.

There was Dimitri, who probably hated him now that he'd sent the man's sister home ruined and in the middle of the night. If Dimitri did come he could do nothing. He was a man without power here. He could only make things worse.

The others were too far away, as well. Ruslan was living incognito in France with his bride. Illarion and Dove were on a never-ending honeymoon somewhere in Europe. Maybe. They could be in Japan for all he knew. Perhaps Preston Worth would come, somehow learning a smuggler had set up shop in his house. But that was hardly a promising outlet. Worth would side with Denning.

There was Nikolay, who was in London, but

still too far away. Nikolay was oblivious to all of
this, as he should be. His wife was expecting a
child this spring. The thought of restless, reckless Nikolay becoming a father brought a faint
smile to his lips. He would not see the child.
Denning would have dispatched him long before Klara gave birth. Stepan hoped it was a son.
Nikolay deserved a son to ride with, to practise swordplay with. His heart clenched at those
images. How long had he himself longed for a
father to do those things with? Nikolay's son
would be lucky. That boy would have the dream.
Might he have had a son of his own one day?

That was a dangerous thought. He'd been careful with Anna, but not as careful as he might
have been. It had never occurred to him not to
marry her once he'd taken her to bed. Regardless of his misgivings, honour was honour. He'd
meant to discuss it with Anna the next morning,
but the morning had taken a very different direction than the one he'd intended. It was possible Anna was carrying his child, *their* child.
The thought warmed him. A piece of him might
indeed be left behind.

'Do you think it will be today, milord?' Joseph

stirred, moving closer to him, shivering. Stepan wished he had his hands free so he could hold the boy. He would take his coat off and wrap him in it.

'Oh, no,' Stepan said with a confidence he didn't feel. He simply didn't know. Denning might let them linger for weeks, he might even give them a trial if the man's conscience woke up in time. Then again, Denning might just do it today and make a timely example of them to suit his purposes.

Across the cell, Oliver woke up against the wall. 'Does hanging hurt very long?'

Stepan managed a smile, trying to take their minds off the macabre. 'You and Joseph don't need to worry about it. They aren't going to hang boys.' At least he hoped not. Feeling the boys' eyes on him was galvanising. Even at the last, there were people who needed him. These boys were counting on him and he would not fail them. He had to keep his spirits up for their sake and his wits. He would bargain with Denning for them if the time came. He would try to spare them. Then he sobered. 'You will probably be transported, though.'

Who knew if he'd have a chance to speak with them again in detail? 'You must promise me you will stay together and watch out for one another. You must be like brothers. You will be all the other has.' He gave Oliver a long look. 'Do you understand? You will have to be strong. Transportation is not the worst thing to happen to you. You will get a chance at a new life, eventually.' With luck, it might even be better than what they could have hoped for here.

'They will hang you, though, milord.' Joseph was serious.

'Yes.' He would not lie to Joseph about that. Stepan had spent his life saving others and now there was no way out for himself. That was not entirely true. There was one way out. He could take his own life and cheat Denning of his prize. Denning wouldn't be able to make an exhibition out of him. Instinctively, he knew Denning would resent him challenging his power even at the last.

Ruslan's father had taken his life in prison before the Tsar could execute him. At the time, Stepan had been ashamed of the man's decision.

He'd seen it as weak and cowardly, although he'd never said as much to Ruslan. He saw that decision differently now. Perhaps the man had feared his son trying something rash to save him and had done it to protect his boy. Perhaps the man had seen the act as a chance to rob a petty tyrant of his power. Maybe those were the reasons Denning had brought the boys—to prevent just such a turn of events. Perhaps Ruslan's father's final moments had taken more bravery than Stepan had originally understood. But his bravery would have to take a different path. He would not leave the boys alone, not when their fates were uncertain and there was a chance he could do something about them.

'We could fight them, if we lured the guards inside when they brought our food.' Joseph began to plan. 'We could lock them in and you could run.'

'No,' Stepan said sternly. 'There will be no heroics on my behalf, Joseph.' He didn't want anyone dying for him. Not Joseph, not Oliver, not Anna-Maria, not Dimitri. He wanted them all safe, otherwise what had any of this been for? He might as well have stayed in Kuban.

* * *

It was a long day. The boys jumped and exchanged wild-eyed glances every time the door opened, even though he assured them if one wasn't hung in the morning, they were safe another day since the British army insisted on morning hangings. But if the truth were told, something in him leaped, too, when the doors opened. Apparently, his hope wasn't as dead as he thought it was. But it was only guards bringing their meals. He had to remind himself there was no one coming. 'This is merely Denning playing with us,' he told the boys. 'He knows waiting can be its own kind of torture. Waiting for the unknown even more so.' One never knew if one should want time to hurry up so that the outcome would be clear, or if one should beg for time to slow down because at least for now one was alive.

The boys drifted off to sleep after a bread supper, Joseph still shivering with fever. Stepan stayed awake, keeping watch for what it was worth, the way he'd kept watch all those nights on the journey from Kuban, all those nights in London waiting up for Nikolay and Illarion to come home, to know they were safe. It was what he was good at: standing vigil.

Anna-Maria kept watch with him in his thoughts, the image of her burning bright in his mind. She was safe now and so was the child that she might carry. *A son.* The possibility no longer filled him with trepidation and he marvelled at the revelation. There was even elation with the thought that he might be a *father*. That he might have taken a boy fishing, or bought him his first pony—a docile, fat little beast with short legs and a thick mane. He let his mind conjure up a hundred scenes of ponies and piggyback rides, the boy on his shoulders, Anna-Maria at his side.

When had this happened, this loss of fear, this desire to love? He knew the answer. It wasn't a when that had changed him but a who. Anna. Anna had given him back love, given him back himself, here at the last when it was too late.

There was a soft squeak of the main door opening, someone coming to collect supper dishes, finally. He looked up when the key turned in the lock. There were two guards this time instead of one. His senses were on alert, the drowsy lethargy leaving him. 'We've brought paper and ink, Shevchenko.' The one man spoke quietly out of deference for the sleeping boys. The other held up a key for the shackles. 'You can write if you like.'

Stepan struggled to his feet and swallowed as he held out his hands. He knew what this meant. Denning would not have allowed the concession on its own. 'Tomorrow, then?' He rubbed his wrists as the shackles fell away. He would have a night of freedom before they were put back on in the morning to lead him away.

A chance to fight, came the unbidden thought, a remnant of his ghostly vigil with Anna. *A chance to live.*

'Yes.' The men were solemn, polite. 'The captain wants to wait until the town is awake to watch.' After breakfast, then. Well, now he knew.

'And the boys?' He nodded towards the sleeping forms, his heart pounding. He had two boys left to save and he would if it was the last thing he did. The expression wasn't just words any more.

'They will be hanged, as well.' The men shuffled their feet uncomfortably.

The warrior in him woke. 'They are children.' His stomach clenched in desperation. He had to save them. 'I want an audience with Denning. I want to bargain. I want them transported instead, if not set free outright.' He racked his brain for options. He had money—perhaps he could buy their freedom as long as Denning had one man to hang. Denning was not the most scrupulous of men. 'Tell him!' Stepan said when the men remained silent. 'They are children, dammit. They are just trying to survive.'

The door locked behind them and Stepan stared at the paper and ink left with the little writing desk. Reality claimed him. He was down to last things. He was thirty-one and this was all the time he would get. When the boys woke, their needs would claim the rest of his time and strength. There was only this time left to reflect on his life and settle his affairs and yet he could focus only on Anna-Maria.

Did she know that he loved her? That he was capable of loving and she'd been the one to show it to him? There'd been times throughout his life he'd been ready to lay down his life for his friends, for Anna-Maria. But now, he wanted to live for her, for what they might have had. Never had he felt the tang of life so completely as he did now—thinking of Anna, watching the boys rest. He was needed alive.

That settled it. Determination replaced desperation. He would not go out in the morning and simply let Denning put a noose over his head and pull the lever. He would fight every step of the way. If he had to die tomorrow, he would die trying.

Each passing moment was a hellish torment for Anna as the carriage stopped yet again in the crowded streets of Shoreham. She hit the side of the carriage with her fist in frustration. They were so close and they would be too late at this rate. They'd arrived last night and gathered at Seacrest; Dimitri and Evie, May and Sir Liam, Jonathan Lashley and his wife, Claire, even Anna's father had come, all from Little Westbury. Nikolay had ridden ahead of the Worths from London on his warhorse, Cossack, eating up the miles with enviable speed and had already been waiting at Seacrest, already gathering information, none of it good. Anna wished she could have ridden with him.

She managed a peek out the window, but it did nothing to ease the knot in her stomach. It had been there since Nikolay had brought back his report last night. He'd ridden down to the barracks and asked to see Stepan, but had been turned away. Stepan would hang in the morning in the town square. Anna had gone to pieces then. To her amazement, it had been her father who had carried her from the room and sat with her through the night, holding her with great tenderness, murmuring empty assurances as she cried. Even now, his words remained imprinted on her mind. *'There, there, my darling girl, let it all out. I know what it is to lose the one you love.'*

Now the morning was here and time was flying again. There had been too much of it in the night and now there wasn't enough.

They'd left early from Seacrest, but apparently Shoreham hadn't had such a grand entertainment as a hanging in ages and everyone had turned out for it. Not everyone was pleased by it, though. She sensed the anger in the crowd.

She heard it in the calls that went out whenever a soldier passed. Perhaps the men could turn the crowd and use the chaos to free Stepan?

Dimitri poked his head inside. 'We won't get any closer,' he informed them.

'We have to,' Anna protested. 'What are we going to do?' How many times had she asked the question? Surely this time there would be an answer.

'They're bringing him out now.' Dimitri ignored her question and her stomach lurched. If she couldn't go forward, she could go up. Stepan was out there and she was going to see him. If the worst happened, he would see her at the last. Anna shoved past her brother.

'Where are you going, Anna?' He grabbed for her, but she wrested away, climbing up to the driver's seat. She clambered up on top of the carriage to the luggage rack.

Dimitri scrambled up behind her. 'Anna, this is madness! Get inside where you are safe. The crowd might riot.'

'No, he has to see me. He has to know I am here.' She calmed for a moment and searched her brother's eyes. 'Don't you see, I love him and he loves me. He gave himself up to save me and now we have to save him.' She didn't try to hold back the tears. She wasn't ashamed to love Stepan.

Dimitri held her gaze, the full significance of her words settling on him. A wry smile quirked at his lips. 'I was so afraid you'd fall in love with the first man who showed you any adventure and I was right. I just never dreamed it would be my best friend.' He paused. 'You do know if we're successful today, he won't be able to come back? He'll have to leave England.' If she went with him, she'd never be able to come back either. It would mean leaving Dimitri.

'I know,' she whispered. 'Let's see him free first.'

The ominous drums rolled. Stepan and the boys were brought out. Her heart clenched. Even at a distance, they looked haggard and dirty. Denning had not allowed him any quarter even in death. Denning couldn't risk it. No one wanted to hang a clean-shaven, well-laundered man who looked every inch the prince he was. There was little of the prince in his face today, though. Stepan's face was cut, there were new bruises and he was heavily guarded by three men, as if there'd been trouble earlier. Anna hoped there had been. She hoped Denning was paying for every step Stepan took towards the noose.

'Stepan!' She called his name over the crowd and watched his posture go alert.

Look at me, she begged silently. *I will hold you with my gaze until it's over. I will not let you go.*

The crowd faded, the world narrowed to just the two of them.

Chapter Twenty-Three

Anna was here! Stepan's head turned towards the crowd, scanning it quickly and finding her atop a carriage, Dimitri beside her. Despite the grimness of the situation, his heart soared at the sight of her. His brave Anna here at the last. Her eyes held his over the crowd, over the noise.

I will hold you with my gaze until it's over. I will not let you go.

He wished suddenly that he looked better for her. She would see his bruised face and she would worry. He was a battered specimen indeed. There had been fighting this morning when the guards had come. He'd fought again when he'd been brought before Denning, this time in chains. He'd managed to get his chains around Denning's neck before the guards had reached him. It had delayed the hanging. Denning insisted on changing into clean clothes, but it had not stopped it.

So intent was he on Anna, he nearly missed the commotion at the front of the scaffold as Preston Worth, flanked by the imposing form of Sir Liam Casek on one side and Prince Nikolay Baklanov on the other, approached the scaffold and contained chaos broke loose. His Anna had not come alone. Stepan shot a quick look at Joseph and Oliver at his sides, a look that said to be alert.

'What is going on here?' Preston's voice carried over the crowd, silencing them as he approached Captain Denning. 'Since when do we hang men without a trial?'

'Since they've been caught smuggling and confessed to it,' Denning answered smartly. 'I have his vodka as proof.'

'We were coerced.' Stepan spoke up, rapidly, forcing his hoarse voice to carry. 'He threatened a lady's virtue if I did not confess to his charges. I am a gentleman. I would have confessed to anything to save a lady from rape.'

He watched Worth nod, his eyes narrowing in

speculation. 'Is that true? Are there witnesses?' Worth turned his gaze to him and Stepan had the suspicion Preston Worth was making this up as he went with only a very loose idea of what he was doing.

'I would not ask a lady to incriminate herself in something likely to be scandalous.' Stepan hedged, his eyes darting across the platform at Nikolay and Liam, ready at their stations. Worth couldn't truly think he'd reason his way out of this if he'd brought them. 'You have only my word, as a prince of Kuban.'

The crowd oohed, enjoying the drama. 'Ah, yes, another consideration, Denning,' Worth pressed his case. 'This man is not a British citizen. He is not subject to our laws. He is a royal prince. He cannot be tried and convicted here.' He spread his hands. 'It seems the evidence for hanging is shaky indeed—a foreign national with no obligation to keep our laws and an account of coercion.' Worth tapped a hand against his thigh impatiently as he scolded, 'This is not the finest hour of the British legal system, Captain.'

Was that true? Stepan wondered. Was he not

subordinate to English law? For a moment, he thought Worth's case would carry weight, that it would be enough, but it was Denning's hand that lay close to the fatal lever. Even if Worth was right, actions would speak louder.

'A condemned man will say anything and there is no witness,' Denning snarled. He raised his hand. 'Let the hanging commence!' A hood was slipped over Stepan's head without warning and all went dark. Stepan struggled. No, this could not be it. He wanted to see Anna, freedom was so close, he could feel it, taste it. Nikolay and Liam were just feet away.

He could sense movement in the crowd. 'Stop, you have a witness!' It was Anna. He wished he could see. Her words came fast, a sure sign Denning's hand was at the lever. 'I'm the woman he saved. Denning threatened me to force a confession.'

Jeers and hisses went up, the crowd was starting to turn against Denning and Stepan understood the brilliance of Preston's plan and Anna's sacrifice. They were all close now: the carriage, Anna, Dimitri—Dimitri who had once thrown a knife to save Evie's life. The import of that took on new meaning. Stepan stopped fighting and stood still. He wished he could tell the boys the same, but that would expose too much. He forced himself to breathe deeply, calmly, to put his trust in his friends. Nikolay would save Joseph. Liam would take Oliver. And Dimitri would throw for him. He had simply to wait and be ready.

'Cut them down. They all must stand trial first. We have a witness.' Worth's order came loud and clear. The end game was in motion. Stepan steeled himself. Denning would comply or Denning would pull the lever. It would all be over in a matter of seconds.

Denning spoke, rage evident in his tone. 'Shevchenko has no power here. He is not above the law.'

'Nor he is below it,' Preston answered. 'He is in limbo, he is neutral. He can be neither innocent nor guilty. He must be returned to Kuban and face his justice there, if I am right. If you are right, you may try him for his crime at that time, but not before.'

'He must be made an example of!' Denning

roared. 'He has broken the law.' Stepan strained his ears. The crowd was silent.

Worth made the most of that silence. 'What say you, people of Shoreham? Will you support this tyranny? This man has been given no trial, he has been given no justice by those who are supposed to protect you. If it can be done to him, it can be done to you. If you allow this man to hang today, you will be next whether you're guilty or not. Nothing will stop Denning, nothing except you. This is your chance. Will you take it?'

The crowd's volume began to rise, the sound of rotten fruit being thrown filled the air. Denning swore, his voice only reaching those on the platform. 'You think you're powerful, Worth. I will show you real power.'

Instinctively, Stepan knew this was the moment. Time stopped in a scream—Anna, he thought. For a moment there was air beneath his feet, the tightening of the rope about his neck, he began to choke, then came the *thunk* of a blade into the knot above him and he was falling.

Beneath the gallows, Stepan was frantic. He had to get the hood off, he had to see, he had to stand up, almost impossible to do with his hands tied and there were only seconds before the soldiers found him. Then, someone was there, familiar hands, old hands, pulling off the hood, 'My son, quickly, to the carriage.' Christof Petrovich shoved him forward, Stepan could see the wheels of the coach and he went, stumbling on weak legs. His strength was giving out at the last, when freedom was just feet away. But Christof caught him beneath the arms and half carried him the rest of the away, his voice rough with emotion at Stepan's ear. 'Don't you dare give up now, not when my daughter loves you.' At the coach, he barked orders through the chaos, 'Daughter, drive! I have him!' Stepan looked up with his failing strength to see Anna at the box, reins in hand as he and Christof tumbled inside. For the moment, he was alive. For the first time in two days he let himself believe in the impossible: he was going to live.

Anna chirped to the horses, setting the big Friesans into motion, the coach pushing its way through the roiling crowd by sheer dint of its bulk. 'Come on, get on!' She spied Preston and Liam fighting back to back, cutting a path through soldiers towards the coach, Dimitri and Nikolay each with a boy following behind him. Beatrice and Evie reached out hands for the boys. Nikolay scrambled up beside her, taking the reins. The other men grabbed on to the sides of the coach, ready to defend the carriage from soldiers intent on giving chase. The crowd helped there, barring the soldiers' way with their mass and righteous indignation.

'To the docks!' Anna-Maria cried to Nikolay. The *Skorost* was their best way out. A carriage carrying a surfeit of passengers would easily be run down on the roads.

The *Skorost* was ready, the captain and crew having returned early this morning under the cover of darkness at Nikolay's instruction. It was short work to be on board. There was no one to give pursuit. Denning and his troops were caught up with the crowd and would be for a while. But Anna stood at the rail, keeping vigil just in case. She would rest easier once they were out on open water.

'Anna.' A hoarse voice spoke behind her. She closed her eyes, savouring the sound of it. 'You came for me.' Stepan's arms closed around her and a lone tear of happiness slid down her cheek.

'Of course I came for you. I love you.' She'd nearly lost him today. She would never take the feel of his arms, never take the time they had together for granted. She'd seen the lever slip, seen the noose tighten about Stepan's neck for one horrifying moment. It had been too close. Nothing was guaranteed. 'I didn't do it alone, though.'

'I know.' The simple words said it all. She could feel the emotion in him at the realisation. For a long while they didn't speak. There were no words adequate to describe what they felt. They simply stood at the rail, watching the English shores fade, and let the grace of the moment flood them.

Anna turned in his arms, lifting her face to his, her eyes shining with tears. 'When you give your love to others, you have to let others love you back the same way. Otherwise it's not fair.'

'It was too dangerous,' Stepan began to protest. She smiled. Stepan would always protest. But his protests would have to wait. The others surrounded them now. She would have to share him for a while.

Dimitri's hand was at his shoulder and she watched Stepan turn towards his best friend, uncertain. 'Are you angry?'

Dimitri shook his head. 'You saved my sister and my father when I asked you to do the impossible. I could want no better man for her than you.'

Then came Nikolay, 'You got me out of the Tsar's dungeons when I was unconscious and wounded. I would have died in there if not for you. If Illarion were here, he'd say the same thing. You've saved each of us, watched over each of us as a brother, always ready to give advice we didn't necessarily want to hear and always ready to back us up even if we didn't make the decisions you wanted. Of course we came for you.'

Stepan wiped at his eyes and Anna pressed close, her arms about his waist. She was never going to let him go. Preston Worth cleared his throat. 'Now that we've got you, the question is what to do with you. You do understand you can't stay in England?'

She looked up at Stepan to see him smiling. He caught her gaze. 'I have it on good authority

I'm to rebuild my fortunes in America. I have everything I need right here.'

'Except a minister,' Dimitri mentioned with a clearing of his throat. Her brother might condone their love, but he'd want them wed.

Stepan laughed. 'There are plenty of those in Calais, I'm told. I will marry your sister as soon as we reach land.'

Oh, no. This was not how their life together was going to start. Anna jabbed him in the stomach with her elbow. 'Perhaps you should ask me how I feel about that?'

'You're absolutely right, my dear.' Stepan dropped to one knee and took her hand before all their family and their friends. 'Anna-Maria Svetlana Petrova, will you do me the greatest honour of my life and be my wife?'

Anna's face broke into a beatific smile. 'Yes, just as soon as we reach land.'

They wasted no time, no fussing over dresses or flowers or a grand church. In fact, Anna didn't even leave the ship. Stepan left with Dimitri long enough to find a priest. When one had come seconds from death, one didn't want to squander another minute of life. That wasn't to say there were no preparations, however. Stepan refused to marry his bride in gallows clothes. He did bathe and shave and change into fresh clothes. Bea did Anna's hair in an intricate dark braid and Evie spent the crossing fashioning a veil from a scarf, insisting that Anna have something bridal to mark the occasion.

To Stepan, it might have been the finest wedding he'd ever attended, because it was his and she was his. He waited for Anna at the prow of his ship, at the end of a little aisle marked by rush-light, Dimitri at his shoulder, his friends gathered about him as Anna walked towards him on her father's arm. It was a glorious sight to see them together, father and daughter, a new peace between them. In the background, a sailor's fiddle played a slow ballad to mark their progress.

No cathedral, no swelling organ, no French-designed gown could have made the occasion finer. Anna was beautiful in a clean dress of blue muslin with a white-lace collar and Evie's hastily made veil on her head. When Stepan pushed the veil back and looked into the topaz depths of her eyes, he saw his life there, the past, present and his future, whatever it might hold. Grace filled him. How blessed he was to have Anna, a woman who knew who he had been, who was the keeper of all the stories of his life and who believed in who he might yet be: a husband and, God willing, a father, a *good* father. He could be that. He knew that now. Anna had shown him it had been in him all along.

The priest intoned the service in French, as it happened. But Stepan caught the parts that mattered. *'With my body I thee worship...'* *'Until death do us part'*—that had new meaning after today—and, best of all, *'You may kiss your bride.'*

He kissed her long and sweet as the sun set and the waves began to roll, a reminder that time waited for no one. There would be goodbyes now. Their party could go no further with them. Nikolay, Dimitri and his father, Preston, Liam, Jonathon and their wives needed to return home to their children and their dreams. Irish, Joseph and Oliver would go with them—Irish with Sir Liam who knew a little something about being an Irish boy growing up on London's streets; Joseph with Preston; and Oliver with Dimitri, who was already making plans for the boy's help as a secretary. A boat waited to take them all home to England, the captain eager to catch the tide. But after that…hmmm. Stepan shared a secret smile with Anna as they faced their guests. After that, the night would be theirs.

Christof took his leave first, sharing a private moment with them at the prow of the ship, their hands in each of his. 'My children,' he said softly. 'Stepan, you've been a son to me since the first time Dimitri brought you home. Now you've become my son in truth. I've always been proud of you, even when you disagreed with me. But today, you became a man. You have taken a wife and you will have a family soon.' He turned to Anna. 'My daughter. I have not always been fair to you. You've borne the weight of my grief for so long. Forgive me. You're so much like her, like your mother. She was all goodness and light and so are you, I see it in you when you look at your husband.' He joined their hands. 'Today, you've made an old man happy. Now, spend your lives making one another happy.'

'Thank you, Papa,' Anna whispered. They

could not linger overlong with Christof. There were other guests to see to and other farewells to make. It would be a while before they were all together again and they were in no hurry to rush these final moments filled with tears and smiles.

Dimitri was the last to leave the gangplank of the *Skorost*. He hugged Anna one last time. 'You are a beautiful bride, Sister, and you've married a good man, the very best of men.'

Then it was Stepan's turn. He embraced Dimitri. 'This is only goodbye for now. We will see you again, my friend.'

Anna slipped her hand into his as they watched Dimitri's straight back walk down the gangplank to join the others. A sailor pulled the plank up and the *Skorost* pushed away from the dock, their friends fading from view. 'What are you thinking?'

'That this tale has ended quite well.' He smiled. 'The last prince of Kuban is sailing into the sunset, his princess by his side.'

Anna wrinkled her nose. 'The end? Do you really think that? This is just the beginning. Once upon a time a princess married her prince and they made love all their days and lived happily ever after.' She smiled. 'By the way, it's a very *long* story and it starts tonight, just as soon as I can get you naked.'

* * * * *

LET'S TALK
Romance

For exclusive extracts, competitions
and special offers, find us online:

f facebook.com/millsandboon

⊙ @millsandboonuk

🐦 @millsandboon

Or get in touch on 0844 844 1351*

For all the latest titles coming soon,
visit millsandboon.co.uk/nextmonth